CW00505127

MAGIC GONE WILD

THE WITCHES OF HOLLOW COVE
BOOK THIRTEEN

KIM RICHARDSON

FABLEPRINT

FablePrint

Witchy Little Lies, The Witches of Hollow Cove,
Book Thirteen
Copyright © 2023 by Kim Richardson
All rights reserved, including the right of
Reproduction in whole or in any form.
Cover by Kim Richardson
Printed in the United States of America

[1. Supernatural—Fiction. 2. Demonology—Fiction.
3. Magic—Fiction].

BOOKS BY KIM RICHARDSON

THE WITCHES OF HOLLOW COVE
Shadow Witch
Midnight Spells
Charmed Nights
Magical Mojo
Practical Hexes
Wicked Ways
Witching Whispers
Mystic Madness
Rebel Magic
Cosmic Jinx
Brewing Crazy

THE DARK FILES
Spells & Ashes
Charms & Demons
Hexes & Flames
Curses & Blood

SHADOW AND LIGHT
Dark Hunt
Dark Bound
Dark Rise
Dark Gift
Dark Curse
Dark Angel
Dark Strike

MAGIC
GONE WILD

THE WITCHES OF HOLLOW COVE
BOOK THIRTEEN

KIM RICHARDSON

CHAPTER
1

How does a witch plan a wedding when a god wants her dead?

Very carefully.

Not only did I have to try and make things work with my mother and Katherine, Marcus's mother, but I also had that constant throbbing pressure of being watched, always looking over my shoulder, wondering if today was the day the Creator of Storybook offed me.

It had been ten days since he showed up at my mother's doorstep, telling me he wanted to kill me. I'd just stared back like an idiot, too shocked for my brain to catch up. There might have been a bit of drool.

And then he'd just up and left. No, vanished. Just like Lilith had done many times.

So naturally, I'd been a total spaz since.

It didn't help that I'd had to keep any emotion from showing on my face that night as I walked back to my mother's kitchen to join them and did my best to give my mother the dinner she deserved. All the while, my stomach was in knots, and Marcus's lasagna kept getting lodged in my throat. Add the four glasses of wine, and by the time the night was over, I was a mumbling, incoherent fool.

The Creator of Storybook wanted me dead.

Why? I'd never met that god before. Trust me. I'd remember that pale bastard if I'd ever seen him. It just didn't make sense. Had I insulted him somehow? Usually, when gods wanted you dead, it was because you did something to offend them. But how could that be when the first time I'd laid eyes on him was when he'd appeared on my mother's porch?

He'd basically told me he'd created the portal. He'd brought over Captain Hook's ship as well as the Nutcracker soldiers, and we'd lost lives. Not to mention those eight paranormals who had crossed through, including Scarlett, and were lost to us forever.

I hadn't uttered a single word about the god that night. Or a week later. I'd wanted to talk to Lilith first. But the goddess was ghosting me.

I knew I'd have to tell Marcus, my aunts, Iris, and Ronin, eventually, but I'd busied myself with the wedding plans to keep from thinking about it.

Speaking of said wedding plans... That night at my mother's place, after Marcus had helped me with making lasagna for a surprise dinner, I'd been so distraught that when my mother decided we should have the wedding soon—as in ten days—I'd agreed to it without thinking it through. And Marcus just consented to whatever I wanted, assuming that a wedding in a mere few days was exactly what I wanted. It wasn't.

Who planned a wedding in ten days?

This witch.

So now, I was getting married in three days. Yeah. What a giant clusterfuck.

I sat at the kitchen table of Davenport House, watching the toaster and waiting for signs of clattering, my hands wrapped around a hot cup of coffee. House had given us back power days ago, and thankfully he hadn't removed it again. Yet.

Seeing that most of our Davenport relatives and relations were paranormals and didn't believe in modern technology, which was basically the old landline phone, Iris and I were on message card duty this morning.

Staring at the toaster, I was hit with the tremendous feeling of déjà vu. I'd been on card duty before, just like this, when Beverly had been engaged to the dirtbag incubus Derrick. It had been a ruse, a plot to get him to remove my magic for Lucifer.

Although Beverly had recovered from the ordeal, I didn't want to bring it up, just in case it upset her.

My mother had wanted us to have the reception at the Sunset Seashore Resort & Spa, the most prestigious hotel in Cape Elizabeth, but it was fully booked throughout the summer. So were all the other hotels she tried. Having a wedding in such a short amount of time, the only other logical place that could accommodate many guests was Davenport House. So obviously, we opted to have an outdoor wedding on the house grounds, which my mother happily boasted had been her idea all along. Of course it was.

The truth was, it was a relief to have it here at Davenport House. Outdoor weddings were my favorite and the prettiest, in my opinion. And as a garden wedding, we could take full advantage of the manicured gardens and lush, mature trees and fruit trees. They weren't in season, but Ruth had said she had a few potions that could make the apple and crabapple trees blossom like spring.

I had no doubt she could pull it off. I just didn't know how we would pull off a massive wedding in three days. Even with magic, it sounded insane.

The toaster shuddered, followed by a clattering sound from the inside.

Hildo, the black cat familiar, lunged on the table with his rump up, head down, pupils dilated, and ears low while he wiggled his hind legs back and forth. He looked like he was ready to swat the toaster off the table.

With a sudden pop, a white card fired out of one of the toasting slots like a bagel. Hildo leaped off the table, caught it in mid-flight with his claws, twisted around, and landed expertly with the card clasped in his mouth like he'd just caught a bird.

"Not bad," I told the cat. I was impressed. Wish I could do that.

"I know," said the cat with the card still in his mouth. He blinked, his yellow eyes gleaming. He looked smug, if a cat could actually *look* smug. He padded over, his tail high, and deposited the card next to me. He returned to the spot next to the toaster and lay down, watching and waiting for his next card victim.

I flipped the card over:

FREE BOOZE (AND A WEDDING)!
TESSA & MARCUS
RSVP
Kindly respond by Thursday, June 27, by
phone or any *magical means of communication*
of your choosing.
Mr. and Mrs. Wallbanger accept with pleas-
ure
Seats at the cauldron: 2
Magic: Dark magic

"What's the matter with you?" Iris eyed me
from across the table. Her pile of RSVPs was
slightly higher than mine.

"What do you mean?"

"You've been acting weird lately."

I shrugged. "I'm the definition of weird. Haven't you noticed?" I placed the card on the
"Accepts" pile, which was now my only pile.
No one had declined the invitation. Well, not
yet.

The Dark witch's pixie-like features twisted
in what I could only guess was annoyance.
"You're doing it again. I know something's up."
She leaned forward and whispered, "Are you
getting cold feet? Because that's totally normal.
I mean, you're about to tie the knot with a guy
forever. I'd be a little freaked out too."

She thought I had cold feet? "No. That's not
it. Getting married to Marcus is like… it's like a

6

dream come true." Which was exactly how I felt. "I never thought I'd meet someone like him. Never thought I'd be so blissfully happy."

Iris stared at me momentarily, her dark eyes rolling over my face as though trying to decide if she believed me. She leaned back with a satisfied smile. "So there *is* something. What is it?"

Crap.

A loud explosion sounded from the potions room off the kitchen, saving me from telling Iris.

Ruth came rushing out, gliding over the hardwood floors like an expert slider from the local curling team, her face smeared with pink...frosting maybe? Her white hair was sticking out on end as though she'd just been electrocuted. The white apron tied loosely around her small frame with the words IF YOU CAN'T FLY WITH THE BIG GIRLS, STAY HOME was splattered with more of that pink stuff, along with speckles of blue and purple stains.

"I'm fine. I'm okay. No need to worry," said my aunt. We heard a pop, and her hair sizzled and smoked. Knowing her, she'd probably stuck something there temporarily and forgotten about it.

I frowned, looking her over. "What's going on in there?"

Her grin deepened the lines at the corners of her blue eyes and mouth. "Your wedding cake!"

She clapped her hands, sending pink slops on the floor and the walls.

If she didn't look so delighted, I would have felt bad. "How is that going?" Ruth had offered to make the cake, and knowing her cooking and baking abilities, I would have been a fool to refuse. Not only because of my aunt's extraordinary culinary skills did I accept, but we were also on a time crunch. Brooms & Brew and The Crone's Pastry Shack would help with the appetizers and hors d'oeuvres while my aunts took care of the main courses and the wedding cake.

But Ruth had been at it for days. Surely she should have been finished with the cake by now?

"It's going great." Ruth scratched her nose. "Don't you worry, Tessa. I'm going to give you the *best* wedding cake the paranormal community has ever seen. You just wait."

"Hopefully, it'll be edible," muttered Hildo, staring at his witch companion as if wondering whether he'd made the right choice pairing up with her.

Ruth's face fell. "Are you worried about the cake? You think it won't taste good?"

I glared at the cat. "Of course not. I have absolute faith in you, Ruth. I wouldn't want anyone else making my wedding cake. I promise."

It was apparently the right thing to say, as Ruth's face brightened, and she straightened her shoulders, looking proud. "It's going to knock your socks off!" And with that, Ruth spun around and rushed back into the potions room, her bare feet slapping hard on the wood floor.

I laughed. I loved my Aunt Ruthy. Seeing her this happy, hell, I should ask her to bake me a cake every day.

I would have been perfectly delighted ex- cept... except for that dark cloud hovering around me.

The Creator, or whatever his real name was, hadn't shown his face again. Maybe he got bored and moved on to someone else. Perhaps he returned to his Storybook and decided I wasn't worth the hassle of killing? If only I were that lucky. I didn't know the reason why I hadn't seen him yet. But I didn't think he would easily forget. Not after that threat.

I really needed to speak to Lilith. If she was ghosting me the usual way, I'd have to make her an offering. Maybe then she'd come and talk to me.

"You still haven't answered my question," said the Dark witch, an expectant arch to her brow. "If it's not the wedding, then what? What's gotten you all tense? Tell me."

I'd already blabbed, so I couldn't lie to her and say nothing was bothering me. "It's not im- portant."

"Like hell it isn't."

"I'll tell you later." At her glare, I added, "I promise. I'll tell you everything. Just... not right now." I shifted in my chair. "How many do you have in your accepted pile so far?" I asked Iris, wanting to steer her away from what was really bothering me. I knew I would have to tell her, just not right now. It wasn't the right time.

Seemingly having accepted that we would talk more later, Iris patted the top of her pile like she was tapping the top head of a child. "Thirty-two."

"Thirty-two?" I leaned over and fingered through my pile. "That's about fifty people so far. I don't know fifty people." I felt a heavy chunk of dread fall into the pit of my gut. "Whatever happened to the small wedding I wanted?"

"It's not about what *you* want." My mother appeared in the kitchen with a box and set it on the table beside me.

"It's not?" I eyed her. "Last I checked, it's *my* wedding. Marcus and me."

"It is," said Dolores, who emerged after my mother, bags in her hands. Beverly strolled in behind her with an equal number of bags. Dolores set her bags on the kitchen counter. "Don't let your mother bully you into anything. You know how she can turn this into *her* affair."

My mother picked up Iris's accepted RSVP pile and placed them in her box. "I'm not bully-ing her. It's important to keep up appearances.

You don't want to skip out on inviting important people. That's just bad etiquette."

"I thought we were just going to invite the family," I said, unease creeping into my gut.

My mother moved her hand around the table like she was looking for something. "I don't see any declines. How many have declined the invitation?"

I looked at Iris before answering. "None, so far."

My mother smiled like she'd won the lottery. "How fabulous."

I groaned. "No. Not fabulous. That's way too many people, Mother. I don't even know a quarter of them."

"Your mother is right," said Beverly as she dropped her bags next to Dolores's. She turned around and walked over, her red kitten heels clicking. She was rocking those skinny jeans better than any young woman. Add that low V-cut blouse, and she put us all to shame. "This is a big day. Not only for you but for the Davenport witches."

I blinked. "How so?"

Beverly smiled, making her look years younger. "Because we're Davenport witches, darling. *Everyone* wants to be like us."

Oh boy. It took some serious effort not to roll my eyes. But I was astonished that Dolores hadn't commented on that remark. In fact, she looked like she agreed.

Beverly flicked a finger at me. "You don't want to anger the wrong people. Especially the powerful witch families."

"I don't?"

"No. Besides it's tradition among paranormals. The general rule of thumb is when an influential family member marries, the other important families expect an invitation. It's just how things go."

"I never got an invitation," I blurted. If their theory was true, how come I hadn't been invited to anything since I'd been here?

"No weddings apart from…" Dolores held her tongue as she eyed Beverly, whose face had gone stiff for a second. "Apart from yours, Tessa. There're rumors of a possible match between Lavinia Devonshire and Maddock Le Doux, but we won't know for sure for another month or so."

I met Iris's eyes across the table, and I could see by the way her facial muscles were twitching, she was trying hard not to laugh.

Beverly let out a happy sigh. "Weddings make me horny."

Here we go.

She whirled on me, throwing that manicured finger in my direction again. "Don't forget tonight."

"Tonight?" Oops. I had no idea what she was talking about.

My aunt slapped me hard on the shoulder with strength that reminded me of Dolores. "Your bachelorette party, silly. I've been planning it for days."

"Oh. Right. Yay." Oh. Hell. No.

Beverly had appointed herself chieftess of the bachelorette party before anyone could object. I stiffened, thinking of Beverly's "inner vagina" party a week ago. I didn't want any male appendages served as dessert. But knowing her, it was probably already in the works. Possibly worse.

"It's all been taken care of," said Beverly. "You're going to have the time of your life. Ooooh, I'm *so* excited."

"We've noticed," snapped Dolores.

"No strippers, I hope." Not that I didn't enjoy seeing fit, muscled, half-naked men as much as the next warm-blooded female. I just wasn't in the mood.

Beverly looked like I'd just told her she had to remain celibate for the rest of her life. "I'll pretend I didn't hear that."

The doorbell rang.

"I'll get it." I leaped from my chair before anyone could stop me and hurried down the hallway. Yes, Beverly had arranged my bachelorette party. I just wasn't in the mood to go. Would it be so bad if I didn't?

I pulled open the door. A young male stood on the porch. Angry red pimples marred his youthful face, and dark chest hair peeked from the collar of his shirt. He smelled of wet dog. Werewolf—a young one who looked like he hadn't beasted out into his animal form yet. He clasped a long, rectangular box in his hands.

"Delivery for a Tessa Davenport," he said, looking slightly embarrassed.

"That's me." I took the box and watched the young male enter his beat-up Toyota Tercel and drive away.

"What is it?" Iris's shoulder bumped up against mine.

"A package for me." I took my parcel and made my way back into the kitchen.

"Wedding gift?" asked my mother as she came over.

"Possibly." I placed the package on the kitchen island, wondering who would send me a gift. I lifted the top of the box, and my temporary happy feeling deflated.

A dozen black roses lay in the box. Scratch that: a dozen *dead*, black roses.

"What the hell?"

Dolores's arm hit mine as she leaned forward. "Those are dead flowers. That's an evil omen."

"Why do you say that?" My voice was low, almost a whisper because I already knew what she would say.

14

Dolores glanced at the flowers and said, "Dead flowers mean death. Black, dead flowers mean the worst possible death."

I was the lucky witch, then.

My mother looked at me, her eyes worried. "Who would send you dead roses? Have you been having an affair?"

I gritted my teeth, exasperated. "No, Mother."

My heart slammed in my chest, and I forgot to breathe for a few seconds as fear danced over the back of my mind. I picked up the small card in the box. There were only two words and a signature.

Tick, tock.

It was signed only with the letter C.

The Creator.

CHAPTER
2

What does a witch do when a god sends her a dozen dead, black roses? She panics. She panics *a lot*.

Fear chilled me, and I felt an iron-cold band of dread clasp around my neck as though the god himself had wrapped his hands around me and was squeezing. I couldn't fill my lungs with enough air, as though the room were suddenly small, like a coffin, with me in it.

Worse was that he'd sent the flowers *here*. Not the cottage. Which could only mean he was watching me.

I felt fingers interlace with mine and saw Iris brush up against me. She squeezed my hand

and then let go, no doubt seeing me having a minor, no, major panic attack. So much for the god having forgotten me.

"Tessa? Who would do this?" My mother had the RSVP box clasped to her chest, looking more affronted by the fact that someone dared send me dead flowers.

"It's the Wanderbushes," said Beverly. "They're jealous because their old, saggy bodies could only pique the interest of morticians for coffin fitting. They don't want any Davenport witch to be happy."

The cousins, which I remembered very well, were like my aunts' doppelgängers. I wanted to tell her she was the same age but decided against it.

"Don't touch them! Don't touch anything!" Dolores leaned over the box of flowers and spread out her arms. "This here," she said, with a confident sparkle in her eyes, "is a curse. The kiss-of-death curse." She blinked and added, "Or it's the plague-enchantment hex. Either way, it's not good."

Too late. I'd already grabbed the card. And it was still in my hand.

"What's a hex?" Ruth appeared standing next to Dolores. She looked down at the box of flowers, and her face scrunched up. "Oh. That's a bad omen."

It was a lot worse than that.

"Judith Nutter received a box of dead flowers once," said Ruth, a faintly troubled expression on her face.

"And?" prompted Iris.

I still couldn't figure out how to make my mouth work.

Ruth shrugged. "She died the next day of a heart attack."

"Thank you, Ruth," snapped Dolores. "That's not exactly helping."

My mother scoffed. "Tessa is in perfect health. She won't die of a heart attack."

"If she gets cursed, she might," muttered Ruth.

"Ruth, I think you need to shut up now," hissed Dolores. "It's fine. Tessa didn't touch the flowers. So we can assume..." Her eyes snapped to the card I was holding. "You *touched* the card? Tessa! You *never* touch the card of the person who sent you dead flowers. All witches know this."

Finally, my mouth seemed to work. "I didn't know." Though I was pretty sure the flowers nor the card were cursed. Witches, warlocks, and wizards used curses. Gods didn't. They didn't have to. They could kill you just by snapping their fingers or blinking you into oblivion.

"I didn't know either," said my mother, though it didn't bring me any comfort.

Dolores yanked the card out of my hand. Guess she figured since I was holding it and I hadn't been struck down in death, it *wasn't* cursed. Therefore she could touch it. "I don't understand. Tick, tock? Who is C?"

I felt all eyes on me, even Hildo, who'd stopped staring at the toaster like it was a yummy turkey. This wasn't how I'd planned on telling them. Hell, part of me wished I never did. How does one tell their family that a god out there wants them dead?

So I decided just to wing it and hope for the best.

I took a calming breath, or at least I tried to. "There's something I haven't told you. Haven't told anyone."

My mother took the card from Dolores. "Does it have to do with who sent you these horrible flowers? Really poor taste."

Dolores crossed her arms over her chest, sending a scowl my way. "Spit it out, then. If you know who this C character is, you better tell us now. Because dead flowers mean death."

I stared at the dead roses for a beat longer and then looked up at my mother. "The night Marcus and I came over. The night we surprised you with his lasagna?"

"Yes," answered my mother, a frown forming on her pretty forehead. "I thought it was a wonderful evening. Didn't you?"

"Yes. But someone came over. While you were in the kitchen getting all the plates."

"Who?" asked Dolores, and I could see everyone waiting for me to answer.

I swallowed and said, "The one they call the Creator. The god who made Storybook and the portals. He was there. On my mother's front porch. He told me he was going to kill me." I waited, watching their expressions as they went from confusion and disbelief to finally utter fear.

"That can't be," said Dolores. "Why would a god want you dead? Must be someone playing a trick on you. We all know gods don't have time for our mortal affairs. You must be wrong."

"I wish I were. I'm not. I felt his power. It was him." I remembered the pulsing of magic, of power, like I'd never felt before except on Lilith and Lucifer.

Dolores shook her head, her expression set in a frown. "You're mistaken."

"Why didn't he kill you?"

We all stared at Iris.

The Dark witch shrugged. "He said he wanted to kill you. Why didn't he? He had the opportunity, but he didn't. Why?"

Good question. I glanced at the dead flowers. "To play with me a little bit before he kills me." I knew it to be true when the words left my mouth. I didn't like it. But there we had it. "Like a cat does with a mouse."

"They ask for it," meowed Hildo, his attention back on the toaster. "Just saying."

We settled into a silence, all lost in our thoughts. My mind worked over the events, trying to make a connection, and a stir of fear hit me. Something was wrong here. Things just didn't add up.

Finally, Dolores cut the silence. "And you think this C is the god that Tinker Bell called the Creator? You believe he sent you these flowers?"

Sadness crossed Ruth's face at the mention of the fairy. I knew she'd wanted me to bring Tinker Bell back with me, but the fairy had stayed. Maybe she had a good reason.

"Yeah. It's him." Dread chewed in my gut like an ice cube pressed against my belly. "I don't know anyone else with that initial. It's a message. A very clear message. My time is up." The bastard god was going to kill me.

They'd all gone quiet again with the same fear emulated in their faces.

"Wait a minute here." Dolores pressed her hands to her head like she thought it might explode. "This doesn't make sense. Why would this god want you dead?" Her eyes bore into mine, and she got right up to my face like she was trying to open my forehead to get to my brain. "What did you do?"

A slap of irritation hit me. "Excuse me?"

"Well, you must have done *something* to anger the god. As I said before, gods don't care about us. We're insignificant to them."

"Unless we offer them naked fools," sneered Beverly. "There's nothing insignificant with naked."

"This god didn't even know of your existence until recently," Dolores was saying. "So what did you do? Think, Tessa. This is important."

"Nothing. I didn't do anything." Okay, now she was pissing me off.

"You must have done *something*." Dolores's face was set in resolve. "Tell us. No matter what it is, we won't judge."

"Sure we will," added Beverly.

I gritted my teeth, feeling my blood pressure rising. "Listen. I didn't do anything. I woke up that morning a few weeks ago and found that portal, just like you. I went in to retrieve Marcus and returned with him and Beverly. That's it."

"And you dumped the virus on his tree," said Ruth, and I remembered telling her and my aunts about my trip to Storybook. "He's mad because you made his world sick."

"That would have made sense if he hadn't made the portal *before* I went there." I gripped the counter's edge, wanting to punch something. "He wanted me to cross over. That was his goal from the start." And I still believed that. I glared at Dolores. "I didn't do anything. So drop it."

Dolores frowned at me, a scowl that might have had me backing away from her a year ago. Now? Now I met hers with my own.

"Leave her alone, Dolores." My mother, holding on to that box of RSVPs like it was a newborn, bumped into my side. "Can't you see she had nothing to do with this?" She placed the card back on the kitchen island, and I snatched it up and stuffed it in my pocket.

"Fine." Dolores crossed her arms over her chest. "Then tell me why a god wants your daughter dead if she didn't *do* anything?"

"I don't know," answered my mother. "I just know it's not Tessa's fault."

From the way Dolores's eyes were spinning around in that big head of hers, I knew she wasn't going to let it go. I understood her logic. Hell, it didn't make sense to me either why a god wanted to kill me when I hadn't done anything. Was it my connection to the ley lines? The fact that I was a Shadow witch? Who knew what was going on in that god's head?

"Why didn't you say anything?" My mother was observing me carefully. "Your father was there, and so was Marcus. They could have helped."

I shook my head. "Shock. Denial. All of the above." Plus, I didn't want to ruin the dinner. The look on her face when we'd first arrived, the emotions I saw there, I didn't want to spoil that because of a god who was pissed at me for whatever reason. It wouldn't have made a difference if I had said something to them. The god had just vanished, leaving me too frightened to move for a whole thirty seconds.

"What does Marcus think? He must have an angle," prompted Beverly, glancing around as the silence stretched. "He was in Storybook, like me. Maybe he saw this Creator character?"

"I haven't told him either." I wasn't looking forward to that conversation. Just thinking about it had my stomach spinning like a washing machine.

"He's going to be very angry," said Iris, looking grim.

"I know." God, did I ever. I pulled out my phone from my pocket, not liking how my fingers trembled as I texted Marcus.

Me: *I need to tell you something. You're not going to like it.*

I saw the three dots appear as the chief wrote back.

Marcus: *Are you okay? Is it the wedding?*

Me: *It's not. Try not to be mad. Remember that you love me.*

Marcus: *What did you do?*

He sounded like Dolores.

Me: *Let's talk when you have a moment. Gotta go.*

Marcus: *See you after work.*

This might be the first time I wasn't looking forward to seeing the chief step through our cottage doors. Iris was right. He was going to be furious. Hopefully, this time, he'd take his temper outside. I didn't want House to throw him out on his ass again, like when he'd thrown a fit and smashed the walls and floors with his big gorilla fists.

"We should cancel the wedding," said Ruth, just as some pink icing slipped over her left eye and proceeded down her cheek. She scraped it with her finger and stuffed it in her mouth. "Mmm. Raspberry."

My mother whirled on her, thrusting the box of cards at Ruth's stomach. "Are you mad? I'm not canceling anything! Do you know how hard I've worked these past few days for this wedding? Do you? Tessa *is* getting married in three days, and that's *final*."

Ruth's face screwed up in a frown, but she said nothing. Instead, she just took a step back from my mother's box-assault.

Only my mother would see it that way. "Ruth's right," I said. "We should postpone it for a few days. It'll give me time to try and figure out who he is."

"Well, if you had told us sooner, we wouldn't be in this mess," accused Dolores, and I flinched, her words like a slap from one of her man hands across the face.

I bit down my anger, my fear, my frustrations. The last thing I needed was to start a fight with Dolores. At the moment, I wanted nothing more than to duel with that tall witch, but I didn't. I needed her brain. I needed her help if I wanted to live to see another day. Like my wedding day.

"Do you have a plan?" asked Iris, eyeing the dead roses with curiosity, and I knew when we weren't looking, she was going to grab one.

"How does one hide from a god?" I asked.

"You can't," snapped Dolores.

Ignoring her, I spoke to Ruth. "I thought maybe if we knew his true name, we could find a spell that could keep me hidden. Not forever. Just to give me enough time to figure this out." I remembered asking for something similar when we knew Lucifer was on my ass.

"For your wedding," said my mother, like that was more important than my life.

"Without a name, there's not much we can do," offered Ruth.

I let out a breath, feeling my neck tense up with stress. "Lilith knows. She knows who he is."

"Then why don't you ask her?" Beverly stared at me like I was the stupidest person on the planet that I hadn't thought of that.

"I have." I let out a sigh through my nose. "Many times. She's ghosting me."

"Then we'll just have to make her listen." Ruth's face had gone serious with faint, pensive lines between her brows. "We'll perform an offering she can't refuse, and she'll come."

I gave my aunt a forced smile, knowing she was trying to help. "Maybe. But that won't make her tell us the Creator's real name." The fact that she was ghosting me, and in her reaction to my questioning the last time she seemed to be protecting this god, I knew it would be tough just to get her to come.

"We should still try," continued Ruth. "Lilith is a nice person."

"She's a *goddess*, you nitwit," hissed Dolores.

Ruth made a face. "Still a nice person. She'll listen. I know she will. She'll come if we ask nicely."

Dolores snorted. "She's not a well-behaved golden retriever, Ruth. She's a goddess. She doesn't care if we ask nicely. She does as she pleases."

Ain't that the truth.

Ruth set her jaw in determination. "She'll come. I know it. I'll start with the offering ritual as soon as I work out a final, small detail in your wedding cake."

A pang squeezed my chest. I was already making Ruth work around the clock on this cake, this wedding. Now she was going to try a ritual to invoke a goddess who didn't want to be summoned, whose celestial phone was off.

"Thanks, Ruth. But I want to help. You're already doing so much. Let me help."

"I'll help too," offered Iris, and she smiled at me. "And Ronin. You can count us in."

"Okay." Ruth rubbed her hands together. "We're summoning a goddess tonight!" she chirped. It was hard to stay angry when you looked at Aunt Ruth. She was so damn cute and happy. Part of me wished I could have brought Tinker Bell back with me.

"I'll look into my private book collection," said Dolores, surprising me. "I have a list of god names. Maybe we'll find one with a penchant for fairy tales and stories."

"Thanks." I was still angry with her, but she made me realize I should talk to my father. He could give me a list of names of gods. Or he could ask around in the Netherworld, something we couldn't do.

"We'll do it tonight as soon as the sun sets," said Ruth.

"Sounds great."

"You better make it quick," said Beverly. "We have your bachelorette party tonight. You can't be late for what I've planned for you," she added with a sly smile. "Trust me."

I stared at Beverly, seeing the same narcissistic qualities in my mother at the moment, like my wedding and this damn bachelorette party were more important than this god who wanted me dead.

A wedding right now sounded ridiculous. Especially when a god could just pop by, snuff the life out of me, and pop right out. I mean, what was the point of all the preparations if I wasn't going to live long enough to enjoy married life? What was the point of anything?

I felt my downward spiral hit. The self-pity party that was about to commence.

But I wouldn't let it.

I was a strong, grown-ass woman, witch, who wouldn't drown in despair. Yes, a god out there somewhere wanted me dead, but I wasn't dead *yet*. And I would find out who the hell he was.

I glanced at the box of dead roses. Maybe this was exactly what he wanted, for me to feel anxious and hopeless. If he did, he didn't know me at all.

Dolores brought up a good point. Maybe I *had* done something? I just couldn't remember what. What could I possibly have done to offend a god? Well, I just had to find out what.

And I would. I'd start with a list and go from there. If I knew, maybe I could bargain with him. Gods bargained. That I knew for a fact, just thinking of Lilith as an example. She'd give me anything for some time in the sack with Marcus. I was willing to bet that if I could offer the god something in return, maybe, just maybe, he'd let me live.

"What about the flowers?" I eyed the box, hating the flowers and wishing they'd never been delivered.

Dolores looked at me. "Burn them."

And so I did.

CHAPTER
3

"How's the list going?" Ronin came to sit next to me on my couch. He spread out his long legs over the coffee table, a beer on his lap. His brown hair was styled in that perfect blend of modern sophistication, and his eyes were alight with curiosity and possibilities.

I sighed. "Not great." I'd been at it for about four hours, thinking of everything I could that "might" upset a god since I returned to Hollow Cove a little over a year ago.

And so far, I'd written the word *List*.

My half-vampire friend leaned over to look at my piece of paper. He snorted and leaned back. "You've got nothing."

"I know."

"Not even one? You can't think of *one* reason why this god is after you? Not one?"

I narrowed my eyes at him, not appreciating his tone. "I've been racking my brain for hours. The only thing that makes sense is what Ruth said."

"What did Ruth say?" Ronin gulped his beer. He tapped his bottle with his fingers, waiting for me to answer.

"That this Creator was pissed because I poisoned his tree, which would make sense if he hadn't already created the portal and wanted me trapped in it." It was my father's theory. He'd brought it up that time Marcus was taken through the portal. And I was going with it. "I only went in there to get Marcus and to stop the portal from spewing out other fictional characters that could hurt us."

"Like those Nutcracker soldiers," said the half-vampire. A strange smile materialized on his face. "They were fun to kill. Just saying."

I shook my head. "Maybe for you. But they were a threat. And that god let them in. He wanted this to happen." I tried to visualize a smug smile on the god's face, but I couldn't. All I remember was his deep loathing for me, his disgust that had radiated from him in near-palpable waves. It was impossible to imagine him with a different face.

I also had a lingering fear that this Creator would create another portal to another world again. And maybe this time it wouldn't be filled with unicorns and fairies and talking bunnies but something fouler, darker, and much deadlier.

So far, he hadn't. But that didn't mean he wouldn't.

So why wasn't he? To toy with me. Because that's what gods liked best. Toying with us miserable mortals.

"I think this god is having a blast right about now," I said after a moment as I placed my pen on my blank paper. Might as well stop. It was pointless.

"Why do you say that?" Iris came over, balancing a tray of two margaritas and a plate topped with tortilla chips and her guacamole dip in the middle. I hadn't eaten all day. I couldn't. I was a mess. But that dip looked pretty damn good to me right now.

I sighed and leaned back on the couch. "Just a feeling. He sent me those dead roses today to scare me. To instill fear. To show me that I'm just a soft, squishy mortal, and he's a big, dangerous god. But if he plans to kill me, why didn't he kill me when he popped up at my mother's place?"

"Good question," said Ronin, his fingers drumming over his beer bottle. "Maybe he's waiting for something or the right moment."

I flinched, and a tiny spark of fear kindled in my gut. I'd already come to that conclusion, but hearing it out loud made it all the more ominous and real. My denial position was quickly diminishing.

"That's not really comforting, Ronin." With her leg, she kicked Ronin's feet off the coffee table and placed the tray of goodies on it.

Ronin glanced from Iris to me. "I'm not here to comfort Tess. I'm here to give it to her straight. Fact is, a god out there wants to kill her. She needs to prepare herself."

He was right. "How do I do that?" As far as I knew, I couldn't do much to protect myself from a god. I mean, the guy had created a *whole* other world. Me? I could bend ley lines. I could bend *two* ley lines at the same time. Yay me. But that wouldn't save me from a vengeful god.

Ronin took another swig of his beer. "No idea. Sorry."

Of course not. It wasn't every day that we mere mortals were the subject of a god's interest. "I just wish I knew what the hell I did to the guy."

"God," interjected Ronin.

"You should have seen the way he was looking at me." A nauseating mix of dread and fear shook my knees, and I clamped my jaw, shaking away those feelings.

"Like you were hot?" inquired the half-vampire, winning him a smack from Iris. "What?

Maybe she's his type. We've all heard the stories that gods like to have sex with mortals. It's not like it's never happened before."

Yeah, like the way Lilith kept insisting on having some sexy time with Marcus.

I shook my head. "It's not that at all. He looked at me like he *despised* me. Like my very existence offended him. It was the weirdest thing." And it scared the crap out of me.

Ronin leaned over and grabbed a handful of tortilla chips. "Gods are weird. You can't try to understand them. It's useless. The worlds revolve around them, literally."

"I wish Tinker Bell were here," I said, smiling at the memory of that tiny fairy.

Iris took the spot on the couch between Ronin and me. "Don't tell Hildo that," laughed the Dark witch. "He keeps chasing butterflies in the yard, yelling, 'I'll kill you, you flying rat.'"

I laughed, feeling some of my earlier tension loosen around my shoulders. "Well, she might have been able to help me out with this. She didn't know his name, but she could have found out if she knew I was looking for it. But there was no time. We barely made it out." The idea of being stuck in Storybook still made my chest tight. Why did this god want me in that world? If he wanted me dead, why not kill me? It didn't make sense. A lot of this didn't make sense.

"Say you find his name? Then what?" Ronin chewed his tortilla chips. "How is his name going to change anything? It's just a name."

"You can do a lot with a god's true name," said Iris. "You can bind them; make them do your bidding."

I wasn't exactly sure about that part. It might work for demons, even demons in the higher demon ranks. But this was a god. Not sure those same rules applied.

Very true. "My aunts could make wards to protect me from him." Or so I hoped. Not sure that would work since Dolores had made wards to prevent Lucifer from appearing in Davenport House, and he'd still shown up in my bedroom. "The only one who knows his name is Lilith." And she wouldn't tell me.

"So ask her." Ronin grabbed another handful of chips.

"I did."

"Ask harder."

I glared at the half-vampire. "It's not like I haven't tried. I've been trying since the first night I saw him." When Marcus wasn't around, of course. Which had been a few trips in the middle of the night to the backyard while he slept. I called out to the goddess with my arms stretched out, flailing and facing the moon. If any neighbors had taken a peek out their windows, they'd probably concluded I was trying to fly.

But none of it worked.

"Don't worry. Ruth is preparing a summoning ritual for Lilith," said Iris, a confident smile on her face. "It'll work."

"Doubt it." Ronin looked at me. "No offense to Ruth's abilities in the witching department. Just don't think she'll listen. I think you have a better shot. You've called her before, and she's appeared, right? So try it now. Do it."

Part of me wanted to smack him over the head with his beer bottle. But I knew he was only trying to help. "Fine." I let out a breath. "Lilith? Lilith, I need to speak to you. I know you've been avoiding me. I know you can hear me. Lilith?"

Ronin crossed his legs at the knee. "If I were Lilith, that wouldn't drag my goddess ass out of bed."

I clenched my jaw. "Lilith?" I tried again, trying not to visualize myself punching Ronin in the face. I failed. "I thought we were friends. You told me so. I need to speak to you… as friends." I waited, not that I believed she'd appear.

Ronin pursed his lips. "Still not trying hard enough. A bit more conviction in your voice. That's the ticket."

"I *am* trying," I hissed at him. I was seriously going to punch him. I knew it.

Ronin slanted me a bland look. "Are you? Doesn't feel like it. I mean… do you want this god's name or what?"

"I do."

"So deal with her like you would most gods."

"What do you mean?" asked Iris.

Ronin pulled his eyes away from his girl-friend, and they settled on me. "Give her something. You can't just expect her to show up if you're not offering something in return. She's a goddess. She's expecting favors, gifts, human sacrifices. You know the drill."

"I thought that's what Ruth was doing," said Iris, sounding a little confused.

Ronin leveled a stare at me. "Give her something she *wants*."

Ah. I knew precisely where he was going with this. And I knew *exactly* what Lilith wanted. "Lilith," I raised my voice again. "If you come here right now, and let me have a conversation with you, and if you give me the god's name, I'll agree that…" I took a breath and said, "you can have time with Marcus."

Shit. I can't believe I said that.

Iris sucked in a breath, looking mortified, and slapped her hands over her mouth as though *she* had just offered her man to the goddess. Ronin was nodding like he thought that was a swell idea.

It wasn't a great idea. It was a stupid idea of colossal proportions. No way would I let Lilith spend time alone with Marcus—not even a minute. It was a big ol' lie—a test. I wanted to see if she'd come.

Lying to a goddess was probably number one on my list of the stupidest things I'd ever done. But there we had it. I'd done it. Too late to take it back. She could be angry with me afterward, burn me, torture me. I didn't care. I needed answers.

The three of us waited, all seemingly holding our breaths now, waiting for the goddess of hell to appear in my cottage. All my muscles were taut, and I was wound up like an elastic band, stretched to its limits and ready to snap. I could only imagine the storm of emotions that would consume the goddess when I confessed my lie. Maybe she'd take Marcus away from me out of spite. Shit, I hadn't thought about that.

"She's not coming," I said after what felt like twenty minutes but was most probably only sixty seconds. "I really thought she'd come." But part of me was glad that she didn't. I hadn't thought this through. If she'd taken Marcus away with her, I'd never forgive myself. And I was silently thankful she didn't show. It wasn't wise to play with the emotions of a goddess, especially Lilith, who I knew was a tad unhinged after being kept in a prison for so long.

"Me too." Iris's cheeks were high with color. "We all know how much she wants to ride him. Doesn't she, like, try every time you see her?"

"Yeah." It was irritating as hell. Yet another part of me thought she'd appear. "And she didn't show up. Huh."

"Well, that was a bust," said Ronin, sipping his beer. "Can't say you didn't try."

"There's still Ruth. Ruth will make Lilith appear to us. I know it," said Iris. I didn't believe it, but I didn't want to burst her happy bubble.

The fact was, knowing what I knew of the goddess, if dangling Marcus like a piece of meat hadn't tickled her deity fancy, Ruth's little summoning wouldn't work.

It only strengthened my belief that she knew this god, the one who wanted me dead, and she was protecting him. Why, though? Was he one of her lovers? Did they have a thing? She'd told me that she and Lucifer had an open relationship. Maybe this guy was someone she truly cared about: a frightening thought, when she was an egotistical, slightly mad goddess who only cared about herself. Perhaps I was wrong about her. Wouldn't be the first time. Lilith was a complicated creature.

"Here. Have a drink. It'll cheer you up." Iris lifted her margarita, waiting for me to do the same.

I picked up the margarita, and we clinked our glasses together in a toast. "Cheers." I took a sip. "Mmm. Good. Thanks." The alcohol burned my throat. There was too much in it for my liking.

Iris probably wanted me to relax and opted for more.

Ronin tilted his head and drank more of his beer. "Well. You have this bachelorette party to look forward to. Crazy, horny women throwing their bras and panties to dudes onstage," he said, his expression sly. "Too bad I can't come."

Not sure that was my definition of a bachelorette party. But it was probably Beverly's. I didn't think throwing a party was a good idea, but it wasn't as though I could live in a protective bubble for the rest of my life. I had a life—a good life. And I'd be damned if I let that psycho god take it from me. If I knew why the bastard had it in for me, I'd have something to work with, but I had nothing.

"What are you wearing tonight?" Iris was smiling, and I knew she wanted to change the subject. She looked way more excited about this party than I was. The whole idea made me want to hurl.

I shrugged. "Clothes."

Iris raised a brow. "Seriously? You can do better."

I shrugged again. "Clean clothes?"

Ronin laughed. "I'm free tonight. Your man's bachelor party is tomorrow night. Too bad I can't join you." He wiggled his fingers. "Females-only kind of thing. Right?"

I glanced at Ronin. "You're coming tonight."

"I am?" Ronin blinked at me, clearly surprised. "But I thought only ladies were allowed tonight? Isn't that the tradition?"

I looked at Iris and said, "You're my bridesmaid." And then my eyes fell on my half-vampire friend. "And you're my *bridesman*."

Ronin spat the mouthful of beer. "Excuse me? I'm a what?"

"My bridesman. You're my two closest friends." I waited to see if they'd refuse, but they both had broad smiles plastered on their faces. It was so damn cute and emotional, I had to pull my eyes away at the moisture I saw in Iris's eyes so I wouldn't start my own waterworks.

"I need to shower and change." Iris leaped to her feet, her cheeks pink from the margarita. "We'll meet you there. Beverly gave me the address. And wear something nice. It's *your* party. Remember that. Come on, Ronin." She grabbed his hand and pulled him to his feet.

Ronin held his head high. "Bridesman? Yeah, I like the sound of that. The first half-vampire bridesman in history. The vamp of honor."

Laughing, Iris pulled her vampire across the living room and out the front door. I smiled as the front door shut, feeling a little happiness crawl inside me. I hadn't felt happy in more than a week.

I shook my head, trying to rid it of the morbid thoughts that wanted to take over. I grabbed the tray of now-empty margaritas and what was left of the tortilla chips and headed to the kitchen.

"What the hell do I wear tonight?" I set the plate on the counter next to the sink. It's not like I had been shopping lately. I'd had more important things to do, like getting ready for my wedding in three days.

As I turned on the faucet to wash out the margarita glasses, the sound of the front door opening drew my attention.

"Did you forget—"

Mounting levels of fear followed the realization that Iris and Ronin were not in my doorway like I'd first thought.

It was the Creator.

CHAPTER

4

The margarita glass I'd been running under the tap slipped and crashed into the ceramic farm-house sink.

The Creator, the god, looked just like I'd seen him last when he appeared on my mother's porch. Not like I could forget the face of the god who'd threatened to kill me. It was imprinted on my retinas.

He had the same distasteful sneer on his handsome face, staring at the inside of my cottage like it was a chicken coop and he didn't want to soil his expensive white leather shoes.

I really hated the guy. If I wasn't scared shit-less, I would have told him so.

His blond, slicked-back hair glistened under the entrance light. This time around, a white, three-piece suit clung to his lean frame completed by a white tie. Over his shoulders hung the same black cape of some sheer material that reminded me of a child's magician costume. Maybe that was the look he was going for.

With the similar yet irritating ageless allure, just like Lilith and Lucifer—the only two other two gods I could compare him to—I realized I was staring at a being who was most probably thousands of years old. But I couldn't stop staring at his cape. It was an odd outfit choice.

His expression turned sour as he walked through the entrance. The door slammed shut behind him, making me jerk.

I knew right away that the god had closed the door with his divine powers and not House. The floor beneath my feet trembled, like House was trying to resist the god's power but couldn't.

"Here to kill me?" I was shaking, literally shaking, but I wouldn't show this god fear. I was too stubborn and most probably foolish. There went my wedding. My life. And just when it was finally going somewhere, this asshat showed up to take it all away.

Yeah, that made me angry.

Should I call out for help? Seemed like it was too late for that. The only thing between this god and me was the kitchen island.

The god took another few steps until he reached the middle of the space, between the kitchen and living room, and stopped with that same repugnant expression about his face, his black eyes roaming.

"Strange what mortals find comfortable in these wooden hovels," said the god.

"Cottage," I corrected, my blood pounding in my ears. "*Farmhouse* cottage. House, his name is House." Yeah, I was crazy to address a god this way, but I was proud of my cottage. I loved it. I wasn't about to let him insult me.

The god flashed me a lazy smile that chilled my blood. "The magical entity cannot save you. I made sure of that."

Did he mean House? "Did you do something to House?" Bastard. I wanted to rip off his cape and shove it down his throat. But now that he'd mentioned it, I couldn't feel House's magical pulses. Nothing. It was like he was on strike again, but I knew that wasn't the case.

The god cut me a cunning smile. "Let's just say I put it out of business."

My anger flared. "You're a piece of work." If he'd slain House, if that was even possible—probably was for a god—I would go all Rambo on his ass.

The god gave me a blank stare. "Tessa Davenport."

"Yes. I know you know my name. Said so the last time you saw me. What's *your* name?" I figured I would give it a go. What did I have to lose at this point?

Amusement flickered in the god's gaze, but his eyes blazed with a cold fury. His body pulsed with power: a crap load. I could feel the dangerous buzz like the hum of high-tension power lines.

He was going to kill me.

I channeled the energy from the elements, willing them to me and bending them to my will. The air crackled with the sudden inflow of magic. My power was negligible at best next to a god's. I knew it was hopeless, but a girl had to try.

"Your magic is pointless." The god stared at me like the fool I was.

I shrugged. "Instincts."

"Instincts," he repeated, staring at me like I was no better than an animal.

"Thanks for the dead flowers, by the way. Nice touch."

His black eyes met mine, and a smile twitched his lips. "Glad you liked them."

"I didn't. But why bother?" At least I knew for certain he'd sent them, and I didn't have some twisted secret admirer. "You said you wanted me dead," I told him, still hanging on to my magic. One never knew. I might surprise him with my badass magical moves. "What are you waiting for? Better yet, why don't you ex-plain *why* you want me dead? What the hell did

I ever do to you? I've never seen you before. And trust me. I think I would remember you." My eyes rolled over his suit to his cape. Yeah, the cape was just weird.

The god frowned at what he saw on my face. "You're an impudent female." His right eye started to twitch. That was weird too.

My heart thumped like it was wrestling with my lungs. "I'm an acquired taste. Don't like me? Acquire some taste."

For a moment, I thought that was it, the god would snap his fingers and break my neck, but he just stood there, looking more pissed than before, his right eye twitching away like it was line dancing.

It almost seemed as though he was struggling with something. "You can't do it. Can you?" I said, not moving away from the kitchen island. Though it was no real barrier, I used what I had. But what if I was right? Maybe he *couldn't* kill me? But that didn't make sense. He was a god, a being who could create worlds. Surely he could kill me... right?

This god had created a beautiful world with unicorns and other creatures, albeit the fictional characters were a little strange. How could he be truly evil when he could make something so lovely?

The Creator gave me a lazy, fiendish smile. "I have better things to do than to waste my valuable time and energy slaying a skinny, mortal female."

I blinked. "First, thank you for calling me skinny. And second, I won't let you kill me. Give me some credit." I'd fight him with everything I had, even if it was pointless. I'd rather die fighting than just give up.

A playful smile appeared on his hateful lips. "We shall see."

"Oh, you will." Yeah, this fight would be over in about a blink of an eye. "So what's your name?" I tried again. "If you don't tell me, I'm going to have to make one up."

Still nothing.

"Fine. I'll go with Big C. Or I could call you Dick?" Sounded about right.

The god dipped his head, that distasteful expression appearing on his pallid face again, like the mere fact that he was standing here was giving him gas.

"I don't understand what Lilith sees in you," said the god. "You're nothing special. So you can bend ley lines? So what? Witches have been bending ley lines for centuries."

"You know Lilith?" Of course he would. They probably all had drinks at their local god country club. When he didn't answer, I pressed, "You want me dead because you think I'm rude? Is that your thing? Going around the worlds killing those you don't like?"

"I do."

What a douche. "Nice."

The god exhaled in a bored kind of way. "Like I said, I don't waste my time with mortal creatures such as you. I have things to attend to."

"Like creating other worlds with unicorns and butterflies. Got it." I held on to my power, tapping into my demon mojo, too, because why the hell not? "So if I understand correctly, you're *not* going to kill me. If not you, then who?" I asked, my nerves making me shake. No way could I hide that from him.

"I have a parting gift for your wedding. Though, after tonight, I'm not so sure you'll be able to attend."

"Because I'll be dead?" I didn't think so.

With an evil grin, the god raised his arms slowly, like he was about to raise the dead or something. I did not want to see rotten strips of flesh all over my clean floors.

Energy hummed in the air, my hair lifting and floating around my shoulders as the god's magic glided over me, whispering of power and domination. Yup. That was some serious power.

A thin sheen of black mist rose from the floor in the middle of my living room. The acrid scent of cigarette ashes burned my nose. My pulse quickened as shapes materialized from the mist. First, I recognized legs, torsos, and arms as though they were being created from scratch. Was this how he did it?

A second later, the mist resolved itself into humanoid figures about seven feet tall each. And judging by their sheer size and build, I'd have to say, males. But that's where the resemblance ended. The one on the right had straw instead of skin covered by old, weathered clothes, endless black pits for eyes, and just a slit for a mouth. Branches and twigs sprouted out where you would imagine their fingers and feet should have been. A scarecrow, I realized: a hellish scarecrow.

The one on the left was dressed in a coat and breeches, one side red, the other black. He wore a bright red, three-pointed, floppy hat with a jingle bell on the end of each of its three points. His face was stretched into a scream, showing his sharklike teeth, and his eyes were like bloodshot orbs and gleamed with a demented awareness.

"A scarecrow and a jester. Seriously?" It was clear to me now that this god had some serious issues. First, with the fairy tales and now these… what? Urban legends? Yet it didn't explain his hatred and the want-to-kill-me thing.

When I pulled my eyes back to the god, he was gone.

CHAPTER

5

I barely had time to prepare myself as the scarecrow came at me. Remember, my cottage wasn't large, so that gave me about three seconds to get ready.

"Fulgur!"

A bolt of white-purple lightning fired out of my hand and hit the scarecrow's chest.

Hay and twigs exploded from the creature as it took a step back. I could see right through to the other side through the gaping hole in its chest. Good. At least I knew my magic affected it. Much better than with the Big Bad Wolf. Why was that? My only reasoning was that these guys were created or transported here by the Creator. They hadn't used a portal to cross over.

I didn't understand the logistics, but right now, I didn't care. I just didn't want them in my home.

You'd think a hole like that would stop it. It didn't.

I stared, shocked, as hay and twigs pulled inward along the gap's edges, stitching and repairing itself until the hole was gone.

"Well, *that's* not good," I muttered. I glanced over to the jester, expecting it to charge me, but it just stood there at the same spot where it had materialized or was created, like it was waiting for the scarecrow to tag it or to see who would win this fight.

"I will tear you apart, *little* female, and I'm going to enjoy it!" said the scarecrow, its voice like a thousand locusts. Creepy.

I looked down at myself and patted my wine gut. "And here I thought I'd gained weight."

The scarecrow rushed me again.

But I was ready for it.

"Inflitus!" I pulled on my elements as kinetic force shot through my hand, aiming for the scarecrow.

But the bastard leaped sideways. My magic hit the wall with a boom and exploded in chunks of plaster, dust, and wood splinters.

Before I could move, the scarecrow flung its arm at me. A shoot of branches spread out of where its hand was, stretching until it wrapped around my middle.

My feet left solid ground, and the branches lifted me, flinging me across the kitchen like a rag doll. I hit the cabinets, groaning as pain flared up my back. My concentration vanished. I stumbled and whirled around, blinking the black and white spots from my eyes. Ouch.

I rolled onto my stomach, clenching in agony. My sight went gray at the pain, and I nearly passed out.

The scarecrow held me there and pinned me. I stared as more of these branches and twigs grew and multiplied until my arms and legs were pinned against my body. It was like a damn insect cocoon.

"Let go of me, twigman," I barked, struggling against my restraints, but all I managed to do was let go of a nervous fart. Those twigs might as well have been made of steel.

"I like this world. Much more fun than in Storybook," said the scarecrow, still holding me up with its unusually long extended limb. "More variety for my snacks. Human flesh and salt. Nothing better."

"You're from Storybook?" I wheezed. "Do you know Tinker Bell?" I didn't like the fact that this thing originated from Storybook.

"Kill her," came a new voice. It was high-pitched, similar to when you inhale helium from a balloon. My eyes moved, and I saw the jester with its hands on its hips, its nightmarish face twisting. "The Creator wants her to die. He said to kill her. If we don't, we won't get our reward. You want that reward. Don't you?"

"Yeah," answered the scarecrow.

"Do it," said the jester, around a mouth full of sharp yellow teeth that looked like it could chew through metal.

"But I want to play with her first." The scarecrow made a weird clicking sound with its jaw like it was warming it up to eat me. "I like it when humans bleed. The ones that come to Storybook always bleed the most. All that glorious blood." Its features, if you wanted to call them that, twisted with malice, as though inflicting pain on others was its favorite thing.

"Hurry up, then." The jester shook its head, sending the tiny bells ringing. "I'm hungry for a fairy."

Tinker Bell? These things ate tiny, cute fairies? Oh hell, no.

I strained against the branches, but it was useless. They were unnaturally strong. "Don't you touch her," I threatened. "Don't you dare."

The scarecrow moved closer. It opened its mouth, showing off twig-like teeth instead of fangs, and laughed, which was all the more eerie. "We've been trying to catch her for years. Nothing tastes better than fried fairy."

"Very true," said the jester. "With a bit of salt. Everything's better with salt."

"Can't forget the salt," agreed the scarecrow.

I nearly threw up in my mouth. "I'll kill you if you hurt her. I'll fry *you*!"

At that, both jester and scarecrow laughed. It was the vilest, most horrific sound I'd ever heard, and I never wanted to hear that again.

The scarecrow lifted its head and sniffed. "Wait. What is that smell?"

"That was me," I told it. "I just blew you a kiss from my bottom."

It threw its gaze around my cottage, and then it made that clicking sound with its jaw again, reminding me of an insect. "I think I smell salt. Yes. There's salt here. After we kill the human, we'll take it with us."

"Agreed," said the jester. "She won't be needing it after she's dead."

I might not have been able to cross over to Storybook again to save Tinky, but I could do something about these ugly bastards right here.

I knew what I had to do. I didn't want to do it at first, well, because I didn't want to damage my cottage. But it didn't look like I had a choice.

What's the one thing that destroys wood?

Fire.

All righty, then.

I pried open my fingers, wrapped them around the branches that were pinning me to make sure I had contact, and felt them warm, as though blood pounded through those sticks. It was so gross, I had to stifle a shiver.

And then I yanked on my magic, and cried, "Accendo!"

Bright yellow and red flames fired through my outstretched fingers. The fire hit the branches, spreading quickly, like I'd doused them with gasoline.

The scarecrow wailed as it thrashed me around like a rag doll, but I never let go. I pushed out with my magic, harder and harder, thrusting out more flames until I felt a release on my neck.

I fell to the ground on my knees, coughing. I gasped for air, my lungs burning like I'd swallowed acid. My body hurt like I'd done a few cycles in the dryer. The scarecrow screamed as my fire continued to burn it.

Ha! I'd gotten it good.

The scarecrow flailed its arms as it threw itself against the walls of my cottage. The creature's screams were terrifying, and the smell of burnt wood, like a campfire, filled the air.

I smiled, happy to see it burn. Now it would think twice about attacking me again with its creepy-ass twig arms.

The scarecrow flung over the couch, and the couch sprouted in flames. So did my beautiful linen drapes.

My smile faded. "Oh shit." I leaped to my feet in a panic, searching for the fire extinguisher but then realizing this was a magical house. We didn't need those. House would normally put out the fire himself, but I couldn't feel him. The god had done something to House.

"Damn you, twigman!" I shouted. I didn't want to have to extinguish the scarecrow, not after it tried to kill me, but if I didn't, my cottage would burn down. With me in it.

The scarecrow whirled around, flapping its flaming arms. It tripped, going for one of my upholstered chairs.

"Not the chair!" I howled. Marcus *loved* that chair.

Crap. I needed water. I rushed out of the kitchen, yanked my magic around, tapped into the elements, and cried, Cata—"

A fist came out of nowhere and hit me in the side of the head. It threw me hard to my left, and if I hadn't planted my legs at the last minute, it would have thrown me to the ground. And then I'd have been finished.

I blinked at the jester. Seems like it finally decided to join the fun.

"Amateur little witch," snarled the jester. "You'll have to do better than that if you want to defeat us with your little witch tricks."

"Oh, I've got lots of tricks," I told it. "Can you put on eyeliner while driving? Or eat an entire large pizza by yourself?" I hooked thumbs at myself. "This witch can."

The jester cocked its head to the side. "We should bring your body back to Storybook and let the others feast on your flesh. It looks scrumptious."

Ew. "There are more of you in Storybook?" That was a horrid thought. And I was glad I hadn't run into them.

The jester's lips stretched into a smile. "Yes. Many more."

"Quick tip," I said, pointing my finger. "You should never reproduce."

The jester wiggled its fingers at me. "I'll make it a quick death. What do you say?"

"How about… uh, *no*." The jester just stared at me, so I kept going. "Why did your Creator not try to kill me himself? Is it because he *can't*? Is he weak?" If he had a weakness, I needed to know about it.

The creature shrieked in laughter and shook its head, the bells from its hat chiming. "The Creator is all-powerful. He is not weak."

"Then why didn't he kill me himself?"

The jester dipped its head low. "Because he wants *me* to do it."

My head throbbed with pain. "Don't mess with me, clown. I haven't slept in days. I'm a little *unstable*."

I could still hear the scarecrow's screams as my fire continued to eat at it. Tears leaked from my eyes as smoke rose and wafted into my nostrils.

Then I heard a peal of mocking laughter. "Nothing tastes as good as a small drop of pepper on human flesh," said the jester. "I like my meat rare, bloody. It's the only real way to eat meat. With salt, of course. Always with salt."

"Fuck off, you cannibal clown. No one is eating me."

The jester's shoulders shook as it laughed. "We'll just see about that."

It came at me, spinning like a top. The sounds of bells threw me off for a second. It was also disturbing.

Fury surged through me, so scarlet and bright that I could hardly believe it was mine. I drew in my will, focusing it on the creature and my sudden rage, and tapped into my demon mojo.

A jet of black demon magic erupted from my fingers. The jester got it in the heart. Did it even have one?

The force of it threw the creature back and up into the air. It was held there momentarily, wreathed in a halo of black energy. The jester thrashed and howled, its limbs flailing and kicking.

And then I brought my hands together.

The jester exploded, not in a mess of blood and guts but a cloud of confetti.

Confetti sprinkled down to my feet and covered the floor in a blanket of tiny multicolored pieces of paper.

"Not nearly as gross as I'd expected. But definitely weird."

I blinked and turned around. My living room was a wall of seething fire. If I didn't do something quickly, only ashes would be left of my cottage.

"Cataracta!" I shouted.

A curtain of water rose and crashed into the living room, hitting the walls, the couch, and everything aflame, even the scarecrow.

I heard a loud hissing, like pouring water over a hot pan. Mist rolled over my living room, and when it dissipated, all that was left of the fire were black, scorched walls, a couch, a chair, and the floors.

I exhaled. "Great."

The jester was in pieces, but the scarecrow was lying on the ground in one piece, albeit still smoldering. Red embers burned through its wood-like body.

I edged closer and, for good measure, kicked it.

The body exploded into hay: all over me, of course.

That's when the front door swung open.

"Tessa? Why do you have confetti in your hair?" Ruth stared at me, her jaw hanging open. "Is this part of your bachelorette party? Am I too late?"

I spat out some hay. "I need a drink."

CHAPTER

6

"**Y**ou smell like a campfire," said Dolores, eyeing me in the rearview mirror of the old Volvo, the engine's hum steady.

"That's because her house was on fire," laughed Ruth, next to me in the back seat.

"What were you thinking using your fire magic inside?" Dolores took a sharp left turn, sending Ruth and me sliding along the back seat.

"Uh, I was thinking I didn't want to die? I told you. The Creator, or whatever his name is, sent a couple of gifts. I had to defend myself." I had taken a shower, but I guess the air still stank.

"A witch *never* uses fire as a means of defense in her own home," said Dolores as she took a fast right turn, sending us all to the left. "Every witch knows this."

"I didn't." And I didn't appreciate her rubbing it in. Her condescending tone didn't help brighten my already irritated mood. The only thing that did help was that as soon as I'd defeated the scarecrow and the jester, House came back on, so to speak. Within a few minutes, he'd managed to "refurbish" the damaged walls, floor, and even the furniture.

I held my breath as I watched House do his thing. Part of me had been terrified that the god had killed the magical entity that was House. But thankfully, he'd managed only to paralyze him while his goons tried and failed to kill me.

I was sure the Creator would find out soon that I wasn't dead. Made me wonder what else he'd throw my way.

"But you got them. Didn't you, Tessa?" Ruth smiled proudly at me.

I matched her smile. "I did." She had on a blue blouse paired with a flowing skirt. Looking more closely, she'd also tried to match her eyeshadow to the same blue as her skirt, a pearly blue that she had smeared over her upper lids. Her fluffy white hair was kept in place with green butterfly clips resembling fairies, much like Tinker Bell.

The thought that the scarecrow mentioned he ate fairies, possibly wanting to eat Tinky, didn't settle well with me. Here I thought the most dangerous character in that world had been Aunt Beverly as the Queen of Hearts. I was wrong. Was she in danger? When I killed those guys back at the cottage, were they *dead* dead, or did they materialize back in Storybook?

I didn't have the heart to tell Ruth what I'd learned about Tinker Bell. I knew it would devastate her. She'd been a bit upset that I hadn't brought the fairy back with me, and if now she found out that Tinky might be in danger, it would destroy her.

Not to mention that Ruth had been slightly put off after barging into the cottage earlier.

Unfortunately, Ruth's offering-ritual to the goddess didn't work. Lilith never showed up after all her hard work. This explained why she hadn't heard the commotion in my cottage. She'd been too busy trying to get the goddess to listen.

Hell, if Lilith wasn't listening when I'd offered her some time with Marcus, I doubted any offers would tempt the goddess at this point. Lilith was making this hard.

I sighed and looked out the window. Passing cars flashed their headlights, and streetlights clicked alight as Dolores barreled down the highway.

"It's not over. He's not finished with me. He's still going to try." I didn't understand. If the god truly wanted me dead, why didn't he just follow through? The only logical explanation was that perhaps he couldn't, but that didn't make sense. What also didn't make sense was why this god wanted to kill me in the first place. I still couldn't figure it out. What the hell had I ever done to him? Nothing, as far as I knew.

"I wouldn't worry about it." Beverly pouted her lips as she stared at herself in the sun-visor vanity mirror. "It's fine. Maybe he just wants to play with you. You know how gods are," said my aunt, like that was supposed to cheer me up. "If he *really* wanted you dead, you'd be dead. Plain and simple. So stop whining and put a smile on your face. It's your bachelorette party, for cauldron's sake. Act like you're happy about that."

I raised my fists and shook them. "Yay." I should have stayed in Storybook.

Beverly turned in the front passenger seat to look at me. "You could have *tried* a little harder," she said, her eyes traveling over my clothes with a disapproving frown.

I looked down at myself, at my dark jeans and black top. "Hey. It's clean. I even took a shower. That's making an effort." But the real reason I didn't put in any real effort was that I thought this was pointless. And possibly dangerous. I shouldn't be going anywhere when I had a god on my tail. What I should have done was put my foot down and stayed home, that's what.

Beverly sighed. "I guess it'll work. You do stink." She turned around and continued to admire her perfect features in the mirror. "The owner gave me a *really* good deal on this place."

"Why? Because you offered him favors?" sneered Dolores. Then she laughed hard at her joke.

Beverly looked at her sister. "Dolores. I'm only going to say this once. Eyebrows. There should always be two."

Dolores's hands gripped the wheel tighter than necessary, but she didn't say anything.

"As I was saying, before I was rudely interrupted by a sasquatch..." said Beverly. "I used to date the owner. It lasted for only a little while because he had an incurable disease."

"Cancer?" I asked.

Beverly shook her head. "Stupidity."

"Good to know." A beep came from my phone. I pulled it out of my bag and saw Marcus's name. Funny how just seeing his name on my phone made my pulse rise.

Marcus: *Have fun tonight.*

Me: *Unlikely.*

Marcus: *What's wrong?*

Me: *That thing I needed to tell you about? It can't wait. Can you meet me after this party?*

Marcus: *Yes. Try to have some fun. I'll see you soon.*

After about a half-hour drive, Dolores pulled the Volvo into a neat driveway. A redbrick building with rows of neatly trimmed boxwood hedges welcomed us. A large sign above black double doors read Cape Elizabeth Ladies' Club.

"Come on, ladies." Beverly sprinted out of the Volvo like a band of bachelors was waiting for her inside.

I rolled my eyes, and with tremendous effort, I popped the door open and slid out.

"Here." Beverly came around the Volvo to my side. Before I could react, she looped a sash over me. "There. Now we can go in."

I grabbed the sash, trying to read what it said upside down. My lips parted when I made the connection. "*SAME PENIS FOREVER*? Are you crazy?"

Ruth snorted. "I'm glad I'm not wearing that."

I shook my head. "You expect me to wear this?" I was going to choke her with it.

Beverly let out an exasperated sigh. "Yes. Stop being a child. We all had to wear one before we got married."

"No, we didn't," said Dolores, giving me a look that said she felt sorry for me. Or maybe that was just the face of someone who was glad *she* didn't have to wear the sash.

I wanted to rip it off, but I knew Beverly would be upset if I did. She had been in charge of organizing this after all. It was just one night. How bad could one night get? Really bad.

"Let's go." Beverly grabbed my arm and hauled me through the club's front doors.

A tide of loud music came crashing over me as we walked in. The air was hot, stinking of cigarette smoke, booze, and some musk-like scent that reminded me of body odor at the gym.

A male who had muscles that would put Arnold Schwarzenegger to shame stood at the entrance. His arms were like tree trunks, crossed over his hard chest.

He blinked. And for a moment, his light eyes had vertical pupils like a cat's. Then he blinked again, and his eyes returned to their human shape. They traveled over my sash, and I saw a smirk twitch on his lips.

I frowned at him. "Don't even start."

"This is the bride-to-be, Bruno," said Beverly to the bouncer, stroking the big man's arm with her free hand. "Call me." She winked, squeezed his arm, and yanked me with her down the hallway, where it opened into a larger room. Red lights flashed and swayed in synchronicity over a small dance floor. The pull of paranormal energies prickled over my skin. My gaze traveling the length of the club, I spotted only a dozen or so females I didn't recognize, most probably human, some sprawled on red couches and only a handful sitting at the bar.

A hand waved, and I saw Iris and Ronin sitting at a long table. One look at my sash and Ronin's head fell back as he laughed. Yeah. I wasn't going to hear the end of that one. I spotted my mother next to Iris, applying lipstick. She reminded me of Beverly, that one.

A gorgeous woman sat across from them. She looked to be in her early fifties. Her dark hair was pulled back into an elegant low bun, accentuating her high cheekbones, perfect straight nose, and oval face. Her gray eyes filled with contempt at what she read across my chest.

My heart thrashed. "You invited Katherine?" Crap. I hadn't seen her yet. Hell, I hadn't seen her in months, and from the glower on her face, she didn't appear to be pleased with her future daughter-in-law.

Beverly plastered one of her fake smiles and whispered, "I didn't have a choice. Come on."

Music blared suddenly. My legs felt like they were made of steel as my eyes traveled over to the stage, wishing I could walk back out as six male strippers came out dancing and thrusting their hips.

Screams and cheers assaulted my ears—Ronin the loudest of them all—as women clapped. Some jumped from their chairs.

Holy hell.

The strippers came out only wearing pants, their bare chests gleaming in the lights of the stage, I suspected with the help of body oil. But that's not what had me rooted to the spot.

They all... had experienced their sixtieth birthday a while ago.

I blinked. "Holy crap. It's like Seniors Gone Wild."

Beverly beamed. She tossed her hair like she was in a hair dye commercial. "The Silver Fox Strippers. They were the only ones available on such short notice."

My gaze flipped back to the male strippers. "I'm not surprised. That one looks like he needs his oxygen tank."

"Wow." Ruth's eyes bugged out of her head. She was smiling like someone who'd never seen a group of half-naked men thrusting their hips in a sexual manner. Come to think of it, she probably hadn't.

Dolores's face had darkened a few shades, but she had her game face on like she didn't want us to think she was bothered by the scene.

Hell, *I* was bothered by the scene.

Ronin whistled. "It's like Chippendales, the golden years. I love it."

Beverly hauled me over to our table. "Here she is. The bride-to-be. Say hello, Tessa."

I raised a hand and gave a lame wave. "Hello, Tessa."

"You're late," said my mother. "We've been waiting a half hour in this... this place." Her face was screwed up like she was afraid touching anything might give her an STD.

I looked over at Marcus's mother. "Thank you for coming." *Thank you for coming?* How stupid was that? The wereape female looked like she was about to tear apart one of those strippers if he got too close. She probably could.

The fact that she didn't answer made me feel worse. I didn't want her to think this was *my* idea. Not that anything was wrong with male strippers. They just weren't my thing. Hers either, apparently.

"Sit." Beverly pushed me into the chair at the front of the table as Ruth and Dolores took their seats. "I'll get some drinks." She strutted through the tables and chairs, waving at some of the customers, and headed for the bar.

Iris leaned over and said, "Is this what you thought your aunt would come up with?"

"No. This is worse."

The Dark witch giggled and sipped an orange-colored drink that looked like a bloody Caesar. "I'll admit it's a little eccentric."

"That's not the word I'd use." More like mortifying.

Shouts rose, and I looked over to the stage. The cowboy stripper, because he was the only one with the cowboy hat, ripped off his jeans in a flash, like something I'd seen Marcus do countless times. But he wasn't my glorious wereape.

Cowboy grandpa stood in only a teeny-weeny G-string.

"I feel like my IQ just dropped twenty points."

Ronin whistled. "Take it off! Take it off!"

I was going to kill that half-vampire.

Another stripper with long gray hair and beard, let's call him Gandalf, followed his senior pal and yanked off his pants, showing off a midnight-blue G-string. Another one did the same until they were all on stage in only their tiny, tight underwear, gyrating and thrusting their hips.

Grandpas in G-strings. I could never unsee this even if I tossed bleach in my eyes.

"I think they're going to need some hip replacements after this," I said.

Iris snorted as she took another sip of her bloody Caesar. "I think they're in pretty good shape for their age."

"They are," said a wide-eyed Ruth. "Look at all those muscles."

"Oh please," said my mother. "They're nothing special. Bet they're spelled to look like that."

Maybe. Maybe not.

"Tess." Ronin leaned over. "How's it feel? Being that this is one of your last days of freedom?" He stared at the sash over my chest. "Says it right there."

Iris leaned over and smacked him on the arm. "Watch it."

The half-vampire laughed. "What? I'm the bridesman. I'm supposed to tease her a little bit. Just having a little fun before her life is over— ow." The half-vampire rubbed his arm where Iris had hit him again.

We really shouldn't be here. "I feel fine. I'm happy to be getting married to Marcus." I looked over at his mother, hoping to open a conversation with her, but she was glaring at the stage like she was contemplating leaping on it and putting all the grandpas out of business.

"Here we are." Beverly arrived with a tray of shooters. She placed the tray in the middle of the table. "Bottoms up, ladies."

"And bridesman," said Ronin with a smile. He was totally loving this.

"I hate shots." It was totally true. I didn't like hard alcohol. But when Beverly sliced a glare my way, I picked up one of the tiny shot glasses filled with clear liquid.

I was surprised to see Katherine pick one up.

"Smiling is free, Katherine," said Beverly, having noticed the wereape's attitude.

"So is having some class, Beverly," answered Marcus's mother. "If your dress was any shorter, it would be a belt."

Kill me now.

Beverly ignored her comment as she grabbed her shot glass, pretending like the other woman didn't exist. Katherine looked miserable. I guess she didn't agree to having strippers as a part of a bachelorette party. I was beginning to think that Beverly had organized what *she* would have wanted. Not what I would have liked.

I knew the two women had a history, something to do with Marcus's father. Looked like that history was still ongoing.

Dolores held up her glass. "To Tessa and Marcus. Never go to bed mad. Stay up and fight."

"To Tessa and Marcus," everyone chorused, making my face flame. God, I hated the attention.

Feeling all eyes from the club on me, I put the glass to my lips, tossed my head back, and chugged it. I winced. "Damn, that's horrible. Like drinking rubbing alcohol."

Iris laughed. "The second one will be better," she said, and I suspected the flush on her cheeks wasn't because of the half-naked seniors and more because of what she'd been drinking.

"… It's tradition in our culture," Katherine was saying to my mother, and I turned my attention to them.

"It's not *our* tradition." My mother raised a defiant brow at Marcus's mother. "I'm not having Tessa wear a secondhand wedding gown."

Oh shit.

Katherine's face was stone cold. "My mother-in-law's dress is made of the finest silk."

I opened my mouth to tell my mother to shut up, even though I agreed with her and did not want to wear someone else's dress, but I was interrupted by a waiter.

"This is for you," said the dark-skinned waiter, who was about my age. He placed a square napkin on the table and covered it with a glass of red wine.

"Uh. I didn't order this," I told him, thinking of asking him to take it back. Maybe Beverly had ordered it, knowing I didn't like shots.

"I know. It's from the gentleman at the bar." The waiter straightened and pointed to a man leaning on the bar. His black eyes pinned me. He flashed me a cold smile as he held his glass of red wine in a toast.

My muscles locked, and my blood went cold. He was no gentleman.

It was the god, the Creator.

Chapter

7

My stomach reeled as I stared across the club at the god that had just tried to eliminate me with his goons. His sharp features molded into what I could only describe as disdain. It was obvious he hated being here. We had that in common. He set his glass of red wine on the bar without touching it. I doubted he would drink anything from our world. Our peasant wine probably tasted like piss to him.

My tension had my blood pressure rising, and I pulled on my magic. His presence was a threat. Did he want to kill me here? Now? In front of all these people? Possibly. What did he care? He was a god.

"He wanted me to give you this," said the waiter as he handed me a card.

"Tessa? You've got an admirer?" Beverly was all smiles as she looked over my head and around the club. I didn't have to look at Katherine to feel the scowl on her face. "Where is he?" When I didn't answer, she bumped her hip against my shoulder as she leaned over me, trying to read the card.

Ignoring my aunt's proximity, I read the card. *WANT TO PLAY A GAME?*

Clenching my jaw, I crumpled the card in my trembling hand as blood pounded against my temples. What the hell did that mean? Was my life a game to him? Why did gods think it was okay to play with mortal lives? I hated this bastard. More so now that he'd shown up here when I had my family with me.

It meant he was going to do something to me. Right here. Right now.

"Who gave you that card?" My mother was staring at me, a curious frown on her face. I still wouldn't look at Katherine. "Tessa? What does it say?"

I swallowed. "Not important." My mother was already a basket case with the wedding approaching. I didn't need to tell her this.

Instead, I looked over my shoulder at the bar, but the Creator was gone. Well, I couldn't see him at the moment, but that didn't mean he wasn't here, watching, waiting, and enjoying seeing the fear on my face. I really hated this guy, god, whatever.

"Come to mama!" shouted a voice, pulling my attention to the stage. To my horror, I saw Dolores waving money at one of the strippers wearing a policeman hat who was thrusting his hips at her face. "Come and get it, big boy!"

Yeah, I could never unsee that either.

"Looks like Dolores is having a good time," sneered Ronin, flipping her his thumbs when he caught her looking our way.

"Who sent you the drink?" Iris had leaned over once Beverly had walked away, and my mother started arguing with Katherine over that wedding dress again. I didn't like the fact that there was even a question of me wearing someone else's dress, but I had bigger problems at the moment.

I looked at the Dark witch, seeing Ronin's attention on me as well. "I have to tell you something," I said, my voice as low as I could over the blaring music.

After Iris and Ronin pulled their chairs closer, I told them what had happened after they'd left my place. Of the god visit and him sending his cronies. Seeing their shocked expressions didn't make me feel any better.

"We should have stayed with you," said Iris just as Ruth's voice blared over the music.

"Take it off! Take it off!" she was shouting next to Dolores.

"Girls! Wait for me!" Beverly ran over to the stage to join her sisters.

I caught Katherine's annoyed expression and shrugged. "They don't get out much." At least my aunts were having a good time, unlike Marcus's mom, who could probably kill someone with her icy, predatorial expression.

"Doesn't look like it." Katherine looked away from me, almost as though seeing her future daughter-in-law was painful. I thought she liked me. At least, she preferred me to Allison, or so I thought. Maybe not anymore. At least she'd spoken to me.

When I looked back at Beverly, she was wearing the same sash as me with the same inscription *SAME PENIS FOREVER*. No. Wait. Mine had disappeared, I realized, staring down at myself.

My mouth parted. I didn't know how she'd done it, but Aunt Beverly had stolen my sash and was now wearing it like she was the one about to be married.

I laughed. It looked better on her anyway.

"And you think he's here? In this place?" Iris pressed her hands on her lap, her fingers fumbling, looking for Dana, no doubt, but the witch had left her DNA album at home.

"I know he's here. I just saw him." I handed Iris the crumpled card. "He sent me this. Take a look."

78

Iris's face was tight with anger as she read the card and then handed it to Ronin.

"And he sent you that card," said Ronin, handing it back to me. "Pretty obvious he's fucking with you."

I grimaced and started to tear the card into tiny pieces. "Yeah. I got that part."

"Still no idea who he is, though. Right?" Iris looked at me, her dark eyes filled with worry.

I shook my head and tore off another piece. "No. Ruth's ritual didn't work. I'm no closer to finding out who he is. I tried asking him."

"Did he tell you why he wants you dead?" Ronin put his beer glass to his mouth and took a sip.

"Didn't answer that either." I sighed. "Trying to figure out who he is and why he's after me is pointless. I should look for ways to protect myself instead." I looked between my friends. "And how to trap him."

Iris's eyes rounded. She leaned over and whispered, "Trap him? Are you crazy?" Though I could barely hear her over the roaring music, her lips signage was easy enough.

"Not like I have a choice." And not like I knew if that were even possible.

"You're talking crazy, woman," said Ronin. "You can't trap a god. 'Cause, well, he's a *god*."

"It's been done before," I said, remembering having this conversation with my father about Lilith. "I refuse to live my life looking over my shoulder, wondering when that bastard is going to strike. I can't live like that." I *won't* live like that.

Iris leaned back in her chair, looking a little pale despite the hot air in this place. "That's a very dangerous thing, Tessa. You sure about that?"

"Absolutely. It's not like I have a choice. This god... wants to play games with me. Until he's had enough and decides to kill me. Well, I won't let him. I'll beat him to it." I wasn't about to wait around until this Creator got bored.

I realized talking out loud about trapping a god where I'd just seen him wasn't a smart thing to do. He might still be around. But seeing his reaction to being in a crowded, mortal place, I was pretty sure he came to deliver that message to me, rejoiced at my response, and then split. Yeah. He wasn't here anymore.

"I'll have a chat with my dad when I get back," I said. Hopefully soon. I was pretty sure I'd seen enough grandpa strippers for a lifetime.

"I'll help you," said Iris, and my heart swelled at how lucky I was to have such good friends, knowing she was taking a risk in this plan—a huge one. "But you have one major problem. You need his name for this plan of yours to work. Without his name, you can't trap him."

"Yeah," agreed Ronin. "How are you going to manage that?"

"Lucifer."

Iris and Ronin just stared at me like my scalp had fallen off, wondering if my brain was still intact.

I raised my hand, glad my mother and aunts were all still occupied and not paying attention to us. "I know what you're going to say."

"After what he did to you?" said Iris, looking mad for the first time tonight. "No. You can't. You can't do this, Tessa."

The thought of seeing Lucifer again did make my stomach churn. The king of hell had taken away my magic once. He could do it again. "It's my only shot."

"At getting killed by this god instead of the other?" Ronin shook his head at me. "I think that shot went straight to your brain, and it's doing a little crazy dance in there."

"He's my only chance." It was the truth. If Lilith was ghosting me, he was my next best thing. "He knows who that god is. I'm certain of it. And he'll tell me."

Iris crossed her arms over her chest. "How? I'd like to hear this."

I swallowed, knowing full well what their reaction would be. "I'm going to offer him something in return."

Ronin leaned back, running his fingers through his hair, something he did when he was nervous and anxious. "This is crazy."

"Tessa. Can you hear yourself?" Iris looked like she was stuck between wanting to help out her friend and wanting to clobber said friend with her glass. "Gods are not to be trusted. They don't care about us or our problems. He'll probably trick you into agreeing to something foul. Like giving up your soul or something."

I perked up. "So you *do* think he'll agree."

Iris pressed her lips together tightly. "I hate to say it… but yes. I think he might."

"Hey, hey, hey." Ronin spread out his hands on the table. "No. I don't think so, babe. You can't agree to this. It's crazy."

Iris said nothing, and I could tell she was torn.

"It's the only way, Ronin," I told my half-vampire friend. "I'd rather owe a god a favor than always wonder if today will be my last. That's not living."

Ronin shook his head. "It's fucked up."

"Fine." My irritation flared. "So what would you have me do? You think living like that is normal?"

Ronin's jaw clenched. "I just… don't want to see you get hurt."

"Me neither. But talking to Lucifer is my best chance."

"Marcus probably hates the idea as much as we do." Iris watched my face, and then I saw her realization of what she saw there. "You haven't told him. Have you? He doesn't know?"

"No." And that was not something I was looking forward to. "I'm going to tell him tonight. He's supposed to meet me here later. I'll tell him everything." I would. I wouldn't hold anything back. Not this time.

"She's over here!"

I looked up at the sound of the voice and saw Beverly, Dolores, and Ruth coming my way.

Uh-oh.

Beverly grabbed my arm and pulled me to my feet. "It's time for your dance, darling."

I frowned as she pulled me away from the table to a chair that had been arranged just off the stage. "My what?"

Beverly pushed me forcefully into the chair. She pulled off the sash and fitted me with it once again. "You're going to thank me later."

"I doubt that."

My worst fears emerged as Gandalf-stripper came at me, gyrating his wizard hips and smacking his ass, all the while sending me sensuous smiles and licking his lips.

I was in hell.

Beverly cheered and clapped. "Give it to her, Lloyd."

Why was I not surprised she knew the strippers by their first names?

"Ah!"

Gandalf-stripper pressed a foot on my chair and leaned closer, thrusting his hips and junk in my face.

I was going to barf.

"You like that. Don't you, baby?" said Gandalf-stripper, running his hands down his oiled-up chest.

"As much as a bloodsucking tick."

The older man surprised me as he leaped up and spun around so his back was to me. And then, and then he bent forward. I had a full view of the buttocks area and the tiny G-string fabric that did nothing to hide the foliage around his meat clackers.

I was seriously going to barf.

Gandalf-stripper bounced his butt up and down and slapped it hard.

Holding my breath, I contemplated whether I should blast his stripper ass out of my face. But there were rules about using magic in front of humans. I didn't need to have my Merlin license suspended, not when I needed it most.

I could hear my aunts laughing and, once again, Ronin was the loudest. Okay, so they were enjoying this. Good for them.

"Ah!" I cried as Gandalf-stripper sat on my lap. "Get off." I pushed him off and cringed at his clammy skin.

Gandalf-stripper jumped to the ground, raised his arms, and did some bodybuilder pose, making the women in the club all scream like they were looking at Sylvester Stallone. Hell, I would have gladly enjoyed a dance from the older, hot actor and bodybuilder. But this was *not* Sylvester Stallone. Not even close.

I had to save myself.

I leaped from the chair. "I'm leaving." I didn't care if Beverly was annoyed at me. I was done.

"Oh, no you don't," I heard Beverly shout. "Boys! Get her!"

"What the hell?" I turned to see Gandalf-stripper and a handful of other senior strippers running toward me.

Shit.

I spun and ran. Having thrown myself away, not with any direction, I realized I was staring at the bar and not the exit. I doubled back and headed toward the entrance of the club.

"Stop the bachelorette!" a voice came from behind me, way too close.

Motherfrackers. What was Beverly thinking? This was *not* okay.

My heart thrashed in my chest. I could see the doors. Almost there. Ten more steps—

My face smashed into a wall. Well, not a wall per se, but a hard man-chest.

I stumbled back as the scent of musk filled my nostrils. I looked up into the face of a hand-some man with gray hair and a matching short beard, the owner of the man's chest I'd just mugged with my visage. He was huge, just as large as the bouncer, possibly bigger.

He was a hot silver fox and one of those damn strippers trying to grab me.

I jumped back and pointed a threatening finger at him. "Don't you touch me! You hear me? Don't even think about tickling me with your meat package, you man whore!"

"Tessa?"

I cringed and looked over my shoulder. Marcus stood behind me with a look of pure horror plastered on his face.

"Tessa," said Marcus, stepping closer. He gestured toward the massive man-beast I was still pointing at. "I'd like you to meet my father."

Oh fuck…

Chapter

8

"**H**ere, put this on." Marcus held what looked like an amulet. It was silver with a tree symbol cast in a circle.

"What's this?" I took the amulet, feeling its weight in my hand. A prickling of power came from it. It was quite beautiful. I wasn't one for wearing jewelry, but this I liked.

"It's for protection." The chief's eyes were crinkled, and I could tell he was holding a lot of his emotions back. "I asked your aunts to make it last night. After the…"

"After the scene where I told your father to keep his junk away from my face?" A flush of humiliation rushed from my neck to my face at the memory.

Marcus smiled. "You do make the best first impressions."

I slipped the amulet on, feeling a pulse radiating from it on my chest. "You think it'll protect me from that god?"

My wereape nodded. "I do. Ruth says it can not only protect you, but it'll also warn you if he appears."

After I'd left the male strip club, I'd hopped into Marcus's Jeep. Once I saw his father climb into his gray and black Range Rover Sport and drive away, I told Marcus everything. I'd expected him to be mad. Furious. But he'd been icy calm, which to me was worse. I'd rather know and see what he was thinking so I could better organize my comeback, but he'd been reticent the whole ride home.

"I need a walk," he'd said as he'd parked the Jeep. "Be back soon."

Now I knew where he'd gone.

He was in a better mood when he returned three hours later and climbed into bed, careful not to wake me. I was already awake. I couldn't sleep. Not when I knew he was prowling the streets of Hollow Cove, wanting to break things, especially gods' necks.

I knew he'd barely slept the night before. But knowing him, he stayed up all night to keep watch over me. My heart crushed as though a hand squeezed it. I'd slept maybe four hours, but not profoundly.

"Thank you." I leaned over and kissed him. He pulled back right away, turning his face, which did not make me feel better, or desirable.

"Are you almost ready?" Marcus walked to the front door, grabbing his jacket from the standing coatrack and the Jeep keys from the small entryway table. "Don't want to be late. My mother has a thing about tardiness."

"I'm ready." I'd made a real effort for *this* dinner. I walked to the mirror in the entrance and stared at the woman in the black dress with her hair half up and makeup, making sure I didn't have any lint or cat hair stuck to me. Hildo's fur was black, though, so I doubted it was visible. Sighing, I grabbed Beverly's borrowed black clutch and followed Marcus out to his Jeep.

The chief fired up the engine, and I leaned back into the leather seats, trying to calm my pounding heart. I didn't know why I was so nervous. It was just a dinner with his parents. I'd had dinner with his mother before. But after last night, the way she and my mother argued, and then having my face splattered against his father's chest, I wasn't looking forward to it.

"You're quiet."

"Your parents hate me." The memory of the dislike plastered on Marcus's father's face had my insides stirring like I needed some Imodium.

Marcus frowned as he looked me over. "My parents don't *hate* you. Why would you say that?"

"A feeling." A very *deep* feeling.

A smile tugged Marcus's lips. "You thought my father was one of those strippers. I get it. He's about the same age. Honest mistake. Not your fault."

I wished I could believe him. I pulled a card from my clutch, running my fingers over it.

"What's that? Is that a picture of the cottage?"

I stared at the card. "It's a card I made for your mother. I know she likes art. I thought I'd make something. Sort of a peace offering." Though she was an amazing landscape artist while I was more of a digital artist, I could still hold a paintbrush and paint. So I painted a version of Davenport Cottage on a blank card with all the trees and flowers in bloom. It wasn't much compared to Katherine's landscape masterpieces, but it had taken me all afternoon.

"Did you write something inside?"

I opened the card. "Just a thank-you that she came out last night." It was the least I could do, remembering how uncomfortable she'd looked.

We fell into a heavy silence after that. The notion that I had a wedding coming up, a mysterious god wanted to kill me, and now meeting up with Marcus's parents was all hitting me hard. I realized then how tired I was—emotionally and physically. We'd talked about going to Scotland for our honeymoon. I wanted to visit the Highlands and look for Nessie in Loch Ness after the wedding. But now, with this god situation, I wasn't sure we could go anywhere.

"After this dinner, we'll figure out how to stop this god," came Marcus's voice. "There has to be a way."

Yeah, with Lucifer. But I didn't bring it up. Now that I saw how distressed he was over the god-wanting-me-dead thing, I decided to wait before telling him I wanted to owe a favor to *another* god. Yeah, I sounded insane. Maybe I was, just a bit.

"I thought this was just going to be your parents and us?" My voice was high with emotion as I stared out the car window at the large, three-story, mountain-style mansion and the ten cars filling the long and curved driveway.

"Well, you know my mother," said the chief as he parked his Jeep behind a Mercedes convertible. "She loves to throw parties."

I felt like I was going to be sick. "Oh no."

Marcus killed the engine. "What?"

"I forgot to put on deodorant." I was mortified. How could I forget something as monumental as that? Judging by the sleekness of my pits, I was already sweating. Great.

"You smell great." Marcus gave me a lazy smile, his eyes filled with craving. "And that dress looks amazing on you. Can't wait until I rip it off."

I tried to smile, but I was pretty sure I looked constipated. "Let's get this over with." I slipped out of the Jeep and waited for Marcus to join me on the walkway.

My pulse quickened, my low heels crunching on the gravel path that separated a manicured row of roses and hydrangeas all nestled around perfect boxwood hedges.

Orange light spilled from the many windows as we stepped up to the impressive double doors with my heart in my throat. The sound of music and voices drifted through.

Marcus leaned over and rang the doorbell. No sooner than ten seconds, the front door swung open.

A petite woman in a dark skirt suit with a pair of black flats stood on the threshold. Her short, plum-colored hair gleamed in the light of the entrance.

"There you are! The happy couple at last. Come in. Come in." She ushered us with her hands, the corners of her eyes wrinkling with her grin at the sight of us.

"Hi, Audrey," said Marcus as he stepped inside his parents' house.

I'd met Audrey before. She was Mrs. Durand's assistant and a White witch. She was also charming.

I followed him in. A majestic, double-sided staircase split the mansion in half, surrounded by miles of crafted wood paneling, all polished and gleaming. The walls were decorated with Katherine's paintings. All the furniture was in a cabin style with lots of wood detail yet with clean, modern lines, nothing too unwieldy.

I wanted to say hello to Audrey, but instead, I said, "I thought it was just going to be the Durands and us."

Audrey closed the door behind me, and I could see her brown eyes crinkling at me. "You're nervous. Don't be. You'll do fine," she said, speaking fast.

My mouth fell open. *I'll do fine? What do you mean?* Okay, now I was really panicking. "Marcus? What is she talking about?"

The chief shrugged. "I don't know."

Before Audrey could explain what she meant, a figure stepped into my line of sight.

Mrs. Durand appeared in the hallway wearing a black and white dress that hugged her curves with a classy yet sexy vibe. Her long, dark hair was up, giving us a full view of her glorious cheekbones and facial structure. Her glowing smile reminded me of Marcus's. Eyes bright, they settled on her son without even glancing at me.

Things were going splendidly.

"Ah. There you are." Mrs. Durand came forward and hugged her son. "My strong, beautiful boy.

93

Marcus laughed. "Hi, Mom. Thank you for inviting us." He gestured to me. Maybe he'd noticed how she'd ignored my presence.

Feeling awkward and reliving a moment in high school when no one wanted to pick me to be on their softball team, I thrust my hand at her with the card and blurted, "Ish is frr you." *What the hell did I just say?*

Mrs. Durand stared at me, her features stone cold, and it was impossible to know what she was thinking. She took the card from me and looked it over.

"I made it for you." God, did I sound like an eleven-year-old kid. "I mean. It's nothing compared to your paintings, I mean. Wow," I said, with a laugh, pointing out the spectacular paintings of landscapes and horses, which I'd been lucky enough to have when she'd given one to me as a gift. "Who has the time to paint these days, am I right? Not that I'm implying you don't have anything better to do." Oh God, shut me up now.

"Come," instructed Mrs. Durand as she hooked her arm around her son's. "Our guests are waiting."

I watched, my face flaming and my armpits slippery with sweat as Mrs. Durand walked away with Marcus and disappeared into the living room area to the left of the hallway.

"That went well," I muttered.

"That was very thoughtful, Tessa," said Audrey. Was that pity in her eyes? "Don't worry. I'm sure she loves it."

"Sure. Especially when you say not to worry." What was I thinking, doing something so amateurish? Compared to her talent, I'd basically given her something even a five-year-old could best.

"Come. Let me get you something to drink. I think you need it. Red wine, I think, right?"

I let Audrey guide me into a room to the right that looked like a butler's pantry. She filled a glass with a bottle of red wine, which probably cost more than my monthly wages from Hollow Cove, and handed it to me.

I grabbed it and took a big gulp. "I'll be needing one of those again in about five minutes."

Audrey laughed, and she squeezed my arm in delight. "I was so happy to hear about your engagement. Marcus is very lucky to have such a clever witch."

I took another larger sip of my wine. "I think Mrs. Durand would disagree with you." And Mr. Durand.

I had to stop thinking like that. I wasn't marrying them. I was marrying their son. Okay, so I wasn't their favorite person. I could live with that. I'd just have to put up with them a few times a year. That didn't sound so bad when I was going to live the rest of my life with such a hot male specimen.

That was *if* I lived long enough.

The morbid thoughts of the god crept in, adding another layer of stress to my already over-the-top stressed-out body.

"Hey. Don't worry," said Audrey, mistaking my sudden anxiety overload as being directed solely at Mrs. Durand. "She's hard to warm up to, but you'll see. Mrs. Durand loves her son more than anything. All she wants is for him to be happy. And you make him happy. Happier than I've ever seen him."

I didn't miss the fact that she hadn't disagreed with my previous statement. I stared at my glass of wine. It was nearly empty.

"Here." Audrey tipped the same red wine into my glass. "Not so fast this time. You want to keep your wits about you."

I followed Mrs. Durand's assistant out of the butler's pantry to another room with lots of brown leather sofas, chairs, and dark polished wood stark against the white walls. A massive Persian carpet in deep shades of red, blue, and gold spread out against the wood floors. It drew my eye to the grand stone fireplace across the room, lit with yellow and orange flames.

A dozen strangers stood in the room, sharing happy conversations as they laughed and drank, all to a soft murmur of classical music in the background. None were my age, judging by the white heads and the few gray beards.

"Be right back," Audrey said as she hurried away and disappeared.

I spotted Mrs. Durand, her arm still locked around her son's as she conversed with an elderly gentleman in a suit, next to one of the fireplaces. She wasn't holding my card anymore. A flush of heat burned my face as I imagined her tossing it in the garbage.

I felt eyes on me, and I turned to find Mr. Durand watching me. His face was blank, and I had no idea if he was pleased to see me or if he wanted to throw me out.

I wouldn't blame him. I did say some rude things to him.

I took a swig of liquid courage and walked over. "Hi. I just wanted to apologize again for last night. If I had known you were Marcus's father, I would have never said those things."

Mr. Durand blinked, his big frame imposing, and even though he was older than Marcus, I wasn't sure who would win in a fight.

Feeling nervous that he wasn't answering, I babbled, "Beverly says hi." *Why the hell did I say that?*

I felt Mrs. Durand's head snap in my direction before I saw it twist like that girl in the *Exorcist* movie. Yup. Now I'd done it.

But then Mr. Durand's face spread into a smile, transforming his handsome features to utterly gorgeous, and I could totally understand why Beverly was still swooning over him. Mr.

Durand was a hot tamale. Though his eyes were green, unlike his son's gray eyes, their faces had the same square jaw and straight nose.

"How is your aunt?" Mr. Durand's voice was as deep and rough as his exterior but with a certain sophisticated quality. It was also the first time I'd heard him speak. Since he didn't look like he wanted to bash my head in anymore, I felt myself relax.

"She's great."

"Everyone. Please make your way to the dining room. Dinner will be served shortly," announced Mrs. Durand suddenly, and I had the feeling this was all my doing. Obviously, she didn't want me to talk about my gorgeous, single aunt to her husband. Whooops. My bad.

A rough, calloused hand wrapped around my left hand, and Marcus bumped his large chest into me.

"Stop flirting with my dad," he whispered, and my entire body felt like I'd been doused with lava.

"What?" I whirled around, but Mr. Durand was gone. I glowered at Marcus and whispered, "You shouldn't say things like that when your mother is shooting daggers tipped with poison at me with her eyes." I wasn't Beverly, but to her, I was the closest thing. I'd rather not be murdered by my future mother-in-law.

Marcus laughed. "I know. We all heard you talking about Beverly."

98

"Fantastic." I took a sip of my wine, wishing I could spontaneously combust.

Marcus leaned in and kissed my neck, sending tiny thrills through me. "Come, wife," he ordered, and I think I might have purred.

Voices bustled as I let Marcus pull me into the dining room. Most of the guests I didn't know were already seated. It looked just as sophisticated as the last time I was here. A table that could easily fit twenty was laden with pricey-looking plates and silverware that glimmered in the light of a massive iron chandelier hanging from the twelve-foot ceiling. Four centerpieces of a mix of white hydrangeas and red roses set in open-frame, wrought-iron balls sat over a white with gold etching tablecloth. Katherine Durand knew how to do elegance right. It wasn't tacky. It was perfect.

Mr. Durand sat at the head of the table like a king and looked the part. Marcus led me to the empty seats to the right of his father. I took my seat and stared down at my wineglass. It was empty. "How did that happen?"

"I'll get you more."

Before I could protest, Marcus stood and walked away, leaving me in a room filled with strangers.

"Did you enjoy your party last night?"

I looked up at Mr. Durand, surprised that he was talking to me but more surprised that he was bringing up *that* party in a conversation.

"Not really. But don't tell Beverly that." Crap. I slapped my forehead with the palm of my head. There I went again, speaking the one name that would have Mrs. Durand seeing red.

Mr. Durand laughed, and it sounded just like when his son laughed. "Hmm. Yes. I can see how that kind of entertainment is something she would enjoy."

I snickered. "You sound like you know her well."

Mr. Durand's green eyes held me for a second, and I flinched, feeling like a terrified little bunny looking into the eyes of the wolf right before he ate me. "Tell me about yourself." It was more of a command than a polite conversation where you ask a person to talk about themselves.

I watched as Mr. Durand took his glass of golden liquid and put it to his lips. "Well, I'm a witch."

"So I've been told. What else? What do you do in your time off, apart from seeing strippers."

The guests sitting across from me looked my way as my face took on another few degrees of heat. When I saw the tiniest of smiles on Mr. Durand's face, I let out some tension that had made my neck stiff. "I have my own business. Mostly book covers for authors, and sometimes I create websites."

"So you're an artist."

"Not as accomplished as your wife. But I guess you could say that." I cringed inwardly as I recalled the lame card I'd given her.

"I hear you and my son are living in a cottage. Right next to Davenport House?"

The thought of Davenport Cottage made me smile. "Yes. House gave us a smaller version of himself as a gift." When Mr. Durand's eyes narrowed like I was speaking a foreign language to him, I added, "The house created another version of itself. A smaller version. And we live there."

A body bumped into my shoulder. Marcus leaned over the table and placed a new glass of red wine next to me.

"You and Mom should come over and see it," said Marcus as he took his seat and leaned on the chair's backrest.

Mr. Durand pursed his lips in thought. "Maybe I will."

"Everyone," called a voice, and I turned my head to see Mrs. Durand standing at the entrance to the dining room. "Before we start dinner, I have a surprise," she announced, smiling as her eyes met mine. "A tradition that has seen many generations in the Durand family. One that I know my future daughter-in-law will embrace, just as I did when I was engaged to Martin."

Oohs and aahs erupted from the guests around the table, and then to my surprise, they started to clap. Was I missing something here?

I grabbed my glass of red wine and took a gulp, feeling a little light-headed from the previous glass and a half I'd already drunk in less than five minutes. I leaned over and whispered to Marcus, "What's going on?"

The chief shook his head. "No idea."

"Audrey, if you please," ordered Mrs. Durand, looking over her shoulder.

Audrey appeared in the dining room. She pushed a trolly with a mannequin covered in a white gown. The witch assistant set the trolly next to Mrs. Durand and stood with her hands clasped behind her back. Smiling, Mrs. Durand gesticulated with her hands over the mannequin in a way that would put Vanna White to shame.

Oh. Hell. No.

I gawked at the wedding dress that looked like it crawled its way out of the medieval ages. With so many layers of fabric and lace, it looked like a wedding cake. The long sleeves and invisible bodice were only made worse by the fur. Yup. White fur looped around the dress and up around the shoulders and collar. Yikes.

Knowing her, Ruth would have probably burned the damn thing right here and now. Davenport witches did not wear fur.

I knew this was the dress my mother and Mrs. Durand had been fighting over last night. And now, seeing it with my own retinas, I agreed with my mother. The dress, well, it was *horrendous*. It was the ugliest dress I'd ever seen. This was a joke. It had to be. No one in their right mind would wear something so atrocious. I'd rather go naked than wear something that looked like it could bite me.

"Tessa." Katherine Durand was all smiles when she looked at me. "What do you think?"

"How many white foxes had to die to make that dress." I laughed. She didn't.

As Mrs. Durand's face darkened, the guests at the table all sucked in a collective breath.

"Sorry. Bad joke. Too much wine," I said lamely, lifting my glass and trying to smooth out my comment. I shouldn't have drunk that wine so fast. My head was spinning, and the verbal diarrhea was coming out in spades.

Mrs. Durand took a visible breath to calm the storm I could see brewing in her gray eyes. "You don't like the dress?"

"Uh…"

"What don't you like about it?"

Everything. "It's a bit old-fashioned for me. Umm. Nice, though." It belonged in a museum.

By Katherine's look of pure fury, it was obviously the *wrong* thing to say. Was there a right thing to say?

"Audrey. Please take the gown away," said Mrs. Durand, still watching me. Her eyes flicked to Marcus, and I didn't need to be a telepath to read her mind. It was obvious. She was wondering what the hell he was doing with a flaky, ill-mannered witch such as me. Possibly wishing he'd picked Allison. She would have rocked that gown. She would have plastered on a fake smile and told the room how absolutely divine it felt and what an honor it was to wear it.

But that wasn't me.

I felt small and insignificant in my chair. My only break from Mrs. Durand's constant beatdown stare was when the waiters came in with our food.

I felt like a total ass for the rest of the evening.

And things didn't really improve after that.

CHAPTER
9

I was quiet on the ride home in Marcus's Jeep. I kept replaying the image of Mrs. Durand burning my card in one of her many fireplaces, a smile on her face. It couldn't have gone more wrong if I'd planned it. Mr. Durand was friendly to me, but that was probably just an act so his wife wouldn't make a scene.

Marcus had tried to smooth things over when he'd whispered, "You don't have to wear that," when Audrey dragged the mannequin away. But it was too late. I'd laughed at the dress in front of all her guests, a dress she had worn when she got married.

Good one, Tessa.

105

After that, I doubted there was any way to make things right with Marcus's mother. I just had to accept my actions and move on.

The only good thing about the night was that I'd barely thought of the god, the Creator, wishing me dead.

I clasped the amulet with my hand, feeling its comforting hum and letting it soothe my nerves.

"You okay?" asked Marcus as he took the next right.

"Never better."

"You look like you're about to be sick."

"Don't worry. I won't puke in your car."

The chief sighed. "I'm sorry you didn't have a good time. You can't let my mother get to you. She thought you'd love the dress."

I snorted. "How can I love a dress that's been worn before and looks like it could bite me and walk away on its own?"

"Wereapes do things differently than witches," he said. "It wasn't meant to insult you. My mother wore that dress on her wedding day. So did my grandmother."

"I got that part." And it looked it.

"It's just a silly tradition. You don't have to wear it. You don't have to do anything you don't want. This is your day."

"*Our* day. But I appreciate you saying that."

Marcus cut a look my way. "Did you feel anything coming from the amulet tonight?"

"No." I didn't want to give Marcus a false sense of security. That tiny amulet couldn't do much against a god. But it seemed to make him feel better, so I didn't push it. I was too tired. Too humiliated. Too upset.

Tonight had been a disaster. I just wanted to crawl into bed and pretend it never happened.

Why didn't I just lie? Because I was a lousy liar. Everyone would have seen that. It would probably have been worse to lie.

"You want to cancel the wedding?"

I flinched as the words caught me off guard. It's not like I wasn't thinking the same thing.

"No." There was still the possibility of speaking to Lucifer. I had to hold on to that. There might still be some hope left.

Marcus pulled his Jeep up Davenport House's driveway and killed the engine. I said nothing as I climbed out and dragged my ass to our cottage. Mrs. Durand might not think it grand enough for her son, but I loved it.

I pushed the door open, and my heels clicked to a halt.

Candles littered the floor, the counters, and the table. A few hovered in the air, illuminating the interior with a soft yellow glow. Rose petals sprinkled the floor like scented, lush carpets. Soft music filled my ears. An ice bucket with a bottle of champagne next to two champagne flutes sat in the middle of the table. Golden glitter fell from the ceiling like miniature stars as I stepped forward, a spell of some sort. It was magical. Beautiful.

I spun around. "How? When?"

Marcus stepped in next to me and closed the door. "I asked your aunts to help me out with this."

"I bet they did. They love stuff like this. Romantic surprises." And it was romantic. Lovely. My heart swelled at the effort and thought put into this. My eyes burned as all the emotions from the dinner escapade started to come up, but I pushed them down. I wouldn't let the dinner with Marcus's parents ruin this moment.

I looked at the chief as he crossed the room and went straight for the champagne. "But why?"

Marcus grabbed the champagne bottle and began to loosen the cage. "Because you deserve it. Because my girl needs a break every now and then. I wanted to do something special for you."

Huh. And here I thought it was the other way around, that *he* needed a break and something special for him. I hadn't even given him anything for his birthday, apart from traveling into another world and bringing his fine ass back home.

After a pop, Marcus filled the two glasses with champagne like a pro, not losing a single drop.

He walked over to me with the two champagne flutes. "Here's to our future happiness."

I grabbed one of the glasses. "To us." The thought of chucking down some champagne after all the wine had my liver spitting in protest. But I took a sip like a champ. I'd deal with the migraine tomorrow. A soft, fruity taste coated my throat as the liquid went down. The champagne was good. Really good. Top quality. "This is nice. Tastes expensive."

Marcus's eyes were full of emotion. "You're the best thing that's ever happened to me, Tessa."

I swallowed, taking a moment to downplay what his words were doing to me. "I know. And don't you forget it," I teased, but his words clung to me, sending my heart into fits of somersaults and jumping jacks.

"Now that I have you in my life. I can't imagine my life without you in it. I can't."

"It would be very boring."

"It's you and me, babe. Together."

I didn't know what to say to that, so I just nodded like an idiot.

Marcus smiled and chugged the whole glass in one go. He smacked his lips and set the glass down, took mine and set it down, and grabbed my hand. "Come. I have a surprise for you."

"Does it involve you naked?" A little bit of Marcus naked would wash away all my worries. Perhaps, even his parents regretting his decision to marrying me.

"Better."

I did a little dance. "My hormones want to know, dear sir."

"You'll see, madam."

I didn't have to wait long. The chief pulled me into our bathroom. And I had to do a double take.

"What's this?"

Our modest bathroom, now triple its original size, had a massive Jacuzzi tub that could fit an elephant, instead of the smaller claw-foot tub. Candles were everywhere, and the same glitter fell over us like tiny shooting stars.

"But… how? Did House do this?"

Marcus spun me around and started pulling down my dress's zipper. "Yes. I didn't ask the house, but your aunts did."

My skin riddled with goose bumps as his warm, rough fingertips grazed my skin. "It's huge."

The chief chuckled. "I know. I couldn't fit in the smaller tub."

I laughed as I realized we could have been discussing his considerable manhood, not the tub. I smiled as my dress fell around my ankles. "No kidding." Marcus was a very large, muscular beast of a man. If he tried to sit in the original clawfoot tub, it would smash to pieces. His fingers brushed against my back as he undid my bra. "And you did all this without me knowing?"

"I've got skills. I'm not just a pretty face."

The girls fell loose as my bra hit the tile floor. "Tell me about it." My lady garden pounded as he slowly pulled down my underwear, his lips kissing the curve of my ass and my thighs. When he licked the interior of my thigh, my knees buckled, and I nearly fell.

"You've been a dirty little witch," teased the chief. "So I'm going to clean you up *real* good."

"Everywhere?"

"Everywhere."

Yay me! "This is *so* much better than dinner with your parents," I said, my voice husky and full of need. "Hell, if I'd known this was waiting for me after, I might have put on that dress."

The chief laughed—a sound that I loved so much and would never get tired of hearing.

Solid, manly hands grabbed my shoulders, and I was spun back around. My eyes widened at the gorgeous and very naked man before me.

"How'd you do that?" He'd managed to remove all his clothes while taking off mine and licking me.

Marcus's eyes were molten as he met mine, sending tiny thrills over my skin. I wasn't firm or thin by any means. I was soft with curves and imperfections. And now, with a growing wine gut—my new addition. But the desire in his eyes at the sight of me naked made me feel like a ten. Hell, if he thought I was a ten, maybe I was. Who was I to judge the poor man?

KIM RICHARDSON

"You're perfect," he said, his voice full of need. "You're so fucking sexy."

I swallowed. "Yes, I get that all the time." I looked down at his hard, large manhood brushing against my thigh. I'd never get used to seeing that either.

Marcus caught me looking and grinned at my approval. He leaned in and crushed his full lips on mine, none too gently.

Yup. This was totally what I needed at the moment.

I moaned into his mouth as our tongues interlaced. He tasted of champagne and wine and something else that was just as delicious. I shivered as he dragged his hands down to my hips and then along my thighs. I slid my hands over his broad back, feeling his smooth skin.

"I missed you," he whispered against my mouth.

"I know."

The chief let out a sound between a laugh and a growl, which sent a splash of heat pooling into my core.

"You're gonna get it tonight," he snarled and dropped his mouth over my neck, kissing and licking.

"Will there be spanking?"

"If you want."

"And rubbing?"

"Lots of rubbing."

112

I gave him my bedroom eyes. "I'm a lucky witch." His kisses were like a kind of torture, increasing in intensity and making me lightheaded. I did my best not to drool.

"It's time for your *rubbing*," he said around his kissing. "Right now." His mouth was ferocious and greedy.

"But what about my bath?" I teased around his mouth. "You promised."

But all those thoughts evaporated from my mind as he grabbed my hips, lifted me, carried me over to the giant Jacuzzi, and set me on the edge.

I let my hand fall into the water, testing it. "A girl can get used to this," I said, a massive grin on my face. The temperature of the water was perfect. Not too hot, not too cold. Totally spelled to be that way, no doubt.

Next, he moved his hands and grabbed my knees, spreading my legs apart as he leaned in. "We could do this every night if you want."

"You're such a tease."

"I don't tease. I deliver the goods."

Sweet sassy molassey!

His eyes rolled over my naked body. I'd never been wanted in such a fierce, passionate way. Forget dieting and plastic surgery. If he lusted over me like this, why change? It meant I could have my cheesecake and eat it *all*.

I moaned as his expert fingers found my sweet spot and worked their magic, sending me nearly over the edge. Pools of desire ignited in my core, watching this gorgeous, strong man draped around me and seeing his own craving for me.

He thrust himself against me, driving my pleasure deep. I dug my fingers into his back, making him shudder. Wrapping my legs around his waist, I pulled him against me, never wanting to let him go. We moved together in a jumble of groans, caresses, and emotions.

I let all feelings of reality go. All my problems. The god. The wedding. That horrid dress. All of it. I'd deal with them tomorrow.

Tonight, I'd think of nothing but Marcus and me.

And did Marcus deliver the goods? Oh yeah. Twice.

CHAPTER
10

I woke feeling like a million bucks. I woke feeling like a ten. Hell, I *was* a ten. I mean, who wouldn't after my amazing, coitus-orgasmic night with my future husband?

Husband. It had a nice ring to it as well. Husband. Husband. Husband.

Yeah. It really did.

I was the luckiest woman on the planet. Not only was he incredible in the sack, but he was also attentive, clever, sexy as hell, and beastly strong. Those attributes checked off everything on my list and then some.

Feeling his weight next to me in bed, I turned around to face him, my amulet hot against my skin, pulsing, and I realized I must have slept with it.

My amulet was hot.

Startled, I sat up, my heart thrashing as I looked around the room. No one was there. Just me and Marcus and our huge bed.

I sighed. Guess the amulet was defective. I wouldn't tell Marcus. Not after the effort he'd put into ensuring I was safe after last night.

I lay back down. His eyes were closed, and I watched as his chest rose and fell in a rhythm. I felt lucky. I never got to see him in the mornings. He was always gone by the time I woke up. Judging by the sun shining through our bedroom window, it was surely past seven in the morning. I wondered why he was still here. Maybe I'd tired him out last night? Ha. Wouldn't that be something?

I reached over and cleared a strand of his dark locks from his eyes to get a better view of his face. It was such a lovely face. It deserved to be looked at.

A smile spread over his lips. "Morning."

"Morning, hot stuff." I snugged in closer, enjoying his smell. Was it weird? Possibly.

Marcus's eyes fluttered open and focused on me. "Are you always this pretty in the morning?"

"You bet your ass I am." *I'm a ten.* More like a seven, but who's counting?

The chief lifted his hand and rubbed it against my waist. Then he yanked me closer until our fronts touched. "I love your ass."

"Me too."

"I love your tits too."

"They aim to please."

Marcus flashed me a lazy smile. A growl emanated from his throat as he rubbed his big man-hand over my butt and squeezed.

"You're going to be late for work." I traced my eyes over his lips, wanting to devour them and experience the lovemaking from last night again. Those gorgeous gray eyes rolled over my face, inspecting every inch of it. I felt the world slow to a stop as lust filled my body like a fever.

"Taking the day off." He pulled me closer until I felt his hardness rub up against my lady V. "I want to spend it with you… in bed."

"Sounds good." I couldn't complain. Nope.

His lips found mine, and he kissed me. He tasted like cinnamon and something else I couldn't place, not at all like someone who hadn't brushed their teeth yet. Like me, most probably.

He pulled back. His eyes narrowed, and irritation flashed over his face, but it was gone the next second.

Oh no. It was my breath!

But the next thing I knew, he was on top of me, pinning me down with his hard, heavy body.

117

Again, I couldn't complain.

Lust-filled thrills erupted in my core as he grabbed my wrists and yanked them over my head, holding them easily with one hand while the other trailed down my stomach toward my nether region.

He lowered his mouth to my ear and whispered, "I'm going to fuck you. Going to fuck you hard until you scream."

I frowned, not used to him talking like this. Was this dirty talk? Not sure I liked it. Since we'd been together, he never used words like that. Sure, we had some dirty words in the heat of the moment, but this... this felt *different*.

His hand that pinned my wrists squeezed until it hurt. "You're going to love it."

I stared at his face, not recognizing him at this moment. "You're hurting me. Let me go." I pulled my arms to free them, but the wereape was too strong. My witchy warning flags soared, or it was my woman's intuition. Either way, something was off. Wrong.

His other hand reached down, trying to get to my secret garden, but I clamped my thighs tightly. It was a no-entry zone right now.

"Let me go, Marcus. You're hurting me. What the hell is wrong with you?" I searched his face, and when he looked at me, those were Marcus's gray eyes, but at the same time, they weren't.

They were filled with a deep hatred, a loathing, something I recognized. But not in him.

A thick panic rose in me. "You're *not* Marcus." Shit. The amulet. It had warned me. This was… this was *him*!

Fear surged, and I jerked, instincts kicking in as I tried to tap into my magic.

The god laughed. "I've told you before. Your magic is pointless."

I gritted my teeth. "So you waited for Marcus to leave, and then you what? Climbed into bed with his face? You twisted asshole." A god perv. Fantastic. Of course, these things only happened to me.

The god with Marcus's face sneered. "It's all part of the game, Tessa. Don't you get it?"

"Screw your games," I cried, bucking, jerking, anything to free my hands. I had a god in bed on top of me, pinning me down. This was not going so well. How the hell was I going to get out of this mess?

"Life is a game. Isn't it? Every day you play on a new field and hope to win. Obey the rules, and you live. Disobey, and well… you die. That's how it's usually played."

"I've got a game for you," I said. "Guess which finger I'm holding up?"

A violent light flared behind his eyes. "You're an insolent female."

"If I wanted to sugarcoat everything, I'd be a baker."

Irritation crossed his features. "I understand your obstinance. You've never played a game like this one before. But unlike the ones you know, you aren't allowed to know the rules of this game."

I didn't have time for his crap. I wanted him gone and off me. "Get off me. Get the hell off me."

The god looked down at me, lowering his mouth next to mine. "No. I don't think so. I'd much rather stay *right* here." He planted his lips over mine, and I twisted my face away, wanting to throw up.

"What the hell do you want from me?" No way did this god want sex. I mean, I wasn't horrible to look at, but millions of women were much hotter than me. I was nothing special. "You said you wanted me dead? So why are you doing this?"

Anger flashed over his face, Marcus's face, and it creeped me the hell out. "You need to play the game first. This is my game. And I decide the rules. Then when the time is right, I'll kill you."

"What game?"

He wrapped his free hand around my neck and squeezed. God-Marcus's face swayed as a dizzy spell hit me. Crap. I was going to pass out. I knew it would be the death of me. I needed to do something, and I needed to do it fast.

He leaned over again until his nose was almost touching my face. "Stupid whore of a witch," he sneered, his breath hot over my face.

"You should have stayed in Storybook. You shouldn't have come back here."

"I do what I want. You don't own me," I gasped, my voice hoarse and low, barely a whisper. My head pounded with the effort.

He moved his face next to mine and licked the side of my cheek up to my forehead. I gagged, shivering at the repulsiveness of feeling his tongue against my skin despite the hot pressure around my neck and face. The fact that he was still wearing Marcus's skin didn't help. I was going to need therapy after this.

"I've always wanted to know what you tasted like, the Shadow witch." God-Marcus smiled, showing his white teeth, Marcus's teeth. "What is it about you that's so special? Your magic is mediocre at best. You're average-looking. An average witch with average powers. You're a puzzle."

"Yeah, and what makes *you* so exciting?"

The hand at my throat squeezed harder, and my vision blurred. I wasn't about to let this creep strangle me in my own bed.

So what's a witch to do when a god has her pinned down and choking her?

The only thing she can.

I pulled my knees up and planted my feet on either side of his hips, and I pushed, sliding up to the headboard of my bed. The hold on my neck loosened. And then, with all my strength,

I kicked out and smashed him in the man berries as hard as I could.

I had no idea if a god's privates reacted like mortal ones. But I knew they did when I felt a release around my neck, and the creep rolled off me, groaning.

Without another moment to waste and relish in my new god-cojones-smacking skill, I scrambled out of my bed and slipped away. Coughing, I took deep buckets of air into my lungs, running out of the bedroom and into the hallway. Once at a safer distance, I spat on the floor, disgusted that his tongue had been in my mouth.

"That is *not* okay!" I was going to need to rinse out my mouth with bleach.

A thought occurred to me while I watched him squirming on the bed in pain. He felt pain. Real pain.

I planted my feet. I was going to fry his doppelgänger ass. I realized I was only in a thin T-shirt and underwear. At this point, what did it matter? I might have a real chance at getting rid of him for good.

I doubled back toward my bedroom, pulling on my magic—

A kinetic force blasted at me, sending me soaring across the cottage and crashing into the opposite wall near the entryway.

Okay. Ow.

I slid to the floor on my knees, the back of my head throbbing. When I looked up, God-Marcus was standing in the hallway near the kitchen in only boxer briefs, anger creeping over his face and his right eye twitching.

"That's *not* how the game is played!" howled the god as he stomped his foot, reminding me of a spoiled child.

I wasn't going to let him kill me while on my knees. Ignoring the searing pain in my head, and using the wall, I struggled to stand. "Yeah, well, I'm done playing your stupid games."

The cold expression on his face made him look less and less like the real Marcus. His guise was coming apart. "You're done when *I* say you're done. And I'm not done with you."

I chuckled. "You're barking up the wrong tree, *buddy*. I don't do well when people try to order me around. Just FYI."

His face stretched in a tight-lipped expression of rage. "I am a *god*!"

"That too." I shrugged. "It doesn't matter who you are or what you are. Doesn't work on me." It's not that I wasn't scared. I was terrified. My shaking knees were proof. But I was also angry. Furious that he'd put on Marcus's face and climbed into bed with me, wanting to have some rough sex.

Something was off with this god. His wanting me to play a game was one thing. What struck me as odd was his behavior, the manner of his reaction, his explosive outburst when he seemingly didn't get his way. And again, I got the impression of a pampered child. Obviously, he wasn't used to being told no. He seemed… unstable.

Fury crossed the god's expression. His posture was stiff, like he was trying really hard to stay calm, but it was a tremendous effort. "No. You will do as you're told. You *will* play your part in my game. You don't have a choice."

I shifted uneasily. "I always have a choice."

The god smiled an evil smile, and a chill fell over me. I felt like he'd gripped my neck again. "You won't this time."

Bouts of fear hit me. "Why? Are you going to open another portal and throw Marcus in it?" Was this his idea of a game? Would he toss Marcus back into Storybook? It wouldn't surprise me. He didn't seem capable of being original.

God-Marcus snorted. "Why are you so wound up? You need to relax."

I clenched my jaw. "Telling an angry female to relax works about as well as bathing a cat."

God-Marcus showed me his teeth as his lips curled into an ugly smile. "You are a meddling, insufferable witch, Tessa Davenport. And once you're done playing my game, you will realize that you should have left things alone. You should have never gotten involved." There was that deep hatred again, churning behind his eyes.

I raised my hands. "What are you babbling about? How about you help a witch and tell me why you're doing this? Unlike you, I can't read minds." No idea if gods could read minds, but I wouldn't put it past them. "I don't know what I've done. Tell me what I've done to you that's gotten you so mad."

"Mad?" God-Marcus shook his head at me. "I'm not mad. Mad is a mortal emotion. How absurd to think that I would succumb to such trivial sentiments."

I made hand gestures at him. "Well, you're acting like a spoiled child. What's that if not a mortal emotion?"

His fury at my comment was clearly visible in the wrinkles around his eyes and forehead as well as the tightness of his jaw. I could almost taste his desire to kill me right now, but he controlled it.

God-Marcus's jaw clamped shut. "You should have stayed in Storybook. Everything would have been fine if you'd just stayed there."

"Yeah, you already said that."

God-Marcus lowered his eyes. "You can't escape it. And before you die, you will play your part. You *will* pay for what you took from me."

I frowned. Surely I'd misunderstood. "What?"

The front door smashed open.

Marcus hurried in and halted, staring wild-eyed at his doppelgänger.

Well, this was a conundrum.

CHAPTER
11

Marcus, *my* Marcus, looked at me. His eyes rested on my neck, narrowing, where I was pretty sure was bruised and ugly.

His head snapped back, focusing on the god. He snarled, the muscles over his neck and shoulders popping as he shimmied out of his leather jacket and tossed it. He raised a hand and pointed it at the god. "You dare touch my mate? *My* woman? That was a mistake." The cool venom in his voice had the hairs on the back of my neck rising. The heat of his anger was palpable. He felt the threat to his mate, and he looked like he was about to beast out into his

King Kong alter ego to smash his massive gorilla fists at the god's head.

God-Marcus let out a derisive chortle. "Is that a threat? Though it *has* been centuries since I've had a good brawl, apeman."

"*Wereape*," I corrected. Couldn't help myself.

God-Marcus looked at me, that lazy smile on his face again, making me wish I could kick it off. "The stakes have changed. Now this will be interesting. I trust you won't object to making a few changes to the game. No? Oh goodie. This should be fun." He shook in delight.

My blood went cold at his tone, at the insinuation that this game would be the end of Marcus.

My wereape lowered his posture, looking like a bull ready to plow through his enemy. Marcus was as strong as an ox, a damn bull on steroids, but he was facing a god. Not an ordinary opponent. Not even a demon. This was beyond his skill. Yet he was willing to fight the god. For me.

He radiated an absolute confidence that he could handle any situation efficiently and firmly. It was like he didn't have the slightest hint of doubt that he could kick the god's ass. And that was a problem.

My insides twisted as panic flared up again, making me dizzy. I wouldn't lose Marcus. I had to stop this madness. "Marcus, don't. You can't fight him. It's not a fair fight. Marcus?" I knew it was pointless, seeing only the mad fury re-flecting in his face from the overpowering feel-ing of protection programmed in his wereape brain. It was like talking to a wall at this point. He was too far gone.

"Marcus," I tried again, my heart throbbing in my throat. "Listen to me. Don't do this. He's going to kill you." I knew Marcus was some-what resistant to magic, but he was facing a god, not a wizard or sorcerer. This was a whole dif-ferent type of enemy, one he couldn't beat, no matter how strong he was or how adept his fighting was.

"It ends now." Marcus shifted his body into a predator's stance. A fierce light backlit his gray eyes. He was terrifying on some deep, primeval level, and he exerted that fear like a weapon, us-ing it to stimulate panic. If I didn't know the chief, I would have bolted.

God-Marcus looked over at me and winked. He snapped his fingers, and then he was wear-ing the *exact* same clothes as Marcus.

Okay. Weird.

"Let's do this, apeman," said God-Marcus, a wicked gleam in his eye as he flexed his shoul-der muscles. A cheeky smile spread on his face as he waited, and anticipation brightened his expression at fighting the chief.

Before I could object again, Marcus exploded into motion and rushed the god. God-Marcus was a replica of the wereape, so he matched the

129

chief's strength, possibly more. It was hard to see which of the two was more skilled at fighting, and it was even harder to see which of the two was stronger.

With a fist, God-Marcus hit the chief in the chest. Marcus staggered, his balance off to one side, and I hissed through my teeth, contemplating throwing myself in the fight, but what good would that do? I had zero combat skills.

Marcus shook his head like he was shaking off the punch. He attacked, flexing and hoisting his big, muscled body. He made a fist and smashed it against God-Marcus's head.

God-Marcus stumbled back, laughing like this was all a joke to him. I truly did hate the bastard.

He caught me looking. An ugly smirk skewed God-Marcus's face as he blew me a kiss and then charged.

He hit Marcus like a massive sledgehammer, and the two fell to the ground in a blur of fists hitting flesh and growls. The wereape and god pummeled each other with their fists, breaking into a fervent craze of blows. The floor beneath my feet shuddered and quaked. Each crushing punch sent bile rising up in my throat.

It was the most brutal and primal fight I'd ever witnessed. And it made me sick. Before long, I had no idea who was who. The fact that they were wearing the same clothes meant I couldn't tell them apart. I couldn't help my

Marcus with my magic. I couldn't try my powers in the event that I'd hurt my wereape.

The bastard god did that on purpose.

The fact was not lost on me that they were destroying walls and furniture at the same time. House was going to demand another scumbag cheater to replenish his magic after this.

"What in the cauldron is going on here?"

The sound of Dolores's voice spun me around.

Dolores, Beverly, and Ruth clambered through the doorway, their eyes round and fixated on the scene. Marcus hadn't bothered closing the door, so obviously, they'd heard the fighting from the big house.

"Marcus is fighting the god, the Creator," I said quickly. It sounded crazy when I said it out loud like that.

"Why do they look the same?" Ruth's wild, untamed white hair matched the wildness in her eyes as she held a vial of some potion in each hand. She'd come prepared.

"Because the damn god thought it would be fun to disguise himself as Marcus." The memory of him choking me was still fresh, and I could feel the throbbing around my neck. I didn't want to have to think about what could have happened if I hadn't nailed him in the gonads. When in doubt, go for gonads. *That's* what it should have said on my bachelorette sash.

Beverly stepped forward to join me, her face in a frown as she observed the two men fighting, pummeling fist after fist. The sound set my teeth on edge. "Which one is the *real* Marcus?"

I sighed, the rise of adrenaline making me dizzy. But that could be because I'd smacked the back of my head on the wall. "I don't know." That in itself was terrifying.

"They're like clones. Identical." Ruth was shaking her head, looking as confused as I was.

"We can't just stand here and watch *our* Marcus die. We have to figure out a way to tell them apart somehow," said Dolores, and I felt a prickling of energy in the air as my aunt called on her magic.

I shook my head. "What? Is there a spell? A charm or something you know of?" If we could remove the glamour, we could at least separate them. Marcus couldn't defeat the god, so there was no point in this fight. It would kill him if we didn't stop it somehow.

Frustration crossed Dolores's features. "Not that I know of."

"Quick. Strip naked," said Beverly, pushing me forward. "The one who'll stop is the real Marcus."

Yeah. Doubt that. They didn't know that the imposter Marcus had tried to have sex with me just a few minutes ago.

"That's the stupidest thing I've ever heard," snapped Dolores, her deep frown accentuating the wrinkles on her face. "Only *you* would think of sex in a moment like this."

Beverly made a face. "Got a better idea?"

Dolores set her jaw. "I'm thinking. I need a moment."

"In a moment, it'll all be over." And Marcus won't come out victorious, of that I was certain.

Ruth rushed forward, waving her hands at the two men. "Hey. You! Creator! Yeah, you!" She waited for a moment, trying to catch a glimpse, a sign, or a reaction from God-Marcus. But the two men never looked her way. They were too busy pounding their fists into the other's skull.

"Didn't work," said a disappointed Ruth as she joined me.

"Thanks for trying."

"But…" Ruth's face screwed up. "Why does he look like Marcus?"

Because he wanted to bed me. "Just to trick me, that's all. Pretended to be Marcus. It's all part of this big game he has planned for me." Whatever that was. And after all this, I still didn't know why he had it in for me. Though he had said I'd taken something from him, but what?

Dolores straightened her back. "Well, he needs to be stopped. Before our Marcus gets killed."

I flinched as a fist made contact with Marcus's face, though I didn't know if the puncher was the real Marcus or the god. This was so messed up, it was giving me a migraine.

"I'm telling you. You need to get naked," pressed Beverly, thrusting out her chest. "Real men love curves. Trust me."

Not sure if she was implying that I was fat, but I was still not going to strip down to my birthday suit. Though I was positive if she were me, she'd already be naked.

Dolores's lips moved as she prepared a spell, but she stood there, paralyzed, just as I was, not knowing who *our* Marcus was.

Marcus landed a kick to the other Marcus's knee, sending him down. But he was up in a beat, smashing a great fist across the other's jaw. Blood flew out of someone's mouth. Was that the *real* Marcus? Or did the god bleed as we did? But then he spun, and shock-slapped the other Marcus's face.

Marcus's face, or the god's, rippled in anger as his eyebrows came together. A wild light danced in his eyes. Then both Marcuses hit with terrible ferocity, and I took a step back, though I didn't need to.

One of the Marcuses twisted and kicked the other to the ground. With his face deranged, he locked his hands into enormous fists and brought them down onto the other Marcus's skull like a hammer. Bones crunched.

134

This was absolute madness.

"Your amulet, quick." Ruth stuffed the vials she'd been holding, into the pockets of her long denim skirt, and then she thrust out her hand to me.

I'd forgotten about it, but I did what she instructed, pulling it off my neck and handing it to her. "What can it do?"

"Good thinking, Ruth," said Dolores.

"Strange how that happens sometimes," muttered Beverly.

Ruth pursed her lips. "More than you think." With a determined frown on her brow, Ruth whispered something to the amulet, brought it to her lips, kissed it, and then pitched it in the direction of the two identical men fighting.

I bit my lip as I saw the amulet soar across the room.

And then the strangest thing happened.

The amulet stopped in midair. It hovered just above the fighting men, and then it zipped down and smacked against one of the Marcuses' chests, glowing a bright orange as though a fire burned from inside the amulet.

"There's the bad one," said Ruth, pointing.

"Ruth, you are an incredible witch," I told her, beaming.

Pink colored her cheeks. "Don't tell anyone."

I laughed, but now that I knew who the real Marcus was, I was back in business.

The Marcus imposter jerked back when he noticed the amulet stuck to his chest. Surprise flashed across his face, but it was gone in a second as he continued to pound *my* Marcus.

I'd had enough of this crap.

Power touched my skin like a strong wind gusting—a fierce, mighty current. My aunts' magic.

Their lips moved in collaboration with their hands. Our clothes and hair lifted and carried in an invisible breeze. The hair on the back of my neck pricked at the sudden rise of power—a crap load of it. My skin tingled from its strength.

"Let's get him, ladies," said Dolores, though I was way ahead of her.

And this was *my* fight.

Just as God-Marcus stumbled back from a kick in the stomach from my man, I yanked on my demon mojo because somehow it fit, letting the cold, wild magic rush through my veins as I thrust out my hand.

Black tendrils of demon energy roared forth from my outstretched fingers and slammed into the Marcus with the amulet still stuck on his chest.

For a split second, his eyes met mine. I saw the surprise there and then the recognition of that power. My demon mojo.

I knew it wouldn't kill him, but maybe, just maybe, it would hurt like hell.

The bastard laughed, actually laughed, as the black tendrils wrapped around him, burning and seeping into his skin because we could all smell the odor of burnt flesh.

He twisted with unmatched speed and kicked out hard, nailing Marcus in the gut.

The wereape flew across the living room. He hit the wall with a nauseating crunch and slipped to the floor.

I froze, but Marcus was up on his feet in no time, and his eyes met mine. He was hurt, but with that insatiable fury that burned in his eyes, I knew he'd be back in the fight before too long.

I turned my attention back to God-Marcus. "You son of a bitch."

God-Marcus chuckled. "Boy. *That* was fun. But I must go now. You know. Godly things to do." He grabbed the amulet and pulled it off his chest, leaving a hole in the fabric of his shirt. Through the opening, I could see the imprint of the amulet and the tree branded into his skin. He clasped the talisman in his hand, and when he opened it, ashes fell to the floor.

"Destroying property is a capital offense." I liked the amulet, and it had worked better than I had imagined. I had a feeling Ruth could conjure up another one.

God-Marcus scoffed. There was a sudden blurry quality to his face and body, and then the next moment, instead of the Marcus impersonator, there stood the same pale, blond son-of-a-bitch god with that stupid cape.

He pointed a long, lean finger at me and said, "The game has already started. See you soon."

And then he disappeared.

CHAPTER
12

I sat at Davenport House's kitchen table, my fingers wrapped around a cup of hot coffee as I tried to calm my thrashing heart.

"Here. Put some of this on your neck." Ruth handed me a small jar with orange ointment. "And this is for your head," she said and tipped the contents of a vial with blue liquid that looked suspiciously like ink into my coffee. Who was I to object?

At the mention of my neck, I looked up to find Marcus leaning against the kitchen wall, glowering with his arms crossed over his ample chest.

I was more upset at seeing him fighting the god than finding the imposter in my bed this morning. Not that almost doing the *wild thing* with Marcus's doppelgänger wasn't horrifying. It was. But having witnessed the fight, not knowing if the god would simply kill him, had been a worse kind of hell. Not at all like the times I'd seen him pound a few card soldiers or nutcrackers. This foe was in an entirely different league, which didn't leave me with many options, if any, to get the god off my back.

Peeling my eyes away, I jabbed my finger into the cool mixture and dabbed some on my neck. Not having a mirror, I just followed the pain, which was basically every inch of my neck. I felt a soft tingling against my skin where I'd put the ointment. I could feel a pleasant, cool, soothing sensation, almost like Vicks VapoRub. Thank the cauldron for Ruth and her miracle tonics and healing ointments. I knew Marcus would be a little less edgy as soon as the bruises were gone. Right now, he looked like he was about to go full-on Terminator mode on the god's ass if he saw him again.

His face was blotchy and bruised. His right eye was nearly swollen shut, and his bottom lip was cut, but he'd refused Ruth's aid. Blood marred his torn-up knuckles. He hadn't said a word since the god had left as we all made our way over to the big house.

At least he was alive. It was better than I'd hoped. I'd thought for sure the god would have killed him just for the fun of it, another part of his game.

"Nothing." Dolores slammed the hefty tome she'd been reading shut, making me jerk. She yanked off her reading glasses. "There's nothing here about killing a god. It can't be done. I'm sorry, Tessa, but we must think of something else."

I sighed. I knew that was hopeless. How do you kill an entity that can't be killed? You can't. Which is why I kept going back to my trapping idea.

"So we trap him." It was the only thing that made sense at this point. If you can't kill the thing, at least you can trap it and keep it away from you. Or so I hoped.

"Without his name, it's not going to work," said Ruth, echoing what Iris had said. She closed the jar of the ointment she'd given me. "We need a name."

"Let's work with what we know so far." Beverly joined us at the table with a cup of coffee. She slipped into a chair. "He's male. Arrogant. And he likes to play games." Her green eyes flicked to me. "Right?"

"Right."

Dolores lowered her glasses to the table. "The only god that likes to play games is a trickster god. Like Loki."

"Loki? The Norse god? I didn't get any Viking vibes from him." But that didn't mean it *wasn't* him. What if Dolores was right, and it *was* Loki? It meant I finally had a *name*.

"I have an amazing shield-maiden outfit," said Beverly, leaning forward and giving me a sly smile. She chuckled and said, "It's me naked... with just a shield."

Of course it was.

"Let's say it *is* him," continued Dolores. "It still doesn't explain why he wants to play his games with you, Tessa. Have you ever conjured the Norse god by mistake? We won't judge you."

"Yes, we will," said Beverly, giving her sister a knowing look.

Dolores shrugged. "Okay, maybe we will, but it would only be for a moment."

"Thanks." I sighed. I flicked my eyes over to Marcus, but he was focused on a spot on the floor. "But no. I've never summoned or conjured any Norse god. Wouldn't even know where to begin."

"Hmmm." Dolores pressed her lips in thought. "True. You are still somewhat *undeveloped* with magic."

For some strange reason, I stared down at my boobs.

"But he did say that I'd pay for what I took from him."

142

Dolores's mouth flapped open. "What did you take?"

I shrugged. "Nothing. I have no idea what he's talking about."

"We have a plan of action," said Beverly. "We'll go with Tessa's plan of trapping him. Now that we have his name."

Dolores sighed and pinched the bridge of her nose. "And what if it's *not* him? Then we'll have a very pissed-off Norse god. That's two gods wishing us dead."

"Wishing *me* dead," I corrected. "He's not after you."

"Oh, but he is." Dolores gave me a pointed look. "Coming after you is the same as coming after us. You're family. Your problems are our problems. This concerns us too."

My heart swam with emotions at her comment. I didn't know what I'd do without my aunts. But I didn't want them to get hurt or worse.

Beverly drummed her red, manicured fingernails on her coffee mug. "We won't know for sure until we try. We could offer the god something in return if it's not him. What do Norse gods want?"

"Human sacrifices," said Ruth. "Lots of human sacrifices."

Yeah, I didn't think that was a good option. "Maybe not."

"Well, surely we can think of something," said Beverly. "Right? Dolores? Are you listening to me?"

Dolores gave her sister a comical look. "How could I? We were in the middle of talking about you... for the last two years."

Beverly glared at her sister, but she didn't add anything else.

Dolores pulled another heavy blue tome toward her and flipped it open. "Summoning a Norse god will be difficult, but not as much as trying to trap him." Her eyes met mine. "We'll need some time to prepare."

"How long?"

"Two to three days. Depending on the complexity of the spell. And let me tell you, it is particularly complex."

"But the wedding is tomorrow." I was hoping to do it tonight and have it over with so I could finally relax and have a normal wedding. Guess that wasn't going to happen. "So no wedding, then?" That would kill my mother. She'd been working so hard at getting everything ready and perfect for the wedding, not to mention that wouldn't score me any points with Marcus's family. I was already in the doghouse with his mother. This was a disaster.

"We should cancel the wedding," said Marcus, speaking for the first time, and we all looked at him. Was his face more swollen? "I'm sorry, Tessa. But until we stop this god, Loki, or whatever his name is, it's too dangerous. I don't want to take any chances. Not with you. Not with your aunts. Not when we have family visiting from out of town."

"So you want to cancel the wedding?" I couldn't help but feel a little hurt. It was stupid, but sometimes the heart had a mind of its own.

"Yes." Marcus's tone was firm, final. "I'll let my parents know. It'll be better coming from me."

"You're right." If I told them, Katherine would probably pummel me to death.

Marcus turned his attention to Aunt Ruth. "Ruth, can you make another of those amulets for Tessa?"

Ruth gave him a smile. "Already working on it. I'll have it ready in about a half hour. The metal needs to soak in the potion for a bit for the spell to take."

The chief pushed off the wall, his motions stiff like he was in pain.

"I wish you'd let Ruth take a look at you," I told him.

"I'm fine." Marcus walked over to me and kissed my head. "I'm heading over to my parents' place. I'll be back later. Let me know how the summoning goes."

"We will," informed Dolores.

I watched as my wereape left the kitchen and headed toward the house's front entrance, his gait rigid, and I noticed he wasn't putting much weight on his left leg. Even though I knew wereapes had advanced healing abilities, I wished he'd let my aunt help him. It was almost as though he were punishing himself because he hadn't been there to protect me from the god, Loki, or whatever his name was.

Which was crazy since it wasn't his fault. It was no one's fault.

The mumble of Marcus's low voice reached me. He was talking to someone. On the phone, probably. I sighed at the sound of the front door closing. I couldn't help but envision Katherine's disappointed frown when her son told her the wedding was off. Or maybe she'd be thrilled.

Damn. I had to tell my mother.

I debated calling her on the phone, but this was more of a face-to-face conversation. I owed her as much after all the work she put in. She deserved a frontal exchange, even though I knew this would hurt her. But I didn't have a choice. Marcus was already on the way to tell his parents, and I couldn't have a wedding without a groom.

The cake.

"Ruth. The cake," I mumbled, knowing how hard she'd been working on it.

Ruth flashed me one of her infamous smiles that made her look years younger. "Don't worry about that." She brushed it off with a wave of her hand. "You'll get your cake *and* your wedding."

146

"Not sure about that."

Ruth was nodding. "You will. You'll see. I have a good feeling about this. It'll all work out."

"I wish I could say the same." I wished I had some of her optimism. The truth was, I only felt buckets of dread that were constantly bringing me down.

The sound of bells reached me, and I turned my head as Hildo came padding into the kitchen. Tiny bells hung from his new green collar, and I realized he was the one Marcus had been talking to. But that's not what had me catch my breath.

Attached to his back with a harness were two large, green, sheer butterfly wings.

Oh hell. Ruth had made him into a fairy.

"Hildo," I began, unsure if I should go over there and pull those ridiculous wings off him, but he did look cute.

The cat cut me a look. "Don't. Just don't." He slogged toward the back door, pushed it open with his paw, which technically he shouldn't have been able to open, and slipped out.

I stared at Ruth. "Ruth?"

My aunt shrugged. "He loves it. It doesn't bother him at all. There's nothing wrong with dressing up your familiar. Every witch does it."

Beverly snorted. "No, they don't. Usually because they know if they try, their familiar will curse them. The poor cat looks like you just bathed him."

"He does look miserable." Poor Hildo. No sooner was he getting over his insecurities about Ruth replacing him with Tinker Bell, and she'd gone and made him into a cat fairy. Poor little fairy—I mean, *kitty*.

"He'll get used to it. You'll see." Ruth rubbed her hands on her apron. "He's just a little bit insecure about his looks. Who isn't?"

"I'm not." Beverly smiled, ran a hand slowly down her body, and said, "There's not an insecure inch over this glorious, sensuous body."

"I think I'll need a tetanus shot after that," retorted Dolores.

I rolled my eyes and looked at Ruth. "You're not going to keep those wings on him? Please tell me this is just for a little while. Right, Ruth?"

Ruth ignored me, walked out, and disappeared into her potions room right off the kitchen.

"She's going to lose him." Dolores flipped the pages of her book. "I knew a witch who kept dressing up her dog familiar with kid clothes. They found her body in the town's well."

"Hildo *loves* Ruth," I countered, knowing it to be true.

"Doesn't look like it," said Beverly as she glanced lazily at her perfect nails, looking for any imperfection that wasn't there.

Hildo would never harm Ruth, which I was confident of. But she was inadvertently hurting him, his ego. And I couldn't have that either.

Ruth reappeared in the kitchen as a beep sounded from my phone. I grabbed it and checked the screen. It was a text from Iris.

Iris: *What time do you want us to pick you up?*

Damn. I'd forgotten today was the day I was supposed to go shopping for my wedding dress, which was really whatever they had on the rack. Martha promised she could help me out afterward with some custom-tailor spell to have the dress fit just right.

Me: *Can't. Something came up. We have to cancel the wedding.*

I had barely pressed send when her text came through.

Iris: *OMG. Are you serious? I'm coming over.*

Me: *Okay. But I have to swing by my mother's place first. Meet me at the cottage in an hour.*

That should be enough time to revive my mother.

Iris: *Okay.*

"Here." Ruth slipped another amulet over my head. "It's ready. Though it could have used another few minutes to simmer, but it should be good."

"Another few minutes" and "should be good" weren't exactly the words I found comforting about a protection amulet against a god.

149

But what did I know of potions and magical amulets? Nothing.

I grabbed the amulet and rubbed my fingers over the design, feeling the tingling of its power against my fingertips. "This one's a sun. It's pretty."

"Who cares if it's pretty?" snapped Dolores. "It's the magic that's important."

"Right. But I still like that it's pretty." I slipped Ruth a smile, which she matched. I had a feeling Ruth made these from scratch, carved the metal and everything. Seemed we had more than one witch artist in the family.

Speaking of families.

I stood up and chucked the rest of my coffee for some liquid courage, more like liquid adrenaline. "Better rip off the Band-Aid," I said, thinking of my mother.

"You too?" Ruth showed me her teeth, her eyes wide. "Ooh, I love doing that."

"Uh." Not sure what to say to that. "I'm off to see my mother. You know, to tell her the news."

Dolores snickered. "Good luck with that."

"Thanks."

I needed more than just luck. I needed a miracle to trap the god so I could live my life in peace.

But we all knew miracles didn't exist.

Well, they didn't for me.

CHAPTER
13

The good thing about my mother moving back to Hollow Cove and my father having bought a house here was that I could walk to it. And I really needed to get out and get some fresh air to help clear my head.

But not before I *inadvertently* found a pair of scissors, *accidentally* fell over, and cut the strap that held Hildo's fairy wings. I left the collar on, though the cat wasn't thrilled about it, but he seemed genuinely happy to be wingless.

Ruth would be upset, and I hated to make her angry, but the poor cat had looked miserable. Ruth would eventually see reason. Hopefully.

That fight with the god and Marcus was still fresh in my mind, and every time I thought about it—every few minutes—it sent my heart pounding and my tension rising. The god could have killed Marcus, but I had the impression he enjoyed the fight and enjoyed seeing me going out of my mind with worry for the chief. It's like the god said, it was a game. It was all a game. And for some strange reason, I was a pawn in it—the most essential player.

All because I took something from him... but what?

I sighed and tried to shake off the mountain of trepidation that clasped around my throat, and I could almost feel the god's hands wrapped around it again like phantom fingers clutched to me.

I hated it. Hated that I had no control over this. Hated that I couldn't stop this god or protect myself and my loved ones from him. I had to do something. And I had to do it quickly.

I was so wrapped up in my head that I didn't even realize I'd reached my mother's house until it was right in my face. I'd climbed up the front porch, not even remembering how I got there. Damn, I didn't even remember walking over.

I knocked twice and pushed in. "Hello? Mom?"

"In here," called my mother from what I suspected was the kitchen.

I shut the door behind me and pulled off my shoes. The scent of jasmine, roses, and some other flower I couldn't make out wafted into my nostrils. I glanced into the living room. Jasmine, roses, orchids, tulips, gardenias, and Annabelle hydrangeas, all in different arrays of arrangements, sat in vases on the floor, the couches, chairs, and any spot that had a flat surface. It was like stepping into a flower shop. It reminded me of Marcus's romantic evening with the rose petals and that massive Jacuzzi. Good times.

"What's all this?" I asked as I walked toward the back of the house to the kitchen.

My mother's hair was up in a messy bun, her eyes focused on the strand of cherry blossom in her hand as she snipped off some branches with a garden pruner. More roses and jasmines were scattered on her kitchen island. She stuffed the strand of cherry blossom gently into a tall, cylindrical glass vase with crystals glimmering in the bottom. Next, she filled it with water and topped it with a floating candle.

"Wow. That's gorgeous, Mom." It was, and it made me feel like such an asshole now, seeing the amount of work she was putting into the wedding.

"Thanks." My mother leaned back and wiped her brow. "I think we'll put these as centerpieces for the guest tables. I have something else in mind for our tables. What do you think? You like them?"

"They're gorgeous. Really beautiful." They were. No point in denying it.

My mother flashed a smile. "Thank you, Tessa. Glad you like them. I've always loved arranging flowers. I used to want to open my own flower shop."

"Really? You never told me." My gaze rolled over all the flower arrangements she'd made. They were creative and quite beautiful. I could tell she had a knack for it and loved what she was doing.

A flash of sadness appeared on her face. "No. Well, I was busy with other things."

Yeah, like her idiot boyfriend, Sean. She was probably so busy with booking his band and whatever else his lame musical ass did that she'd dropped her dreams to pursue his. If I ever saw him again, I'd punch him. And then I'd punch him again because it was fun.

"It's never too late to open one," I told her. "You could open one here in Hollow Cove. I'm sure it would be a hit." I didn't doubt that, seeing what she was capable of with just these arrangements.

"No. I don't think I could," she said, dismissing me, but the flush on her cheeks said otherwise. "I think these'll go really well with your garden-wedding theme. Not too much in your face and gaudy like something Katherine would have picked. Bigger is not necessarily better. Sometimes simple yet classy is best."

I swallowed, dreading the words that I was about to say. "About that… I have to tell you something… and you're not going to like it." That was an understatement.

"Can it wait? I have a *mountain* of work to do. Not like Katherine's going to lift a finger to help. She never does. Gets her poor assistant, Abby, to do everything for her."

"Audrey," I corrected.

"Bet she hasn't given Abby a day off work since she started to work for that awful woman years ago. This is her son's wedding too. You'd think she'd be more inclined to do something instead of bossing everyone around. I swear… that wereape…" Her eyes met mine. "Did she try to force that *wretched* dress on you at the dinner?"

I let out a breath. "She didn't *force* it on me, but she made it clear she expected me to wear it." The thought of the dress gave me indigestion.

My mother made a displeased sound in her throat. "I knew it." She slammed the garden pruner on the counter. "The nerve of that woman. I told her not to. I told her my daughter would pick her *own* dress, not some old, raggedy fur castoff. I mean, who in their right mind would wear fur at their wedding?"

"I'm sure lots of people do."

155

"It's not hygienic. Probably full of holes eaten by moths. No. Fleas. That thing is crawling with fleas. It needs to be fumigated with insecticide. Might even have to wear a flea collar if you want to wear it."

That was gross. I was pretty sure Mrs. Durand had the dress dry-cleaned and kept it in pristine condition. But those were my sentiments exactly. I felt a tug on my heart that my mother was on my side and had defended me to Katherine. "She didn't listen."

My mother studied my face. "What happened? What did she do to you?" She lifted the pruners and snapped the air like she wished she could cut a few things off Katherine.

"Well, she did parade the dress right before dinner in front of everyone. How the hell did I know it was some wereape tradition?"

My mother leaned on the counter. "You don't have to wear that monstrosity. You hear me? Don't feel like you have to impress that woman. This is *your* wedding. She seems to think *she's* the one getting married." My mother guffawed. She pulled her eyes back on me. "Burn it."

"Ah. I don't think that would go so well with my future mother-in-law. And even if I wanted to, I can't. I don't have the dress."

"Oh." My mother's face stretched into a victorious smile. "You turned her down? Oooh, I wish I was there to see that look on her face when you told her to shove that dress up her stuck-up ass."

I snorted. "Go, Mom." It was nice and strangely touching to see my mother defend me. "I didn't flat out say that I wouldn't wear it… but I did laugh at it and made some inappropriate comments about it running away." Katherine's angry face would be forever implanted in my mind.

My mother blinked. "You laughed?"

"I did. I thought it was a joke."

"That dress *is* a joke."

I leaned on the counter for support, recalling the event. "She hates me now. I mean, *really* hates me. I think she would have preferred Marcus marrying someone else." Like Allison or just about anyone but me.

"Who cares what she thinks." My mother grabbed the glass vase and carefully set it in the living room on the coffee table next to another glass vase she'd already filled with crystals and cherry blossoms.

"I care. Marcus cares. It's not how I envisioned the dinner going. I don't want to start our life with his parents wishing I'd only been a one-night stand. They hate me."

"I'm sure Martin doesn't hate you," said my mother as she returned to the kitchen. "Men don't care about wedding gowns. That I know. They don't care what you wear. They only care about when they can rip it off."

"Mom." I was not going to have that conversation with her.

She looked at me like I was a daft child. "Well, they do."

I thought about it. "I don't think Martin hates me. He did talk to me at dinner. He was nice." One out of two wasn't too bad.

"I'm telling you," continued my mother as she made her way around the kitchen island and picked up an inflorescence of white roses. "It's that conceited woman. I don't envy you marrying into *that* family. But always remember, you're marrying Marcus, not them."

"But his family comes with him. Just like my strange family comes with me." Though Marcus had already become family to my aunts over the years.

Tension made my shoulders stiff as I watched my mother snip away thorns from the rose stem. "Mom. Put that down. I have to tell you something."

"I can listen to you while I work. I *can* multitask."

"That's just it. You don't need to *work* anymore."

Wait for it…

"What are you talking about?" My mother put down the pruner and rose slowly on the counter, her eyes focusing on me.

I cleared my throat. *Rip off the Band-Aid.* "We're canceling the wedding."

158

"What!"

Take off.

Color flushed my mother's face. "If this is a joke, it's not funny, Tessa. Really not funny."

I shook my head. "It's no joke. Marcus is on his way now to tell his parents. They probably know by now."

My mother closed her eyes as she took a few deep breaths, seemingly trying to calm the storm of emotions brewing inside her. Not sure it helped. "How could you *do* this to me? Do you know how *hard* I've worked!"

Here we go again.

"I know." I glanced around at all the flower arrangements, knowing these took hours and days to create. "I'm sorry."

"*You're* sorry? You're sorry!"

"I didn't have a choice. Let me explain—"

"I've been slaving away for days on these flowers. Not to mention paying for them. Do you know how expensive flowers are?"

"I can formulate an idea."

"Thousands of dollars. Thousands!"

"I'll pay you back." How? And with what money? No idea. But I would pay her back. It might take a whole year, but I would. And I was pretty sure Marcus would help too.

My mother froze, only her eyes moving as they settled on me. "Is this payback? Because of the times you say I *neglected* you? Are you doing this on purpose? Do you want to give me a heart attack?"

Oh boy. "No, Mom. This has nothing to do with you." I guess that wasn't the right thing to say, as her face distorted into something scary.

"What did you say?" Her voice was low. "*Nothing* to do with *me*?"

It was going a lot worse than I had envisioned. "It's not what I meant. Please, give me a moment to explain."

But my mother wasn't listening. She kept shaking her head, muttering, "How could you do this to me, to your mother?"

I knew I'd lost all hope of her focus, so I just dove right in there and gave her an update on the god's latest occurrence, and then the fight just now with Marcus. "So you see… there can't be a wedding. And it's not that I'm not grateful for all your hard work. I am. I really am. But it's not safe right now. Not for anyone. Especially my family."

My mother lost the wildness in her eyes, but her face was still red. "And your aunts can't help you with that? They keep going on and on about what powerful witches they are. Can't they spell him away or something?"

I'd forgotten that my mother was practically human when it came to magic. She didn't possess any magical abilities that I knew of, and she wasn't interested in magic either. "It's not that simple."

"So you're going to cancel the wedding because of some god? Can't you get married and then worry about him after?"

"He might show up at the wedding and decide to kill everyone, including you. I can't take that chance. And neither will Marcus." I watched as my mother hung her head, looking defeated. And that hurt. I never wanted to see her looking like that. "Mom." I made my way around the island and took her hand. "Listen to me. It doesn't mean we'll *never* get married. We will. This is just a temporary setback."

She lifted her head, and hope filled her eyes. "Like a few days? That would work. Yes. I could ask my sisters to put a spell on the flowers so they'll stay fresh. Not all is lost."

The hope in her eyes tugged at my heart. "I'll try." I doubted a few days would be enough. A month would be better, but I knew that's not what my mother was thinking. "If I can figure out how to get rid of that god, then yes. I think we could manage to postpone the wedding a few weeks—"

"I can just leave everything the way it is now," continued my mother, moving away from me and grabbing the same rose. "Nothing will spoil. Yes. That is fine, Tessa. It'll be just fine. I might need a few more days to sort out some stuff. I still haven't decided on *my* dress," she laughed. "Mother of the bride is a big deal in our community."

I doubted my mother cared much about what our paranormal community thought of her. She'd left that all behind years ago when she'd taken off with her human boyfriend, Sean.

"I need to look amazing," she was saying. "Better than Katherine."

There it was. I knew it was pointless trying to make her understand that this god thing would most probably not be over in a few days. But at this point, watching her now, it wouldn't make a difference.

"I'll keep you posted, Mom," I told her as she pruned off a few thorns from the rose stem.

"Please do." She set the stem down and picked up another. Her brows contracted, and I knew a thought had occurred to her. "What about *your* dress. Have you picked one out yet? You know, you won't get a great one since the wedding is only in a few days. It'll be whatever they have on the rack."

"I know. I'm actually going to go shopping with Iris." Just not today. Now that the shopping was canceled, I had something else in mind.

"Not anything with too much lace. It'll make you look too traditional."

"Got it."

"And make sure it's white and not off-white."

"Sounds good."

"And what about your hair?"

162

I shrugged. "What about it?"

My mother gave me a look. "Are you going to wear it up or down?"

"I thought I'd go bald." I laughed. She didn't.

"Be serious, Tessa. If you wear it up, and that's how I think you should, you can pick a beautiful A-line gown or a trumpet. But if you wear a strapless, you should wear it down to cover your wide shoulders."

"Thanks for the compliment, Mom."

"And not too plungy with the neckline," continued my mother as she pointed at me with the pruner. "You don't want to look like a slut on your wedding day."

"No. You wouldn't want that."

She waved the pruner at me. "And stay away from anything mermaid-like. Your hips are too large. You'd look ridiculous in that."

"Always such a pleasure, Mom."

My mother smiled. "You're welcome, sweetheart. Now, go away to hunt your god. I've got work to do."

Yup. My mother. What could I say?

"Thanks, Mom. See you later." I should have told her *god hunting* was not an easy feat, but she was already lost in her creativity. And nothing I told her now would make a difference. The wedding was all she was thinking about.

It should have been me. It was *my* wedding, after all, but how could I when my life was in danger? When my family's lives were in danger?

If I wanted a life, a wedding, I had to do something about this god.

Good thing I knew exactly what to do.

CHAPTER
14

"So the wedding's off?" asked Iris, kneeling on the living room floor next to me.

I sighed, blinking slowly. "It is." At first, I felt relieved with everything that'd been happening. A wedding would be irresponsible and foolish. But now, after I had time to mull it over, I started feeling anxious and wondered if I had made a mistake. Like putting out a bad omen or something. Would Marcus and I ever get married?

"I'm sorry, Tessa." Iris reached over and squeezed my arm.

"It's okay. It's better this way. A wedding now made no sense."

"How did your mom take it?" she asked. "I know how excited she was. More excited than you, I think."

I shook my head. "She didn't. I mean, I told her, and yes, she had a freak-out moment. But then she went into full-on denial mode, thinking the wedding would be back on in a few days."

"Maybe it will," said Iris, and she gave me a weak smile. "If this works, maybe you'll get your wedding in a few days. You never know."

I doubted that. Not the plan part, the wedding part. "I saw Marcus's mother's face when I laughed at that dress. Damn, do I ever regret it now, but it's done. I can imagine she's already packed up and left for her home in France by now, never wanting to see me again." She's probably calling up Allison at this very moment.

Iris shifted on the floor next to me. "Well, if that dress looked as horrible as you described, I would have done the same. No, I would have put a Dark curse on it."

I gave a small laugh. "It's worse in person." Why no one told Katherine the dress was horrid was a mystery. Maybe her circle of friends was too afraid of her reaction to tell her the truth that the dress belonged in a zoo.

"Urgh. And why make you wear it at all?"

I shrugged and said, "Some wereape tradition." That I had soiled with my insensitive comment, apparently. "She wore it. And

166

Marcus's grandmother wore it before her. Anyway. It doesn't matter now. Let's just focus on the plan."

"You sure you don't want your aunts to come and help?" The Dark witch surveyed my face.

"I'm sure. But if you and Ronin want to leave, that's fine. I don't want anyone to get hurt." In case I was wrong. I tended to be more wrong than right lately. I didn't need my aunts for the summoning. That I could handle. "I think I can manage on my own."

I flicked my gaze around the living room. The couch and chairs had been pushed back against the wall to give us enough room to work—not only for the summoning but also in case we needed to fight.

"We're not going anywhere," said the half-vampire, standing a foot away with his arms crossed over his chest. The glower on his handsome face told me he wasn't happy about being here and what I was doing.

"He's right." Iris looked at him. "We're in this with you."

Emotions swam inside my gut. Hopefully, this plan wouldn't kill them, but I still felt a little bit guilty.

Speaking of said guilt, I hadn't told Marcus of this plan of mine either. I couldn't bring myself to tell him. It was wrong *not* to tell him. I got that. But he couldn't do anything to help or protect me from this god.

The fact that he hadn't been able to protect me this morning was tearing him up. I could see it in his face and his posture. He was silent. Furious. More at himself. But it wasn't his fault. No one expected this to happen. How could anyone have guessed a god would suddenly appear and want to kill me?

Worse, this god, this Loki or whoever he was, could transform himself into anyone at any time. He could morph into Dolores, Iris, and even my mother, and I wouldn't be able to tell the difference. That in itself was really disturbing, but it was all just a game to him. And I knew he'd never stop playing until I put a stop to it.

"I have to do this."

Iris nodded. "I know. I would do the same if it was me."

"I still think trapping Loki is a bad idea." Ronin's face was stone cold, his body stiff with tension. "He's a *freaking* god."

"Yes... you said." If I was keeping count, it was the fifth time as of now.

He set his jaw. "And I'm saying it again. I think it's a *really* bad idea. Summoning your BFF Lilith is one thing. But this guy? Who knows what to expect? Your little drawings might not work."

"They'll work." Cauldron, I hoped so because it was my only plan.

Ronin managed to inject his voice with profound skepticism as he said, "But you don't know if that's true. How can you? You've never done this."

I sighed and looked up at him. "It's the only plan I have," I said, irritation flaring. I knew my half-vampire friend was only worried for me, so I couldn't stay mad. When they'd arrived a few minutes after me, I'd told them of my plan to summon the Norse god, Loki, in hopes of trapping him. Then I'd figure out what to do with him.

I recalled a conversation with my father about trapping Lilith and needing to know where to put her once she was trapped. Same thing for Loki. I had to find his cage, his prison, so I could stuff him into it. But I'd already figured out that part. I would ask my pal Jack, the Soul Collector, to lend me one of his pocket dimensions to stuff the Norse god in. Jack would agree. I know he would. But in the case that he wouldn't, that's why I needed to keep the god trapped until plan B surfaced. It hadn't surfaced yet.

"That god, that trickster god, or whatever, did some pretty shitty things." Ronin's face darkened as I was sure he recalled his own dealings with the portals. The voices tricked him into thinking his dead mother was calling him, and he almost went through.

"I almost lost Beverly and Marcus. I can't let that happen again. I can't live constantly wondering if he'll kill me today, or in a month, or a year. It ends now." Anger resurfaced at the mockery I'd seen in the god's eyes.

"What happens if it's *not* Loki? If he's not the one doing this to you? Have you thought about that?" Ronin watched me. The muscle along his jaw tightened with tension. "What are you going to do with him? Say, oops, sorry, my bad. And hope he doesn't kill us all?"

I had thought about it. "He *can't* kill us. He'll be trapped." I pointed to the chalk triangle-shaped sigil I had drawn, hating that my finger was trembling.

"For now," said the half-vampire, not convinced. "You can't trap him forever. And take a guess what'll he'll do once he's free. You want me to tell you?"

Fear tightened my gut. "I know what you're saying. And I hear you. But there's a chance that it's *him*. That this Loki impersonated Marcus this morning because… apparently, I took something from him. But I have to take this chance. I have to know. You would, too, if you saw him fighting Marcus today. You'd be on your knees right now if it was Iris."

A smile pulled the corners of Ronin's lips. "That's where she likes me best. On my knees."

I rolled my eyes and saw the blush rise on Iris's face. "You guys." I gave a nervous laugh.

Because Ronin was right. There was a chance the Norse god, Loki, wasn't the one playing games. Wasn't the one who'd created Storybook and the portals. And I was pretty sure the Norse god would be furious at being summoned and trapped by a mortal witch.

Part of me thought of going over to the big house and asking my aunts for help. But the other part knew they would convince me to stop what I was doing. Then where would that leave me? Exactly where I was before. Scared. Angry. A pawn in this god's game. And I'd had enough of his games.

"Maybe I should have borrowed Beverly's Viking maiden costume," I muttered, sweat trickling down my back, my heart pounding as nerves rose, tightening my gut.

Iris blinked at me. "She has a *Viking* costume? Really?"

I could tell the idea of a Viking costume intrigued her. Maybe Ronin and Iris liked to *dress up* their lovemaking. "Yup. Just the shield and her naked."

Iris laughed. "That doesn't surprise me."

"Me neither." I imagined Aunt Beverly had a string of those *types* of costumes in her closet. And she probably looked damn gorgeous in all of them.

"I got it," said Ronin, his expression serious. "I think you should do it. Definitely more appealing to the god if you *were* naked."

"*Ronin*," hissed Iris.

"Uh… it was just a joke." Wasn't it?

The half-vampire raised his hands in surrender. "No. I'm serious. I'm just saying if he appears here, and one of us is naked, it'll go smoother. I know these things."

"Ronin, seriously?" Iris was glaring at her boyfriend. "This is not the time."

"I don't know if the god prefers women or men," he continued, ignoring the Dark witch. "And I'm all for getting naked."

"We know," I said with a smile.

"But if he's into women, a naked Tess is better than a clothed one. Trust me. You should strip."

I rubbed my eyes. "I can't believe we're having this discussion." I couldn't believe I was *thinking* about it. I was losing my mind.

"Me neither," grumbled Iris. I could understand her not wanting me to strip naked in front of her boyfriend, not that I thought Ronin was implying anything sexual with me. He was genuinely trying to find ways for me not to get killed by the god.

But Ronin wasn't letting his idea go. "We've all heard the stories of pagan gods bedding mortal women. It's happened before. So we know there's interest there."

I pursed my lips in thought. "I'm interested in peanut butter, but you don't see me getting naked when I eat it."

"It'll be a distraction, at least," said the half-vampire.

"Maybe." I wasn't sure Loki would like the naked version of me. And if he'd been in my bed this morning, he'd already seen me half-naked. "But I'm not about to try it." I'd rather be fully clothed if something bad should happen. I didn't want to go running through the streets of Hollow Cove in my X-rated suit. No one wanted to see that.

"Fine." Ronin's face lit up. "You want *me* to get naked?"

"No," chorused Iris and me, making the half-vampire laugh, and laugh hard.

I rubbed my temples and took a breath. This was a disaster. If I couldn't focus soon, it would never work. If I was sloppy because I was distracted, that could end very badly for me, like the god I thought was trapped in his triangle was not trapped at all.

A nagging part of me still didn't believe it was Loki. Seemed too easy. But I needed to find out. He was a trickster god, after all, and if it wasn't him, I was going to ask him who else it could be. Might as well keep the conversation going while he was trapped and forced to answer since he'd be bound to my will. And then… then hope he wouldn't kill us all.

"What's next?" asked Iris.

With quivering fingers, I grabbed a heavy red tome that I had stolen from Dolores's private collection and flipped to the page where I'd put a bookmark earlier. Then I set the book down next to me.

"We're going to do it differently than my aunts. We're not going to do a ritual. We're going to summon the god like we would a demon. And trap him in the triangle. So that's good." At least, that's what it said in Dolores's book.

"That's *not* good," muttered Ronin.

"We need to make protection circles for all of us," I instructed and grabbed the same chalk I used to draw the sizeable triangle-shaped sigil, knowing that Loki would be pissed. "I'll start." Since this was my featherbrain plan, I wrote the name Loki in the center of the triangle, where the summoned god would appear.

Next, I drew a Circle of Solomon to protect the conjurers: me, Iris, and Ronin, though Ronin was just the muscle in case things went sideways. I finished the circle with five archangel names in Latin around it within a coiled serpent.

After I'd done my circle, I handed the chalk to Iris. I watched silently as the Dark witch drew her protection circle about three feet behind the triangle and then crab-crawled over to Ronin and drew his.

"Do I really need this?" asked the half-vampire.

"Yes." Iris closed the circle. "You need to step inside. Now."

Ronin flashed his girlfriend a sensuous grin. "Love it when you give me orders. Love it more when you talk dirty *while* giving me orders."

I laughed. Damn. I needed to focus. I was starting to second-guess my plan of including Ronin. But he would never let Iris conjure a Norse god with me, without him.

Once Ronin stepped into his circle of protection, Iris turned back to me. "We're ready when you are," she said, handing me back my chalk.

"Okay." I took the chalk and stuffed it in my pocket. Then I grabbed the old book and stepped into my circle. Focusing, I drew in my will and concentrated on the incoming energy soaring through me from the elements.

"You ready?" I asked, glancing over at the Dark witch.

"Ready."

I channeled the magic, letting their powers spill into me while I read the incantation. "I conjure you, Loki, god of mischief, to be subject of our will," we chanted in unison. "We invoke you, Loki, god of mischief in the space—"

"Stop!"

I jerked, and the tome I'd been holding flew out of my hands and sailed across the room. I hadn't done that.

I turned to the sound of the voice.

Lilith, goddess of the Netherworld, stood behind me with a murderous expression on her face.

175

CHAPTER
15

"Lilith?" I stared at the goddess.

Her red eyes flared with anger. She looked… she looked like *she* wanted to kill me.

She still had her preferred thirtysomething look with waves of glorious red hair that shimmered like it was on fire. With her designer jeans, short black leather jacket, and knee-high boots, she looked more like she was going out to a club than getting ready to whip my ass.

Lilith, the goddess of hell, hadn't shown up when I'd called her multiple times. Even when Ruth had performed a ritual to summon her, she'd refused to show. And now? Here she was,

right before we finished invoking the god Loki.
Interesting.

Iris sucked in a breath, and from the corner of
my eye, I could see the Dark witch stiffen into a
witch Popsicle. She was afraid. And rightly so.
A sensible person should always be afraid when
a goddess or god showed up unannounced.

But I never said I was sensible.

Ronin cursed. Obviously, he was just as surprised as I was to see the goddess, and he
stepped out of his protection circle and crushed
his body against Iris, using it to shield her.

I shook my head. "You show up now?" I narrowed my eyes at her, but she looked more livid
than I was at the moment, which was a dangerous thing. I didn't care. She stopped the summoning for a reason, and I wanted to know
why. "Why didn't you come sooner? I called
you, you know." Though I wasn't sure that was
the correct term for just calling out a goddess
and expecting her to appear. "Ruth even performed a ritual last night for you. There was
music and dancing. You didn't show."

The goddess raised a perfect brow. "Pagan
rituals aren't my forte. Pagan orgies are."

Gross. But I knew she'd said that on purpose
to throw me off.

"I'm a goddess. I have things to do." She
lacked her usual lazy and bored manner at all
things mundane. She was focused. Alert. One

could even say on edge. I didn't like it. But it spoke volumes.

"I didn't believe I'd ever see you again."

The goddess dipped her head. "Goddesses believe in goddesses. That is to say, power and domination, and then some more power."

"But you show up now," I said, holding her focus. "Right before we could *finish* the summoning." Things were slowly starting to fit together. The way she looked… nervous? Scared? Lilith was involved in this somehow, involved with Loki. "Why? Why don't you want us to finish?"

A lazy smile pulled her lips. "Witches shouldn't be dabbling in things they don't understand. It could end very *badly* for you." She dragged a finger across her neck, smirking.

I wanted to smack the smirk off her stupid goddess face.

"So make me understand. Why? Why didn't you want us to summon Loki? What does Loki have to do with you?"

Lilith stepped closer, and with a swipe of her hand, the summing triangle and the protection circles vanished. So did Dolores's book. Ah, hell. Dolores was going to be pissed.

"Nice." I glared at the goddess. "Why the hell did you do that? That wasn't even my book."

"Dolores won't be happy," muttered Iris.

The goddess walked around us and then snapped her fingers. With a gust of energy, followed by the scent of spices, my living-room set pulled from the wall where I'd pushed it earlier. Everything came forward, placing themselves just as they were before the summoning, like invisible home stagers were arranging a living room. Once the couch, love seat, coffee table, and side tables were all in their proper places, Lilith sprawled out on the couch like she owned the world. Guess she did, in a way.

Glowering, I walked up to her until I was facing her. "A god wants to kill me. Possibly Loki. I've asked for your help, and you've ignored me. I'm starting to think you want me to die."

Lilith crossed her long legs at the knee. She still had that smirk on her face. "I told you. This is for your own good. You have no idea what you're doing. I'm doing you a favor. Trust me when I say… you don't want to get involved."

"You said we were friends." Yeah, I was going to play that card. She was infuriating. "A true friend would help another friend. A true friend wouldn't keep secrets. A true friend doesn't lie."

Lilith gave a mock laugh. "Careful, my little demon witch. You're starting to annoy me. And I've killed those who annoy me, for much less."

"Bull." I was tired of these gods and goddesses and their damn games. Enough was enough.

Her face creased into a wicked smile as she said, "I won't warn you again." A dark glee simmered in the backs of her eyes, unholy and absolute. And then she raised her hand; sparks of power, like currents, danced in the air.

"Tessa? What are you doing?" hissed Iris. The fear in her voice was the only thing that dampened my anger. I didn't want Lilith to hurt Iris or Ronin because I'd lost my temper.

"You should listen to your friend." Lilith flicked a finger at Iris. "She looks smart."

Reeling in my rage, I added, "A god is trying to kill me. We think it might be Loki. You know anything about that?" I watched her face carefully for signs that she was hiding something, that she was holding back. Because I knew she was.

A cigarette appeared in her hand, and she took a drag before blowing a plume of smoke. She smiled at my evident frustration, ticking me off all the more. "I seem to recall… you offering me your mate for a few hours if I helped you."

Fuck me. I crossed my arms over my chest. "So you *were* listening." The fact that she didn't answer my question wasn't lost on me.

Lilith smiled. It was both chilling and disturbing. "See. I've helped you." She waved her hand around in my living room. "I've kept you from imminent death. So I get your male now. Your wereape is mine for… four hours. Not a second less."

Damn it. I'd suffered from a temporary lapse of judgment when I'd voiced that. What the hell did I do? When I screwed up, I screwed up big.

My heart pounded hard against my temples. "I don't know if Loki *would* have killed me." There had been a *very* good chance that he would.

"If you'd been naked, that might have helped," said Ronin. When he saw the glare I cut him, he shrugged. "Just saying. When in doubt, go for naked."

Lilith's eyes focused on Ronin, and she regarded him curiously like this was the first time she'd laid eyes on him. Either that, or she was imagining *him* naked.

"And since you've *removed* that chance, I'll never know." I could just redo the chalk triangle and circles, but something told me she'd keep a watch on me and would interfere again. "I just wanted answers from him. See if he was the one playing these games, whether he created Storybook and those portals. And if he was, I wanted him to tell me why and why he wanted me dead. What was this thing I took from him? That's a pretty reasonable request. Don't you think?"

Lilith's red eyes flashed dangerously as she took another drag of her cigarette. "You made an offering to me. You offered me your mate—a rare and beautiful specimen. With extraordinary stamina." She wiggled her brows. "And now I came to collect."

A fierce feeling of protection flared inside me, and I gritted my teeth. "Yeah, I don't think so. Even if I did, Marcus would never go for it. He'd never be with you for anything. I don't control him," I said, my fury seeping out of me through my pores.

"All women control their males, my silly demon witch." She flicked the ashes of her cigarette on the floor, and I had a feeling she was doing that on purpose to piss me off some more. It was working. "He'll come if you tell him to. Trust me."

I'd never trust her. The strangest feeling was that if my life was in danger, I had no doubt Marcus would do just about anything to save me. Would he spend time with the goddess? Would he have sex with her? To save my life, he would.

I'd really made a mess of things. And I'd gotten Marcus involved. It was a stupid, idiotic thing to do, and I'd regretted it. Deeply. But it was too late. She'd heard.

What would Marcus think if he knew what I'd done? Would he still want to marry me? I had my doubts.

"Not a chance," I told her, seeing her smile fade and knowing I'd done this to myself. I'd offered her Marcus. I did, but I'd lied.

Lilith's upper lip lifted in a half snarl. "You lied to me. You never intended to offer your male." She flicked her half-remaining cigarette onto the floor.

I swallowed hard. "That's right. I lied." Yup. If we had summoned Loki, and he hadn't killed me, Lilith would surely do it.

The goddess looked taken aback for the first time, her expression hard. Her red eyes shimmered with the promise of death, but she recovered quickly.

I strained to keep my composure neutral so as not to show how terrified I was at the moment. My bowels went watery, and I squeezed my thighs, trying not to pee or, worse, let out a nervous fart. Who would fart in front of an angry goddess? Me, most probably.

"Marcus would never agree to it." Ronin had turned his body more to take part in the conversation. "He'd never do it. I know it."

Shit. "Ronin, don't get involved," I warned, knowing Lilith could snap her fingers and kill him in a blink of an eye. I knew he was trying to help, but he couldn't. Not with this.

Lilith snarled, straightening. "I am the queen of the Netherworld. Mine are the screams on the wind and the howling darkness. I am the queen of the night. Shadows bend to my will. You… you are a tiny half-breed. Careful where you tread. I wouldn't think twice about ending you."

A whimper sounded, and Iris pulled Ronin back, pressing him into her.

"Forget him," I told Lilith, focusing on the goddess. "My friends have no part in this. They were just trying to help."

Lilith's features broke into a wicked grin. "If you don't give me your mate, perhaps I'll just have to kill the Dark witch to show you I'm serious."

Fury crossed Ronin's expression. His posture was stiff, like he was trying really hard to stay calm, but it was a tremendous effort. His eyes went from me to Iris and then to Lilith, who was watching it all in a rather clinical way.

I stiffened. My mind blanked, and all I imagined was white-hot rage and Iris's lifeless body falling to the ground. I frowned at the goddess. She was acting weird. Why would she threaten my friends like that? Because she was scared.

"Who are you protecting?" I watched her face tighten again. "Why didn't you want me to speak to Loki? And cut the crap. I know you wouldn't care if he killed me." Okay, I was walking into dangerous territory speaking to her like that. But my gut told me Lilith came here to stop me from discovering something. She *stopped* me. Not *killed* me. And she could have, multiple times.

I also had a feeling she knew I'd lied about Marcus, but she wanted to see me squirm a little bit. That was her nature. She loved to play with things too.

Lilith took a long drag off a new cigarette that had mysteriously appeared. "You don't know what you're talking about. You think you do, but you don't."

It wasn't much of an answer. "Enlighten me. Is it because it's Loki? Is he the one?"

Lilith's frustration was clearly visible in the wrinkles around her eyes and forehead and the tightness of her jaw. I could almost taste her desire to kill us, but she controlled it.

"I need a drink," she said with that same, lazy tone.

"I have nothing to offer you." Not true. I had plenty of wine and hard liquor in the cabinet.

Lilith watched me, seemingly knowing my lie and most probably able to read my mind. She waved her hand over the coffee table, and a bottle of red wine and a glass appeared. My wine. My glass.

The goddess leaned forward, poured herself a generous amount, and leaned back into the sofa.

I turned to look at my friends. Iris mouthed, "What the fuck," and Ronin was posed like he was about to grab Iris and bolt. I didn't blame him. Maybe they should go.

But I wasn't giving up. "Who's Loki to you? Is he a lover? Is that why you're protecting him?"

Lilith giggled, the demeanor reminding me of Aunt Beverly. "I've had many, many lovers. Loki being one of them, yes. But that was a long time ago. You had barely invented the wheel at that point."

"So why are you protecting him? Unless he would have had the answers I was looking for. Am I right? Is he the one?"

Lilith shook her head at me, staring at me like a mother would when her child disappointed her. "Loki would have killed you. All of you. Is that what you want?"

"No. But I think he would have wanted to know why I'd summoned him."

Lilith took a sip of the wine and frowned. "Terrible. You really need to invest in some better wine. This tastes like horse piss."

I shrugged. "I wouldn't know. Never had the pleasure of tasting horse piss."

The goddess glowered, her full lips tight, and a chill fell over me. "Watch it now, my little demon witch. Don't think that I've forgotten that you lied to me."

Heaps of anger replaced my fear and sanity, cementing in my gut. I let out a frustrated breath. "Is it Loki? Tell me."

Lilith set her glass of wine on the coffee table. "I don't think I will."

Fury surged through me, so scarlet and bright that I could hardly believe it was mine. I drew in my will, focusing it through a sudden rage and wanting nothing more than to smack that smug smile off her pretty, false face.

The goddess stiffened. "You don't want to do that."

"Yeah, I'm with the goddess on that," said Ronin. "Tess, you need to relax."

"Relax? How can I *relax* when there's a god out there making my life hell? Threatening my life, my friends, my family. I'm sick of this shit. I want it to end."

"Shouldn't you be preparing for your wedding," said Lilith. "You don't look like a blushing bride. You look red-faced and tired. Not attractive."

My fingernails bit into the soft flesh of my palms as I fisted my hands. "There's not going to be a wedding. It's canceled."

Lilith stared at me, her expression carefully blank.

I stared down at the goddess, feeling reckless and guilty for using Marcus in this mess. "Who. Is. He?" I enunciated carefully.

Lilith matched my defiant glare, and just when I thought I'd done it and gone too far. She said, "It's not Loki. His name is Samael." Her face twisted in distress. "My son. He's my son."

CHAPTER
16

Her son? I had a fleeting brain-fart moment. "Your... *son?*" I watched as Lilith's face went from holding supercilious airs to a downcast, worried complexion, like a parent who worried about their child out late at night. "You have a son?" I repeated.

Lilith stood slowly. Her eyes were bright and brimming with the beginnings of tears. She opened her mouth, her lips flapping like she was about to say something.

Instead, she flicked her finger in my direction. I felt a tug on my amulet followed by the flow of magic heaving my senses. And as I looked down, the amulet burned a bright orange, and then disintegrated into ashes.

"Wonderful."

When I looked back at the goddess, she had vanished.

I cursed. I hated when she did that.

"Well, I'll be dipped in shit, rolled in crumbs, and fried to a deep, golden brown," exclaimed Ronin as he ran his fingers through his hair.

"Oh… my… God," breathed Iris, her mouth hanging open in shock. "It's her *son*?"

"Looks like it." I stared at the spot where Lilith had been. I had no idea she and Lucifer had procreated. The fact that they were still hot for each other and had been around since the beginning of time, there were probably lots of little Liliths and Lucifers. That was a scary thought.

Crap. Things just got a hell of a lot more complicated.

"It makes sense." I looked at Iris and Ronin. "Why she was acting the way she was. I knew she was shielding someone. She was keeping things from me. She's been protecting her kid all along." And why she'd just terminated my amulet.

"*God*," revised Ronin, his eyebrows high. "That's not some cute, chubby, three-year-old kid from down the street with squeezable dimples. We're talking about a g: ruthless, immoral being of unimaginable power. One protected by his mommy goddess. This is so messed up."

I paced the room, racking my brain and coming up short. "Okay, so he's her son. It still doesn't explain why he's doing this to me. I've never met this Samuel. How could I have taken something from him?"

"Sam*a*el," corrected Iris. She moved over to the couch and inspected it. Next, she pulled back something long, red, and glossy pinched between two fingers. "Have to get the name right. It's all about the name."

"Uh. Right. Still, I had no idea Lilith and Lucifer had any offspring. And why the hell does he have it in for me?"

Iris and Ronin both shrugged, their confusion emulating my own.

"And it's not like Lilith is offering any help. She'll never help me. Not when it's been her own son this whole time." I didn't have children of my own, but I could easily understand that mothers didn't betray their children. I wouldn't either. And that was a problem. "Lucifer won't either."

"She might." With the strand of hair clasped in her fingers, Iris moved over to her bag still on the floor, pulled out Dana, and placed the single filament of Lilith's hair on one of the pages. "She might change her mind once she realizes her son is crazy."

"She won't." I had never been sure about anything more in my life than at that moment. "She won't do anything if it goes against her son. She loves her son. He's her *baby*. That's never going to happen." Of course not. She was his mother, and mothers protected their children, even when they were in the wrong.

"Even if he means to kill you?" Ronin reached down and pulled Iris to her feet. "She's an odd one, but she likes you. She could have killed you many times just now, but she didn't. I think she considers you her friend in her screwed-up goddess brain."

"Maybe," I said. "But she won't help. I just wished I knew what I'd done to offend this Samael. What I apparently took from him. Maybe then I could speak to him or apologize." Though for what? I had no clue. I'd never even known of Lilith's existence until I'd helped break her out of that prison, with those creepy Sisters of the Circle, even though I'd heard the stories. So how could I have known about this Samael? I couldn't have.

Irritation flared up at the notion that Lilith knew what her son was up to, and she was *letting* it happen. Would she let him kill me too? Who knew.

"Thank the cauldron we didn't call up Loki," said Iris with a nervous laugh. "Imagine that? The tall, handsome Norse god standing in your living room? How would he have reacted to all of us? And trapped? It could have gone badly."

"We'd probably *all* have had to get naked." Ronin smiled.

I pressed my palm to my forehead. "Lilith did help, in a way, I guess." The Norse god would have been pissed and probably would have wanted to avenge the summoning. So yeah, Lilith had most likely saved all our asses by stopping us. But I'd never admit that to her face. Not when she'd known all along that her son was tormenting me. She could have warned me or something.

Lilith once told me that she wanted to buy a house here in Hollow Cove, which meant she liked our little town. So why didn't she stop her son when he created the portals and had that pirate ship come through?

"At least we can cross Loki off the list. We know who the Creator is." Iris adjusted the strap of her bag on her shoulder. "So what do we do now?"

I cast my gaze around the room. There was not a single smidgen of chalk on the hardwood floor or a single piece of evidence of the summoning we'd tried to do. "I don't know. I need to think and come up with something that's a bit less dangerous." And stupid. The truth was, I had nothing. No schemes. No plans. I couldn't think past the fact that Samael was Lilith's son. And if I tried to do something equally feather-brained, like trap him, Lilith would finish me. Then there'd *never* be a wedding.

I had a name now, his real name. Yet somehow, I was more frustrated than before. Because I couldn't do a damn thing about it.

But I wasn't about to give up, not while I still drew breath. I just had to devise a smarter, better plan, something to free myself of this Samael for good.

"I have to talk to my aunts," I told Iris and Ronin. "They need to know what we've learned. And hopefully, with a name, they'll know what to do." They had loads more experience in these witchy affairs than I did. If anyone could figure out what to do next, it was my aunts.

"I could go for a piece of Ruth's cheesecake," said Iris. "I think I'm experiencing a bout of low blood sugar. Oh, and a glass of wine for my nerves."

I smiled, knowing a sugar boost was always welcomed. "Make that a bottle."

My grin was cut short by the sudden knock on the front door.

"Expecting anyone?" Ronin narrowed his gaze on the door, his body crouched and poised, ready to attack, should this be an enemy.

"No." Instincts hit, and I pulled on my magic, holding it close as I stepped over to the door. I grabbed the handle and yanked it open.

A middle-aged man stood on my porch. He was short, wearing a blue polo shirt with the PARANORMAL PARCEL SERVICE logo and khaki Bermuda shorts that only made him look smaller. He held out a parcel. "Tessa Davenport?"

"Yes." I eyed the package wrapped in brown paper, uneasily, knowing in my gut who had sent it.

"Here you are. Good day."

I held the parcel, watching the man walk away to his van parked at the curb. I glanced at the package, and the words TESSA DAVENPORT, DAVENPORT COTTAGE were written on the address label.

"Who do you think sent it?" Iris had joined me on the threshold.

I tore open the package, my pulse rising as I tossed the strip. "Who do you think? Samael."

"Could be a gift from the guests for your wedding," said Ronin. "Some probably haven't heard yet that it's been canceled."

If only. But I knew it wasn't. I pulled out a small white box inside the soft paper packaging. Stuffing the brown packaging under my arm, I popped open the box.

"What is it?" Iris leaned over, curious, and the scent of her vanilla perfume wafted up my nostrils.

I stared at the contents. "Looks like a card."

"What does it say?" Ronin was on my other side, leaning down until I was sandwiched between the two.

I grabbed the card. It was plain white with only the number 1 stenciled in gold on the front. I flipped it open and read:

When people come to this place, they cry. Here the people all ask why. In this place, the people sleep, and they weep. People's solitude they keep. What am I?

I flipped the card over, wondering if there was more, but it was blank.

"And?" prompted Iris. "Is it from *him*?"

I inspected the card closely and saw a tiny C stenciled on the bottom right corner. Dumbass. He was still signing his name as *the Creator*, thinking I didn't know his real name. Oh, but I did.

There was also a small inscription in the middle that read, *Tick, tock*. Well, I knew what *that* meant.

"It's from Samael." I handed her the card. "It's a riddle. Another one of his games." I knew he wasn't finished with me. I wished I could have a break from his schemes.

I let that information sink in for a little bit. Samael and his damn games. This was another one of his games he wanted me to play. But what the hell did it mean?

Ronin took the card from Iris. "This guy has issues. Boredom. Doesn't know what to do with himself, so he decided to play with you."

"But why? Why *me*?" It infuriated me that Lilith would let her son keep doing this. The least she could do was chat with him and ask him to stop. Or better yet, find someone else to torment. So why wasn't she doing that? It was like she didn't want to. Or, maybe, she already had, and it didn't work. Maybe Lilith couldn't control him. An awful feeling of dismay settled in me, and my gut clenched.

Ronin handed me back the card. "The god's a douche. Playing little kid's games to get off? If I were a god, I'd be surrounded by ladies and throwing the best parties. He's got his priorities screwed up."

Iris laughed. "Bet you would, God-Ronin."

The half-vampire flashed his pearly whites. "*God-Ronin.* It even sounds good."

I didn't doubt that Ronin was right, but Samael was different. He'd created a world to escape to, filled with fictitious characters from children's stories and fairy tales, which for a grown-ass man-god, was concerning. I'd gotten the impression he *was* like a kid. He was certainly acting like a spoiled child: a godling child, no less. And children loved to play games.

But Samael was like... what? *Thousands* of years old? More? It upped my creepy meter to high.

With the card in my hand, I stepped onto the front porch. "I really need to speak to my aunts. Dolores is an expert with riddles. She thrives on this stuff. She'll know what it means. She won't rest until she figures it out." And that's exactly what I needed right now.

I closed the door behind Ronin, and we crossed the grounds, popping in Davenport House's back door a few seconds later.

"Dolores?" I called as I stepped into the kitchen. I glanced into the dining room and then through the living room. No one was here. I moved over to the potions room and poked my head in. "Ruth?" The room was packed with shelves running along three walls. They were all crowded with boxes, glass jars with questionable items, containers with vast magical ingredients, crystal balls, tarot cards, enchanted pendants, collections of every-sized wand, and countless musty old books, journals, and scrolls.

But my tiny aunt wasn't there.

Next, I walked down the long hallway, the wood floors squeaking as I made my way to the base of the staircase. "Beverly? Ruth?" I shouted, staring up at the second floor. "Dolores? You guys up there?" I waited, but all I heard was the constant low hum of the refrigerator coming from the kitchen.

"They could have gone shopping," said Iris, standing in the hallway between the dining room and the living room.

"Maybe." I crossed the living room to the window and looked outside. The Volvo sat in the driveway. "The car's here." I sighed. "Just when I need them, they up and disappear on me. Is there a town meeting I don't know about?"

Ronin shook his head. "Not that I know of. Maybe they went to resuscitate your mother," said Ronin. "That's what sisters do. Right? Probably already drunk too."

"True." However, I didn't imagine Beverly walking over in her heels. *She* would have taken the Volvo.

Something didn't fit. I returned to the kitchen, seeing the coffee machine on and a fresh pot of coffee sitting on the burner, forgotten. An open bottle of wine sat on the kitchen counter, next to an empty glass. Weird. Leaving a bottle of wine unattended was a capital offense in this house.

"Why would they leave a bottle of wine open like that?" I gestured to the wine bottle.

Iris smiled. "Because they knew I was coming over." The Dark witch moved to the counter and poured herself a glass.

"Hmm." My eyes flicked over to the kitchen island. Diced carrots, peppers, zucchini, and onions topped a cutting board, and I noticed an empty baking dish next to them. Ruth would never let whatever she was cooking spoil like that without covering the veggies or putting them in containers.

"Something's off here," I said, turning around. "Feels like they up and left… in a hurry." The cold, familiar feeling of fear settled over me, and my gut clamped.

"You think?" It was Iris's turn to inspect the kitchen. "Why? Because some food is out? Maybe they just forgot to put it away. It can happen."

"Not unless there was an emergency," I answered. "And if that were true, they would have come to the cottage to tell me. They wouldn't just leave like this."

The more I thought about it, the more my tension rose. Where were they?

I spotted a bundle of black fur curled up in a ball on the couch.

"Hildo." I rushed over to the cat. "Have you seen my aunts?"

The cat opened his eyes slowly, his lids heavy with sleep. "No. They were gone when I got here. Can I go back to sleep now? I was dreaming that I was in a field chasing fairies. Good dream."

"How long ago was that?"

The cat closed his eyes and nestled his head between his front paws. "Maybe two hours ago? Don't quote me on that. Now, I'm going back to sleep. Go away."

I pulled my attention back to the kitchen, seeing it messy and abandoned in the middle of preparing dinner. Something was wrong.

I wrapped my arms over my middle, a sickly feeling of trepidation rolling through me. I stood there for a moment, gathering my wits and my thoughts.

Iris came to stand next to me, her face drawn. "What is it, Tessa? You've got that thinking face on. What? What are you thinking?"

I glanced at my friends. "I think I know what the riddle means," I said, as alarm pinched my insides.

"What?" Iris's face held traces of fear, and Ronin shifted next to her.

A fist of fear clamped my chest and squeezed it into a tight ball as the realization hit. I looked at my friends and said, "It's a scavenger hunt. Samael took my aunts, and now he wants me to find them."

Because if I didn't, he was going to kill them.

CHAPTER
17

When a witch has to come clean to her fiancé, the chief of Hollow Cove, it's not pretty. It's gruesome. And it was best to do it alone. No reason to have my friends witness this. I'd rather go down alone in the angry-fiancé zone, thank you very much. No witnesses allowed. It would be too humiliating. Though I did deserve it.

Of course, I'd have to tell him *everything*—meaning the deal of spending time with Lilith I'd offered without his consent, which I regretted profoundly. That was the worst of it.

Or was it calling up a Norse god, Loki, who would have most probably crushed my head into a meat pie? And those of my friends?

All were possible.

But what I was absolutely sure of was that Marcus was going to be livid. And possibly hurt that I hadn't told him. That was worse than him being angry at me. I could handle a few nights of brooding. He was hot when he was doing that. But the hurt part? That's when things got complicated, and feelings and emotions got in the way of making rational decisions. The last thing I wanted was to cause any pain to my wereape. Occasionally I didn't use my head. I was impulsive and sometimes acted without really thinking it through. I blamed my mother for dropping me on my head as a baby. Not sure if she did.

I wasn't happy with myself. I was far from perfect. My temper and my sporadic lapse in judgment, combined with my impulsive nature, was a recipe for disaster. Disaster was my lot in life, maybe my middle name. Who knew?

And apparently, I'd never learn. Not at my age.

I knew Marcus wasn't thrilled about canceling the wedding. Even though he didn't say anything, I could tell. He wanted to be married just as much as I did. He'd kept going on and on about it, calling me "wife" and doing the little things that made me sure. It was an exciting new chapter in our lives, something to look forward to. To grow old together—though I had confirmation that he was going to be a hot grandpa—as we spent the rest of our lives as one unit.

Samael had ruined everything. A reckless, arrogant, spoiled god was a scary thing. I only thought he was out to hurt me, not my aunts. And now he had all three.

Maybe I should have summoned Loki and offered him something in exchange for kicking Samael's ass. But that would have been stupid and enraged Marcus further.

I'd just have to pull up my big-girl panties and deal with it. Which was why a few minutes after I'd left Davenport House, I sat by the curb in front of Marcus's office, my stomach in knots and feeling like I was about to be sick in Ronin's expensive luxury car. That... my half-vampire friend would *never* forgive.

"Stay here," I instructed, feeling a sudden need for fresh air. "I'll be right back." I swallowed, my mouth dry. "Shouldn't take too long." I grabbed the door handle while holding the card in the other, my only peace offering.

Ronin stared at me from the driver seat of his gleaming BMW sedan. "You sure? We can come for moral support. Be witnesses. You might need someone to back up your story."

"He's right." The sound of leather pulled as Iris turned from the front passenger seat to look at me. "You know how angry he's going to be. He's got a temper to match all those big muscles."

"You think Marcus has big muscles?" Ronin leaned his arm over the headrest, flexing his biceps. "What about these babies? They're not puny by any bodybuilding standards."

Iris rolled her eyes. "He'll only be mad because he wasn't there. To protect you."

I nodded. "I know. And it's my fault. But I'll need his help if I'm to make sense of this riddle. I'll need everyone's help."

Yes, he'd be angry, but he'd be more concerned about my missing aunts. And knowing Marcus, that would take precedence over his feelings.

And I'd make it up to him tonight. Many times over.

He'd been in a bad mood the last time I saw him because he hadn't been there when Samael had disguised himself as my Marcus. And after telling his parents about the wedding cancelation, I was pretty sure Marcus was in a bad place.

And here I was, going to add fuel to his temper.

"How do I look?" I glanced up and checked myself in the rearview mirror, hoping a sexy smile could smooth out the tense situation, and frowned at my reflection. "I look like one of those witches in *Macbeth*."

Iris burst out laughing. "You do *not*."

I squinted at her. "Why did you laugh?"

Iris slapped my arm. "Go. Before we change our minds and come with you."

"Be back in one piece," I said as I shut the car door and walked up to the Hollow Cove Security Agency's front doors. My stomach did a few Olympic high jumps with a horrible flat-on-your-face landing as I pulled the door open and strolled through.

He'll be fine. He'll be fine. I kept repeating like a mantra. As chief, Marcus would have no choice but to help me find my aunts. I hoped it was on his own terms and not out of an obligation to his post.

I rushed down the hallway into a lobby. An older woman with white hair and a freshly pressed white shirt sat behind the desk: Grace, Marcus's administrative assistant.

She cocked a brow at the sight of me. "Stop. You need an appointment to see the chief," barked the older woman.

"Maybe. But I don't need an appointment to see my *fiancé*," I told her with a smile so wide, it hurt my face to keep it like that for three seconds.

Ha. Look at me go!

I made for the door on her right. Stenciled on the window was the name MARCUS DURAND with the words CHIEF OFFICER written under it.

Voices carried from behind the door—angry, heated voices. I loved me a good argument.

Especially when *I* wasn't the cause of the discussion. Was that Gilbert in there with him? That would be even better.

Still smiling, I knocked twice and pushed in.

My smile dropped to somewhere near my feet.

Sitting in an office chair facing Marcus at his desk was Mrs. Durand. Her face was stone cold as she beheld me. I had no idea what was going on in her head. Perhaps, just a little something that involved me.

And next to her was a gorgeous blonde, who looked like a princess from some fairy tale, with a face that belonged in fashion magazines: high cheekbones, perfect small nose, and full lips.

And a smile that lacked warmth and sincerity.

Allison, aka Gorilla Bitch—I mean, Barbie.

The card in my hand slipped, and I nearly dropped it, but I did lunge in an unattractive manner to snatch it up, followed by a rip. Damn. I'd ripped my jeans. My ass did get big.

I straightened. My face flamed from embarrassment, anger, and surprise. I was not expecting to see Allison again. Ever. But here she was in all her Barbie, whoring splendor. What the hell was she doing here? Sitting in Marcus's office with his mother?

Sitting in his office with his mother!

Oh crap.

This was it. This was what I was afraid of. I'd laughed at that horrid dress, and I knew it would eventually catch up with me. Katherine loathed me now. She didn't want her son anywhere near a discourteous witch like me. So not even hours after Marcus had canceled the wedding, Allison, the ex-girlfriend, showed up with his *mother*?

I felt the lava pouring out of my ears as I did my best to show no emotion. That never went well.

"Tessa?" Marcus looked up from his chair. I couldn't tell if he was happy or annoyed at seeing Allison again. "You need me?"

Mrs. Durand watched me with a pointed look that said it was rude to barge in on a private conversation even though there had been some arguing. Arguing about me? Why did I get the feeling it *had* been about me?

"Uh, I'm sorry. I didn't know you had visitors," I lied, feeling Allison's stare but refusing to look at her.

Mrs. Durand turned around like the sight of me disgusted her.

"Why do you always look like a homeless person every time I see you?" sneered Allison as she gave a toss of her long locks behind her back. "Showers are free, you know."

I smiled at her. "Allison. You're the reason no one likes you."

207

Lines formed on her forehead as she frowned. "You know, this was a private conversation. You're not invited. How about you be a good little witch and go stir your cauldron."

"I don't care. I have to talk to Marcus. It's important." I knew that sounded rude, and the way Mrs. Durand's shoulders stiffened told me she'd agreed with Allison. I wasn't winning any points back by my rudeness. But my aunts' lives were at stake here, so she could hate me all she wanted.

Allison batted her long, fake eyelashes at Marcus. "Can you please tell her to get out. She's being rude. We were in the middle of something." At that, she turned her head and flashed a smile in my direction.

"If you're waiting for me to care, you better pack a lunch. It's going to be a while." I glanced at the chief, finding his eyes on me. "We need to talk. It's important. It's my aunts."

Allison let out a dramatic sigh and thrust her larger-than-normal chest out. "Yes, your life is *always* above everyone else's. Isn't it?"

"No. But now it is." My heart thumped along with the rising of my temper. I really, really couldn't deal with Allison right now. Too much was at stake to waste a single emotion on that wereape. It didn't help that she was gorgeous, fueling my insecurities, even though I knew Marcus wasn't interested in her. But she just *wouldn't* shut up.

"Please." Allison rolled her eyes in an exaggerated manner. "It's *always* about you. It's like you create problems because you crave the attention. Always flashing your sad, doe eyes. You'd be nothing without all the chaos you cause. Admit it. You're a chaos junkie. You get off on it."

I clenched my jaw, controlling my breathing. "Allison. Somewhere, somehow, you're robbing a village of its idiot."

Allison's face tightened. "Well, only an idiot would mock the Mabel Durand gown. But you wouldn't understand our traditions. You're not one of us. Even though you try and try so hard to fit in, you'll never be one of us."

My bowels churned, and the feeling of throwing up surfaced again. Oh crap. The dress had a *name*? Who names a dress? Damn it. Could I feel any worse about my bout of laughter? Why hadn't Marcus warned me or at least prepared me about that dress?

My eyes settled on Mrs. Durand. She still wouldn't look at me. It was almost as though she was pretending I wasn't here, that I didn't exist.

Allison's face brightened at my constipated expression, no doubt. "I hear you had to cancel the wedding. How unfortunate for you. I'm so *very* sorry."

"Sure you are," I said.

A victory grin spread across her face. "I wonder what you did. Maybe if you ran a brush through that mop you call hair, you would look less like a hobo."

"Allison," growled Marcus.

I had to take a moment to calm down and remind myself that Marcus had asked *me* to marry him, not Allison. The last time I'd seen her, he'd fired her ass. It had been fantastic to watch. Which made me think she'd invited herself with Mrs. Durand, or his mother had asked Allison to tag along. I didn't like the latter. Had Mrs. Durand given up on me so soon? Was she preparing her son for his new bride?

It was pathetic that Allison was still trying to steal Marcus from me. She had perseverance. I'd give her that, though she was wasting her time. But if Katherine was rooting for her and was continuously drilling into her son that I didn't suit him or the family, would he relent and go with his mother's wishes to replace me with Allison? No, I had to stop thinking like that.

Seeing Mrs. Durand's back to me only made me feel worse. Should I have apologized for the dress? Maybe I should have reached out to her. I hated the dress, and I'd never wear it, but I guess I had been unforgivably rude as I tried to see it her way. I basically laughed at her, seeing that she'd worn the dress for her wedding.

Maybe it wasn't too late to make things right. But I'd do it for Marcus, not for me.

I looked at Marcus, his expression shifting apologetically, and I could see he was uncomfortable. I didn't know if it was because of me barging in on a private meeting or because of Allison sitting across from him.

"I wouldn't have come if it wasn't important," I told him.

Marcus's eyes flicked to the card I held, and I could see his realization of who had sent it. I could see the muscles in his jaw tense, even from a distance, but his face was expressionless. Only his eyes held traces of a sudden alarm.

"You'll have to excuse me, Mother." Marcus pushed his chair back and stood. "I need to take care of some things."

I couldn't see his mother's face, but I could imagine the scowl and the disappointment.

"What?" Allison whirled around on Marcus. "You *can't* be serious. You're leaving now? Because of that *witch*?" I knew by her tone she'd wished to use another word.

"Careful, Allison," warned Marcus, making my heart squeeze. He reached his mother and pressed a hand on her shoulder. "I'll call you later."

Mrs. Durand placed a hand over his as she stood. "Of course. You do what needs to be done. I don't want to keep you from your responsibilities."

Allison snorted as she leaped from her chair. And then she plastered that fake smile of hers

211

on her face and looped her arm around Mrs. Durand's. "Let's go, Katherine. There's so much more I have to tell you. Where I've been. What I've bought. The air here has a distinctive stink of *garbage*. Seems like they forgot to take out the trash."

Said trash was me, of course. Before I remembered my mouth had a mind of its own, the words flew. "Maybe you should eat all that makeup on your face, you know, to make you pretty on the inside."

Allison lifted her chin and snickered. "You're just jealous. You've always been jealous of me."

I nodded and propped a hand on my hip. "That's right. I'm jealous of all the people who haven't met you."

The wereape's eyes narrowed. "You think you're smarter than me. Don't you? But clearly, you're not." Her arm around Katherine's tightened, and I knew what she meant by that. The game was on, and she was ten points ahead of me.

I glowered at her before I could control my expression. "I won't be so polite next time. And I won't set my phasers to stun," I told her, smiling at her apparent confusion at my clever *Star Trek* vernacular.

Allison bumped into my shoulder as she and Mrs. Durand left Marcus's office. I had the wild impulse of sticking out my leg to trip her, but then that would make Katherine fall too. And I was already neck-deep in the crapper with her. I couldn't afford any more mistakes if I wanted to win her favor back. How would I do that? No idea.

Even though Allison had left, her presence and words still left a mark. I didn't doubt Mrs. Durand preferred the gorilla Barbie over me. I didn't want to admit it, but it stung like a son-ofabitch.

CHAPTER
18

"You think they're in Storybook?" Marcus stared at the card, not meeting my eyes as we stood on the sidewalk facing the Hollow Cove Security Agency.

"That's the first thing I thought of," I answered, feeling squeamish, guilty, and angry all at once. "But without means to get there—I mean, there're no more portals—that would be impossible. And I believe he *wants* me to try and find them. It's all part of his game, so I figured they must be here."

"You mean in Hollow Cove?" Ronin dipped his head as he eyed me.

"Probably in this town or close to it. Not in another world." Well, that's what I was going with. If he'd cast them off in another world, my aunts were lost to me forever. I pushed the thought away from my mind.

The chief was unusually quiet as he regarded the card. As soon as his mother and Allison had left, I'd told him everything. About Lilith, about summoning Loki, and finally, about Samael and my missing aunts. I sort of just opened my mouth, letting the words fly out in no particular order, which would have been a nightmare to follow and to make sense of for anyone else. But Marcus knew how to sift through my verbal diarrhea.

When I was done, I stared at his face, trying to get clues as to how he was feeling about me at the moment. I knew he was angry, furious, and having Allison show up at the worst possible time didn't help my stress level.

But the chief had kept his posture and expression carefully blank, professional, not revealing as much as a punch in the wall or something.

And somehow, that made me feel worse.

Did he regret proposing? Did he see me in a different light now? I wouldn't blame him. I was an idiot.

We'd walked out of his office in silence to meet up with Ronin and Iris waiting patiently by the car. With one look in Iris's direction, seeing her frown, I knew she'd seen Allison walk out with Mrs. Durand. Her wide eyes were a sign that she wanted the scoop about what had transpired.

Marcus handed me the card, his face hard. "Have you figured out what it means?"

I read the card over again: "When people come to this place, they cry. Here the people all ask why. In this place, the people sleep, and they weep. People's solitude they keep. What am I?" I shook my head. "I don't know. Guys?"

Iris grabbed the card from me, her lips moving in silence as she read it over. "It's a place. Somewhere nearby, maybe? We find the place, and we find your aunts."

"Ticktock," said Marcus. The concern that shone on his face had my pulse throbbing. "He's telling you that you don't have much time to find them." The chief watched me a moment. "Do you think he'll kill them? You think him capable?"

My gut twisted. "Yes." I hated to admit it, but there it was. "Which is why I think they can't be far." I wondered if Samael was here somewhere, watching from the shadows, relishing in my fear of not finding my aunts. He probably was.

"How long do we have?" Iris handed me back the card.

"No idea. But not long." I sighed. "I wished Dolores was here. She's the expert at deciphering riddles."

"I hate riddles," said Ronin. "I prefer when people mean what they say, not dick around with words."

I had to agree with that statement at the moment. But it didn't help us find my aunts either.

Ronin sighed. "That god needs a spanking from his mommy."

"A kick up his godly ass, more like." And worse. I fumbled with the card. "Where can they be?"

"They can be anywhere," said Marcus. "We'll never find them on time if you don't figure out what that riddle means. You can do it. Otherwise, he wouldn't have sent it."

Right. That made sense. I blinked, reading the card repeatedly until I memorized the damn riddle.

"Okay, so we know it's a place," I said, tapping the card on my thigh. "Somewhere where people sleep." I turned on the spot. Fluffy, white clouds blotted out the sun. It was about two in the afternoon, and I was glad about it. It would have been more challenging if I had to search for my aunts at night. "Could be a house or a hotel?"

"There're loads of houses and hotels. Which one?" asked Ronin as he stuffed his hands in his jeans pockets.

"I don't know. I don't think it's a house. It has to be something else." I voiced the riddle in my mind again and then muttered, "When people come to this place, they cry... in this place, people sleep and weep, people's solitude they keep." And then it hit me in the face like one of Allison's fake boobs. "The cemetery." My pulse quickened. "It's the cemetery! They're in the cemetery." That had to be it. It was the only place where people went to weep where the dead slept.

Iris's lips parted. "You're right. That's the riddle. You figured it out. Look at you? Dolores would be impressed."

"Doubt that." I nodded. I'd take the compliment later. Now we needed to find my aunts.

"We'll take my Jeep," ordered Marcus as he hurried over to the burgundy Jeep Cherokee parked at the curb in front of Ronin's BMW.

I looked over at Iris, who was dismissing me with her hand. "We'll follow. Go."

I hustled after Marcus. I didn't mind that he was barking out orders like a sergeant major. At least he was speaking to me and hadn't shut down. There was still hope.

I climbed into the front passenger seat and barely closed the door as the Jeep sped from the curb. The sound of tires tearing up the asphalt followed. My body jerked back into my seat, and I fumbled for the seat belt as we zoomed down Shifter Lane.

We took a sharp left turn. The Jeep fishtailed, recovered, and soared down the road at a speed I didn't think was allowed on this street. I glanced behind me. Ronin's black BMW was right behind us, speeding just as fast. Men and their cars. I'd never understand their need for speed.

I settled back into my seat and cut a glance in the chief's direction. His hold on the steering wheel tightened, his jaw muscles clenching. His closed-off manner was disturbing, to say the least. I'd much prefer him yelling. A fight would be most welcomed.

But he said nothing.

The streets of Hollow Cove were light with barely any traffic and few paranormals walking the sidewalks as we sped through the lanes.

The tension in Marcus's hands on the wheel increased as he made a right turn.

"You can yell at me, you know," I blurted, watching his face. "I can take it."

The chief frowned. "Why would I yell at you?"

"Because I didn't tell you about the summoning? Because I could have been killed if not for Lilith's interruption." I didn't tell him about the offering-him-to-Lilith part. Thought it best to keep that one on the down low. I let out a breath, feeling high on emotions. I could feel my eyes burning. "You've been angry since the *thing* this morning." Just the thought of Samael with Marcus's face made me feel sick again.

Marcus's expression darkened. "That wasn't your fault. You can't blame yourself for a god's twisted schemes. He used you."

"Maybe." I was glad he was speaking to me. Surprised even. "But I wish you'd yell at me or something. I'd feel a lot better if you raised your voice. Come on. Do it."

Marcus looked at me. "I'm not angry, Tessa."

"You're not?"

The chief pulled his gaze back to the road. "I know you well enough to know that you only did what you thought was best. Even if your plan was dangerous."

"And stupid. You can say it."

"I get why you did what you did. You were trying to make him stop." His expression went dark again at the mention of Samael. "We'll find a way to stop him. Together. Just as soon as we find your aunts. I'll keep you and them safe. And then we'll destroy him."

"How?" Did he know something I didn't?

"I know some Dark mages who can be bought for a fee," said the chief. "Like mercenaries. I've heard they're capable of killing a god."

Apparently, there was still a lot I didn't know about our paranormal world. "Are you sure?"

"I did a lot of digging today. Been on the phone with my contacts and informants."

"You have informants?" *That*, I didn't know.

The chief nodded. "Paranormal informants strategically placed in different organizations. One of those informants told me what the Dark mages could do. Their fee will be extensive."

"How much?" Damn, I barely had any savings at all. And with the wedding, even though it had been canceled, it would be a good day if I had fifty bucks in the bank.

Marcus turned his head briefly at me before turning back to the road. "Don't worry about that. I'll do whatever it takes. If we have to sell the Jeep or cash in some savings, it'll be worth it."

It bothered me that we'd basically have to go bankrupt to rid ourselves of the god, but if it worked, it would be worth it.

Lilith.

"If Lilith finds out, we're dead. You do know that. It's her son."

"Then we'll just have to make sure she doesn't know," said the chief. "That's why it's better to go through a third party. Can't be traced back to us."

I hoped he was right. But Lilith was resourceful. She'd be a problem.

Now that Marcus was talking, I was dying to know why Allison had been in his office with his mother. I was still wound up about that. That damn Gorilla Barbie knew how to get to me. But seeing how good Marcus was taking my sneaking behind his back and not telling him about Loki, I thought better of it. Maybe it was just none of my business. Maybe Allison had a legit reason to be there.

And maybe I was Xena, Warrior Princess.

"I'm sorry for all of it." Marcus's tone was much calmer with a tenderness to his voice that implied my actions weren't futile. "Sorry that we had to cancel the wedding."

He was apologizing for that? My eyes burned at the emotions I saw on his face and heard in his voice. "That's not your fault."

"And it's not yours either. I'm just sorry you couldn't have your day."

"But we will. Right?" I waited for him to say something.

"Let's find your aunts and take care of that god. Then we'll make plans."

I sighed internally, knowing that canceling the wedding did bother me more than I cared to admit.

"Why was Allison in your office?" Damn. My mouth had escaped me.

A tiny smile pulled the side of the chief's mouth. "I was wondering when you'd ask me that."

I cocked a brow. "So you knew I'd ask?" By that smug smile, I could tell he knew that had bothered me.

"I did."

"Your mother called her. Didn't she? After you told her the wedding was off."

Marcus looked at me, his brow furrowed. "Is that what you think? You think my mother wants me and Allison to hook up?"

"Doesn't she?" It would explain why she turned her back on me.

The chief pulled his eyes back on the road. The Jeep slowed as he took a sharp left turn. "No. Allison heard about the cancelation from one of my relatives or my mother's close friends. She'd invited my mother to lunch. They were going home and decided to drop by the office first."

Because she's trying to win you over. "To discuss her plan of attack. She's trying to get you back. You do know this. Right?" I was trying not to be juvenile about this, trying not to lose my cool or let my insecurities overpower me.

"She can try. But there's just one girl for me."

Yeah. Nothing could scrape away all the insecurities of a gorgeous blonde better than when your man said something like *that*.

"Don't you forget it," I teased, my heart doing a tap-dance against the walls of my rib cage.

After a short five-minute drive, the cemetery's front iron gate soared into view. Marcus pulled up on the curb, and before he killed the engine, I jumped out of the Jeep. The sound of wheels screeching reached me as Ronin's car parked behind Marcus's Jeep.

I cast my gaze around. Hollow Cove Cemetery was twenty acres of luscious forest, all mixed with headstones, tombstones, and winding paths. Instead of statues of cherubs and angels, this cemetery sported pixies, gnomes, and thousands of cat and dog statues. I always thought of it as a cheery place. And it angered me that Samael would spoil that image for me.

"I hate to state the obvious," said Ronin as he came around his car and joined me at the front of the gate. "But this place is massive. How are we going to find them?"

I sent out my senses and felt a source of magic. It wasn't much. But that could be my aunts.

"This way, I think," I said, starting forward.

"You *think*?" said Ronin, and I caught sight of Iris just as she punched him on the arm.

"Go. I'll follow you." Marcus jogged easily next to me.

Following the trail of magic like a bloodhound on a scent, I rushed down the path and veered to the right, dodging through tombstones and monuments.

They had to be here. They just *had* to be.

We passed a large green headstone that proclaimed, *Here Lies ELEANOR DAVENPORT. Don't stand on my boobs.*

I missed my gran. I wondered what she'd think of me now. Was I a good enough witch, by her standards?

I couldn't help myself. I bounded over, placed my hand on the cold marble headstone, and whispered, "Miss you, Gran."

For a moment, I swear the stone warmed under my touch. But it could just be the pumping of my blood from the running.

And then I was off again, following that faint spark of energy through winding paths that cut through the cemetery.

I tripped over a rock, and if Marcus hadn't been there next to me to break my fall, by grabbing my arm and pulling me upright, I would have pitched forward, face-first in the dirt or smacked my head against a tombstone. Possibly both.

I didn't stop to thank him. I knew we were running out of time.

And I also knew I was heading in the right direction as the pull of magic intensified when I waded through tall grasses in a part where the cemetery wasn't manicured.

I broke out between two tall maple trees that brought me into another section of the cemetery.

And there, hanging spread eagle and unconscious from a large stone monument, was Aunt Dolores.

CHAPTER
19

I halted and spun around, searching for Beverly and Ruth, but I couldn't see them. Still, that didn't mean they weren't here. Yet I couldn't just leave Dolores hanging like a scarecrow while I rummaged through the cemetery, trying to find them.

First, I'd help Dolores and then search the cemetery for them, one dreaded step at a time.

Swallowing my fears, I pushed off at a run again, and only when I got a foot from the monument did I realize how stupid that was. I was most certainly walking into a trap. Samael thrived on games and tricks. But as it dawned on me, it was too late. I was just a foot from my aunt.

"Tessa! Wait!" Marcus bounded next to me, his big shoulder bumping into mine. "Could be a trap." His gray eyes were wild, and I could see the concern across his brow.

I panted, trying to ignore the cramp at my side. "I know. Too late now. I'm here," I said and shrugged.

I waited for a second, my arms out defensively like I was waiting for a magical strike from just standing here. When nothing happened, I let myself relax just a bit.

I glanced at my aunt's face. Her head hung low, and long, gray hair covered most of it, with strands stuck to her sweaty forehead. Her eyes were closed, and a trickle of blood spilled from her nose and the corner of her lips. From what I could see, she was clearly unconscious.

"He hurt her," I seethed, my voice harsh and breathless. "The bastard god hurt my aunt." Fury radiated from me, hot and undulating, and every fiber of my body was ready to do violence. My body shook with unspent power that wanted, needed, an outlet—preferably Samael's head.

Dolores didn't deserve this. Nothing justified having her beaten and strung up like a puppet. He'd humiliated her.

My eyes burned as I felt the angry, desperate tears brimming my eyes. "I'm going to kill him.

I'm going to kill that prick." If what Marcus said was true, I would find a way to pay those Dark mages and kill the god. I'd worry about Lilith after.

A hand pressed on my shoulder, and the scent of musk and a delicious male sweat filled my nose. "I know. And we will," said Marcus, his voice radiating the same fury as mine.

"If she's…" My words caught in my throat as a tidal wave of emotions shook my core, and I was glad Marcus was next to me in case I fell. My heart pounded painfully against my chest.

"She's not," said the wereape, though I didn't know how he could tell just by staring at her. I surely couldn't.

Taking his word for it, I stepped forward. Pinned to her left breast was another card. I'd think about that later. "Help me take her down," I said, my voice coarse and raw.

"I'll cut her ropes." Ronin appeared next to me, his black talons gleaming. And with one swift movement, he slashed easily through my aunt's bonds. The rope ties slipped and fell to the ground. She fell forward, and Marcus was there, catching her easily in his arms. He lifted her as though she weighed nothing, and my aunt was by no means a petite lady. Then he set her on the ground with an incredible amount of gentleness.

Iris fell to her knees and angled her ear next to my aunt's lips. "She's breathing. Thank the cauldron." Iris leaned back as I knelt next to her. She gave me a quick smile. "She's alive."

Alive. My eyes burned, and I blinked quickly, fighting the fit of sobs that wanted to escape my throat. I didn't want to have a meltdown right now. I needed to be in control, focused. Beverly and Ruth were still missing. I'd have lots of time to cry later.

"She looks in bad shape." Ronin stood over us. "Dolores is as tough as nails. On a bad day, she scares the crap out of me. Whatever he did to her... looks like she fought back." Ronin pointed to my aunt's fingers. They were red, blistered, and packed with dirt under her fingernails, and brown stains streaked her white linen blouse as though she'd crawled on the ground.

I gestured to her wrists, my fingers trembling. "Her wrists are bruised. Means she's been here awhile for her skin to bruise like that." Another slow burn of rage took root.

I felt a body brush up against me, and then a strong, wide hand rubbed my shoulders.

"We'll get him, Tessa. I promise." Marcus's strong jaw clenched with emotion. Anger was heavy on him.

The fact that Marcus had come with me meant the world to me. I needed him right now, and I was fine admitting it. Sometimes it was okay not to be strong all the time.

I'd feared he'd been livid at my attempt at summoning Loki, but the chief had surprised me with his calm and understanding demeanor. Guess he was used to my shenanigans. Hell, he wanted to *marry* those shenanigans.

I knew Dolores was dear to him. All my aunts were. Even before I came to Hollow Cove, he'd already formed a strong relationship with them. In a way, they were his aunts too.

To fight off the god, I would need all the help I could get. And the wereape was the perfect ally right now. All my friends were.

"Try to wake her up. We need to know what happened," said the chief, nudging me gently.

"Right." I leaned over and touched her shoulder. "Dolores? Dolores, can you hear me?" I waited. Nothing. Her face showed no emotion. She looked… she looked dead.

"I think she's under some spell." Iris pressed her fingers gently on my aunt's chest and closed her eyes. "Could be a magically induced coma," she said, her eyes still closed.

I scowled bleakly. The thought that we couldn't wake my aunt made my throat tighten. I didn't have a power word or know of a spell to remove a magical coma. "Can you wake her?"

Iris's eyes flashed open. "Of course I can." She swung her bag to her front and gave it a happy tap. "I brought Dana."

Of course she would. The Dark witch never left home without it.

Iris hauled out her large album of DNA she'd collected over the years. She placed it on her lap, flipping through the thick pages and finally landing on one. She picked out a small brown pebble the size of a dog kibble and set it on Dolores's forehead.

"Please tell me that's not dog poop," I asked.

"No." Iris's face was set in concentration. "Better. Hobgoblin stool sample. The best thing to wake someone under a magical coma."

"If the smell doesn't kill you first," mumbled Ronin.

I stared at my Dark witch friend, wondering if this was a joke. Knowing her, it wasn't. "I bet." When and if Dolores woke up, I'd *never* tell her about the hobgoblin poop touching her forehead. What the eye doesn't see, the heart can't grieve.

Next, Iris pressed her hands on Dolores's chest, her lips moving rapidly in a dark chant. The air sizzled and cracked with energy and magic as Iris called upon some demon in the Netherworld to borrow its magic.

"There. That should do it." Iris picked up the tiny brown pebble and placed it back into her album. "You can try waking her up now."

I nudged closer to my aunt. "Dolores?" Her face was still dangerously pale and blank of all emotions. "Dolores? Dolores, it's me, Tessa. Can you hear me?" I waited a moment and shook my head. "It's not working."

"Maybe we should take her back to the house," said Marcus, his voice concerned. "Might be easier than here."

But I didn't want to leave, not yet, not when Beverly and Ruth were still out there somewhere.

I looked over at Iris. "Maybe it didn't work? You want to try it again?"

Iris pressed her lips together in thought. "It worked. You might need to be a bit more *forceful*."

"Like slap her?" The idea of slapping my aunt, who was already down and had suffered severe blows, made me cringe.

"No," said the Dark witch. "Try to wake her up with something that would awaken the mind."

"Like what?"

"What's the most important thing to her?"

That was easy. "Dolores? Your special collection of tomes is on fire—"

"What!" My aunt sat up, her eyes wild. "Quick, get some water. Hurry!"

I clasped both her shoulders, a smile on my face as I tried hard not to laugh. "I lied. Sorry. Everything is fine. They're not burning."

Dolores frowned, confusion heavy in her expression. "Where am I?"

"We're in the cemetery."

Dolores looked around. Her face was streaked with dirt and soil, as were her fingers, giving me the impression that she'd fought. Fought Samael? I didn't know.

"How did I get here?" Dolores looked around, her gaze unfocused. She had a welt on the side of her temple like she'd been struck with a blunt object, and another fit of anger raced through me.

"What's the last thing you remember?" I asked, reeling in my rage.

Dolores blinked and held on to the side of her head like she was getting a headache. "I was in the kitchen. Listening to Beverly go on about some man she had a date with tonight. Ruth was making her kung pao tofu dish."

That explained all the food I saw. "And then?"

My aunt looked at me. "Nothing. Just… darkness… and then here. This now. I don't remember anything else."

"It's okay." It *wasn't* okay. I wanted to know about those few hours missing from her memory. It could help us find Beverly and Ruth, but I didn't want to have to drill her with that. She'd been through enough. Besides, she might remember later.

"But… how did I get here?" she repeated.

"Samael. That's the god's name. He took you. He took you and your sisters."

Dolores flicked her gaze around the cemetery. "Where are they?"

I felt a pang in my insides. "We don't know. Maybe here. Or they could be somewhere else."

Dolores narrowed her eyes. "He's playing his games again. This is all just a game."

"I know."

"What's this?" Dolores pulled off the card that clung to her blouse.

"Another riddle." I looked at Marcus, whose worry reflected my own. I couldn't sense Beverly or Ruth here, which meant whatever was on that card was another riddle. The god was not finished with us. Not even close.

Dolores read the card. Her brows furrowed like she was having a hard time reading it. "Here." She gave it to me. "I don't have my glasses. And I feel a little light-headed." She placed a hand on the side of her head where I'd seen the bump.

I took the card and read, "Darkness, dust, cobwebs, and creaking floors. Secrets, spirits, strange noises, and occasional slamming doors. What am I?" Again, it was signed by the letter C.

"A haunted house," said Iris, and as the words left her mouth, I realized she was right. "It's a haunted house," she said again.

"The only haunted house around here is the Crane family manor," said Marcus.

"We have a haunted house in Hollow Cove?" Not that I should be surprised by that. We were a paranormal town after all. Why should ghosts be any different? Plus, I lived in a haunted house, in a way. Though it was a magical entity, one could count it as haunted.

I perked up. The idea of visiting a haunted house appealed to me.

I sent out my senses again, trying to find another source of energy, of magic, but found nothing. The only source of magic came from all of us. "Beverly and Ruth are not in the cemetery. They're probably in this haunted house. We should hurry." I looked at Marcus. "What's the matter?"

The chief was staring out into the distance. "Something's not right."

"Like what?"

"Too easy." His eyes found mine. "Don't you think finding your aunt like this was too easy?"

"No." Was it? "We followed the riddle, and we found her now. So let's not think about anything else."

"Samael likes to play games," said Marcus, and I noticed Dolores frown in anger. "He wanted us to come here for a reason."

"Yeah, to find Dolores and save her," said Ronin with a questioning brow.

"Save her from *what*? She was just tied here. She wasn't in any danger." Marcus's jaw was tight, as though he was sending out his wereape

235

senses and had felt something. He looked at me and said, "Something's coming," like he'd just pulled the thought out of my head.

"What's coming?"

Fear prickled over me as a sudden burst of energy erupted like it was coming from the ground beneath us.

"Uh. What's happening?" Ronin walked over a few steps, staring into the distance.

"Tessa?" Iris's eyes were round with fear.

The earth rumbled, followed by a deafening crash like thunder, as though the earth itself had split apart. My ears popped at the sudden change in pressure.

I stared in horror as fingers and hands broke through the earth next to gravestones. Mounds of earth tore open as bodies climbed out in a mass of shuffling, twitching humans of every shape and size—at least a dozen of them. But when they neared, I could see their empty eyes staring out from hollow, dead faces.

Zombies.

"Oh crap," I grumbled.

"Right back at ya," echoed Marcus.

Great. I had as much love for zombies as I did for ticks.

And they were coming straight for us.

CHAPTER
20

What was worse than zombies? *Naked* zombies.

They twitched and jerked as they shuffled forward, bits jiggling and swaying. Now *that's* disturbing. I was going to have nightmares for weeks.

I'd encountered recently risen dead folks from our cemetery once before, where they still had a soul and consciousness. So you could have a conversation with them. But this was different.

These were mindless, soulless dead. Nothing more than empty human meat suits, risen from the grave by powerful magic—in this case by the god Samael—and forced to obey their master or whoever created them. They existed to kill and to eat flesh, any flesh, to maintain their decomposing bodies.

"I think I've had this dream before," said Ronin, a smile on his face.

I cursed. "I hate these guys."

"You've fought zombies before?" Marcus raised a brow.

I shrugged. "No. But I can imagine how it goes. Very messy."

"Get the brain." Ronin crouched in an attack stance, his talons wiggling before him like he anticipated decapitating a few zombies. "That's the only thing that'll take them down."

"Speaking from experience?" I asked the half-vampire.

Ronin grinned, looking a bit too excited to be fighting zombies, for my taste. "Nah. I'm going with Hollywood here. Anywhere else, and it's pointless."

I didn't think it was possible to hate Samael more. To raise these poor souls from the dead, naked no less, and use them like this was a form of abuse in my book. Truly he was a disturbed god. These were the actions of a spoiled child, and I'd say it again. He thought this was funny. It wasn't.

The chief pulled off his jacket and caught me staring. "Stay here and protect your aunt. Keep her safe. I can take care of these."

"Always giving me orders."

Marcus flashed me a smile that would have gotten me into trouble if we weren't in a cemetery about to fight a horde of zombies.

And he was in magnificent shape.

"He's here somewhere," I said, searching the cemetery for a glimpse of the god, probably leaning on a tombstone with a glass of some expensive alcohol and enjoying the view. "He can't be far if he's controlling this." I wasn't sure, but I had a feeling he was watching. I wished we had the Dark mages with us so they could find his ass and kill him.

The zombies advanced, chanting and moaning mindless gibberish, for very few of them had functioning mouths. Their decayed legs thrust forward in a steady, slow rhythm that had bile rising in the back of my throat. The grisly sound of bone on bone and the rustle of decomposed flesh was like nothing I'd ever heard before.

"Ew. That's so gross," said Iris, and I had to agree with her.

Dolores tried to stand, but she wobbled. I caught her by the arm before she fell and hurt herself more. "Stay down." I lowered her gently to the ground. "You're no use to us in your state. You don't want to make it worse."

Dolores scowled at me. "I'm fine."

"Sure you are. Iris? Can you come sit next to her?" Iris didn't have defensive magic like I did, and she would be better served next to my aunt, where I could keep an eye on both of them.

"Of course," said the Dark witch, looking a little relieved.

"Hey? Isn't that Mrs. Bamford from Warlock Drive?" asked Ronin. "Yeah. I think it's her. Hey, Mrs. Bamford." Ronin waved at an elderly, naked zombie female who was twitching faster, hearing her name or just a voice as she shuffled toward him.

I couldn't answer as the sound of tearing flesh, and the breaking of bones cut the air, and then in a flash, a four-hundred-pound silverback gorilla stood in the cemetery.

The gorilla bared his sharp teeth in a grin. "Sstaay. Bee bak soon."

I wasn't offended by any means. I knew Marcus didn't mean he thought I was useless. But with the number of undead that kept crawling out of the ground, Dolores would need protection. She was too weak to fight off anything, especially zombies.

The feverish gurgle-moaning rose in volume. The stench of carrion followed, so intense my eyes watered, and I could hardly breathe. I shook off the feeling and focused.

I wasn't afraid of the zombies. I actually felt sorry for them. These were our people, past residents of Hollow Cove, and what Samael was doing to them was unforgivable. And corrupted. I really hated that god.

"Try to make this clean, okay," I told Ronin and Marcus. "Remember, these were people once. *Our* people. They deserve a clean second death." That sounded so strange.

"Don't worry, Tess," said Ronin. "I've got this. I'll barely spill any blood. Well, just a little."

"Marcus. Catch." Iris tossed a silver dagger, which the gorilla caught easily.

"Thanc," said the gorilla, twisting the blade around and getting comfortable with its weight in his large hand.

The nearest zombie, a black male with its lower jaw and parts of its forehead missing, saw me and charged. Feet planted, I channeled my magic, but Ronin got there first.

With a burst of speed, he twisted around the zombie, got behind it, and sank his talons right into the top of its head. He pushed them down into its brain with a soft thud. The zombie twitched once but then was still.

Grimacing, Ronin yanked his talons from its head. "I have to say that was strangely satisfying." The zombie collapsed to the ground in a pile of rotten flesh and cloth.

Gross. "Just don't get killed." I laughed. Damn, I shouldn't be laughing at all.

I heard a deep laugh behind me, and then a gorilla soared into the multitude of the undead.

Marcus moved around a cluster of zombies in an unreal grace, slicing and dicing as he spun around them. Zombies landed at his feet.

Okay. This wasn't so bad. We could do this. From what I could tell, the entirety of the dead in the cemetery weren't coming at us, only a few, maybe forty. We could do this and then head over to that haunted house to find Beverly and Ruth.

A flicker of movement appeared in my line of sight.

A male zombie shambled toward me, a thrashing stick figure with ribbons of rotten flesh. And, of course, completely naked.

I shivered. "Damn, that's nasty. I can never unsee this."

The zombie flailed its arms wildly, striking blindly with heavy sweeps of its limbs.

My magic was limited when it came to zombies in a way; that's if I didn't want to eradicate them completely. I couldn't use fire. That would only turn a zombie into a flaming zombie. You didn't want that. But I thought one power word was worth trying.

I willed my elemental magic to come, lifted my left arm, aimed at its head, and shouted, "Fulgur!"

A bolt of white-purple lightning soared forward toward the zombie.

And, of course, my aim was as good as the aim of a three-year-old child.

The bolt of lightning hit the zombie all right, right in its crotch.

"Ah, hell." Yup. My aiming skills left much to be desired.

I looked over at Marcus and Ronin, hoping they hadn't seen that 'cause *that* would have been embarrassing. But both were engaged in battling a handful of the undead at the same time, too busy to have stopped to watch my super zombie-killing skills.

My reputation was saved.

"Is that what you intended to do?" asked Iris from behind me. "Junk obliterating? That's a first for me, but you should definitely add it to your list of skills." The Dark witch laughed and then laughed harder.

"Nope." I looked over my shoulder at her and Dolores, who was eyeing me with a horrified expression. "But it would have stopped it if he was alive." And that, he was not.

The junk-less zombie kept moving, as though I'd never even hurt it, as though I'd never removed its family jewels.

I tried not to look at the mangled crotch as it shuffled forward, its mouth open in a hollow moan.

I waited for it to be about ten feet from me. If I missed at this distance, I should hand in my Merlin license.

Again, I pulled on the elements around me and cried, "Fulgur!"

Aiming at its forehead, another bolt of white-purple lightning fired out of my hand.

And this time, I hit the mark.

The lightning shot the junk-less zombie smack on its forehead. Its head jerked back, and then it collapsed to the ground in a jumble of limbs.

I stood for a moment, impressed at my zombie-killing skills. Then I made a finger gun and blew my fingertip. "And they said I was a dud."

A sudden wave of dizziness hit as my magic took its payment just as the sounds of flesh pounding flesh reached me. I looked up across the cemetery. My eyes found Marcus, the gorilla, through the wall of zombies between us. He was still fighting well, but he was also fighting off ten zombies at a time. Ice licked up my spine. The other ten remaining were approaching Ronin, who was battling his own three zombies already.

"That's six!" called the half-vampire. He took a moment and flexed his arm muscles like you'd see a wrestler do to try and intimidate his opponent.

"Ayyghht. I still beeet yuu," said the gorilla, as another zombie fell at his feet. In answer to Ronin's show of strength, the gorilla stood up on his legs, flexed his enormous chest muscles, and then proceeded to pound his chest with his massive fists.

"Are they bonding?"

"They are," said a proud Iris. "Aren't they adorable?"

This was a very strange day.

"I should be helping," said Dolores as she struggled to get up. "This isn't right. I'm the Merlin here."

I didn't point out that *I* was a Merlin too. Looked like she really did get knocked over a bit to forget something like that.

I rushed over and pressed her back down until she was sitting again. "They've got it covered. You don't want to exert yourself. Besides, you got a nasty bump on your head that worries me. Just don't move, okay?"

Reluctantly Dolores stayed put. "Maybe that's wise. I am seeing two of you at the moment."

Iris looked at me, her face just as concerned as I was. I knew the double vision was bad after someone suffered a head injury. I wished Ruth were here to help her. Dolores might have been in a magical coma, but she looked like she'd had a concussion. She needed a healer. She needed Ruth.

"Tessa! Behind you!" cried Iris.

I whirled around, a power word on my lips.

Too late.

"Son of a bitch!" I cried out as my left arm flamed with pain.

The scent of carrion hit me just as the weight of another body tried to pull me down from behind. I nearly vomited at the feel of its teeth sinking into my flesh, its rotten tongue tasting my blood. Instincts hit, and I reached over with my right arm and jabbed the zombie in the eye with my fingers.

I will not attempt to describe how gross that was.

The teeth around my arm released. At that exact moment, I whirled and grabbed its arms as I spun and pulled them off me.

The trouble was both arms came right off with a nauseating suction noise.

"Ah!" I cried. "What the hell is this?" I stared at the arms, which were mostly just bone with strings of rotten flesh that hung in my hands. "Oh. That's just wrong."

"Is that not what you expected either?" giggled Iris.

I swung a zombie arm in her direction like a stick. "Do you want me to spank you?"

But that just made Iris laugh harder. At least she was having a good time. This might not have been so bad if it weren't for the still-missing Beverly and Ruth.

I turned my attention back to the zombie as it came at me again, armless, in a shuffle of oozing, peeling skin and tattered clothes. Trying not to puke, I lifted the severed arms and slapped the zombie across the face with them.

"You should go back to sleep," I told it and then smacked it again, making it stumble back.

"It's not your fault. I get that. And I'm really sorry for what I'm about to do."

"Grrrggg," said the armless zombie.

"Grrrggg," I repeated.

I dropped the right zombie arm, yanked on my magic, and shouted, "Fulgur!"

The bolt of white-purple lightning smacked the zombie right between its eyes. It went down like a dead tree.

"Tessa?"

I turned toward the sound of my voice to find a naked Marcus walking over. It was hard, really hard, not to take a moment to admire his delicious physique. But I forced myself to look at his face. Not his manhood. Oops. I peeked.

Behind him came Ronin. Not a single drop of blood on either of them. And not a single zombie was left standing either.

"We're okay," I said, the tightness in my chest releasing as they joined us.

Marcus had a smile on his face. "Why are you holding on to that arm?"

Oh shit.

"Thought the tombstones could use a little dusting." Using the severed arm, I proceeded to swipe the hand part over the top of the closest stone.

Marcus shook his head, grinning. "You are one strange witch."

"That's why you *love* me." I pitched the arm to the ground. "Weird is sexy." Realizing I didn't have any disinfectant, I wiped my hands on my jeans, knowing I would burn them after tonight.

I felt the second card in my jeans pocket. "How far is this haunted house from here?"

"Not far." Marcus was still naked, and it didn't seem to bother him in the least. "Ten minutes."

"We should go. The sooner we get out of here, the better." My aunt needed medical attention, a healer. And the only healer I knew was Ruth. I glanced at Marcus. "Do you know of another healer in Hollow Cove?"

The chief nodded. "Yes. Bronwen. He's a male witch. I've been to see him a couple of times."

"Absolutely not." Dolores, leaning heavily on Iris, stumbled forward. "You're not leaving me behind. Not when it involves my sisters." She pointed a menacing finger at me. "I don't want to hear it. I'm fine. It's just a little bump. And you're going to need me if you're going in that house."

"Why's that?" I went to scratch my face and stopped midair, remembering what my hands had touched a moment ago.

Dolores lifted her chin. "Because I've been inside. That's why." Yanking on Iris, Dolores hobbled through the tombstones, toward the stone path a few feet away, Ronin strolling behind them.

"Stubborn old bat," said Marcus.

"I know." I also knew it was pointless to argue with her. But her gait was labored, and I knew she was in pain. Lots of pain.

Unease fell like a ball of ice in the pit of my stomach. Seeing what Samael had done to Dolores, I could only assume it would be the same or possibly worse for my other aunts.

Hang on, Ruth, Beverly. We're coming.

CHAPTER
21

After another ten minutes of driving through our small, picturesque town, Marcus took the next right and pulled up into a long gravel driveway next to a century-old stone mansion, a three-story brick structure with a mansard roof and tower in the revival-style architecture. The Crane family manor.

He killed the engine of the Jeep, and it made those clicking noises they do. We sat there with the windows rolled down for a second. A warm breeze from a pond whispered through the Jeep, soothing but not enough to calm my nerves.

Marcus stared at Dolores in his rearview mirror and then cut a glance my way. I knew what he was going to say. That is, letting Dolores come with us was a bad idea. But there was no stopping the witch once her mind was made up. A dog with a bone, that one. Before I could convince her to stay in the Jeep while we went to check out the manor, she popped the Jeep's door open and clambered out.

Marcus tapped the steering wheel with his fingers. "Do you think she acquired that hard-headedness over the years, or was she always like that?"

I jerked as Dolores slammed her door. "She was always like that." I was pretty sure Dolores started bossing people around as a toddler.

I stared at him for a moment, wishing our lives weren't so complicated. Wishing we could have our wedding and move on with our lives, our future, the way it was supposed to go. But we all knew where my life was concerned, it never turned out how I thought it would. It was always a disaster of monumental proportions.

My eyes slipped over him, to his black T-shirt, snug against his broad chest, and matching his dark jeans. Marcus always had a change of clothes in his Jeep. Guess you had to when you were constantly ripping the clothes you had on to shreds. I didn't know what possessed me—raging hormones, most likely—but my eyes dipped to his crotch.

251

"See anything you like down there?" Marcus had a smug smile on his face, knowing I liked what I saw and had seen *all* of it mere minutes ago.

I was a perve. My face flamed as I quickly looked away, gathering some self-control. "What? No. I mean, yes. Urgh. Let's just go."

I climbed out of the Jeep, hearing Marcus's chuckle, and joined Dolores on the dilapidated stone walkway with tall grasses growing through cracks. I could imagine the footpath had been lovely at one time. The house had seen better days with its moss-covered roof shingles, peeling paint, and vines covering it like they wanted to suffocate the house. And just like the stone walkway, I was certain it had been beautiful once upon a time.

I turned at the sound of a car door shutting and saw Ronin walking over to us with Iris beside him. Hands on his hips, he scanned his surroundings. "Nice. I've always wanted to sleep in a haunted house."

I looked at him. "Really? I never took you for one of those ghost-hunter types."

"It's more of the adrenaline rush," answered the half-vampire. "Not knowing if someone is right next to you or watching you sleep. Poltergeists are a riot."

I looked at Iris, and she shrugged. "This is new to me."

"Enough with the chitchat." Dolores strode forward, and I was surprised she could walk in a straight line. "Beverly and Ruth are in here. We need to get to them quickly. Come on. Hurry up. We don't have all day."

"Did you give her anything?" Iris leaned next to me, her concern showing on her pixie-like face.

"No." Must have been adrenaline and the need to find her sisters giving her the extra stamina.

Marcus rushed forward and made it to the front door before Dolores. It swung open easily, and we followed them in.

Darkness enveloped us, and I knew this wasn't a normal dark. Not when it was still light outside, and the mansion was filled with windows. They just didn't allow any light. Even with the front door wide open, the light wouldn't penetrate. Weird. And creepy.

The pricks of cold energy were heavy in the air, like we'd stepped into a mist—somewhat close to what I'd felt in the presence of demons but different. Not as potent. Yet I knew without a doubt that multiple entities were here. Friend or foe, I had no idea.

"Can ghosts hurt us?" I looked at Dolores, but her eyes were distant and unfocused like she was still in that coma.

"They can," answered Iris. "They can induce pain and drain you of your soul so that you die and become a ghost as well. I've even heard of a witch who tried to rid a house of ghosts. But she died, and no one could explain how."

"Doesn't make me feel any better."

"This is not Casper, your friendly ghost," said Ronin. "These are angry, lost souls who hate you because you're alive."

"Can we see them?" The thought that I had to fight an invisible foe had a chill roll up my spine and settle around the back of my neck in tiny pricks.

Iris blinked into the darkness. "Only if they want you to. Most of the time, you won't. You'll just see objects moving, like chairs thrown across a room or lamps. Stuff like that."

If Beverly and Ruth were here, had the ghosts attacked them? I sent out my witchy senses and was hit by many different sources of magic. Could be the ghosts. Could be my aunts. There was no telling them apart.

"Here. You'll need this." Marcus held out one of those heavy police-type flashlights.

"Thanks," I said as I took the flashlight, and he handed another to Iris. I knew he and Ronin had no problem seeing through the darkness. But as witches, we couldn't, and if we didn't have a witch light with us, we were basically blind in the dark.

I turned my flashlight on and flicked it around. We stood in a grand foyer with marble floors surrounding us. An enormous chandelier hung from the ceiling with the heads of children with light bulbs coming out of their mouths. It was the ugliest, not to mention the eeriest chandelier I'd ever seen.

"Stay close," ordered the chief as I pulled my eyes away. "Nobody goes anywhere alone. Got it? The last thing I need is to lose one of you."

"Got it, boss," said Ronin, a smile on his face. He grabbed Iris's hand. Yeah, the half-vampire was loving this experience. I just wanted to find my aunts and get the hell out.

But Marcus was right. We had enough to deal with trying to find Beverly and Ruth. One of us getting lost in this house was not an option.

I started forward with Dolores on my right as we followed behind Marcus. Ronin and Iris brought up the rear. The floorboards squeaked under our weight, and water dripped somewhere in the dark. The chief's wide shoulders swung as he crept along a large hallway with doors leading into other rooms on either side. I could barely make out my friends' faces in the dark. Even with the flashlights, the darkness was heavy and everlasting. Colorful tapestries hung on the walls, and plush Oriental carpets decorated the marble floors and the grand wooden staircase that led to the upper levels. The heavy wooden furniture, from the seventeenth century, that occupied the rooms as we walked by was carved into strange, ugly creatures. Life-sized marble sculptures stood against the walls. But the creepiest of all were the portraits.

They were everywhere. Portraits of people I'd guessed were the owners of the house and perhaps the ghosts that haunted it.

One painting showed a relative lying across a red chaise longue, wearing a black dress with puffed sleeves and a corset. Blonde ringlets fell on the side of her face in a style reminiscent of the sixteenth century. The people in the pictures all had the same odd, soulless eyes that seemed to follow you wherever you went. Another portrait showed a woman in a beaded 1920s' dress.

"What's that smell?" Ronin's voice sounded behind me.

"I don't smell anything?" I knew the half-vampire and the wereape had keen senses of smell that we witches didn't possess.

"Rotten eggs," said Marcus, clearly having also smelled it.

"It's the ghosts," came Iris's voice, and I turned around so I could see her face, though most of it was lost in shadow.

"Ghosts smell like demons?" That was strange. I would have never thought.

The Dark witch nodded. "They do. They give off a sulfur-like odor. It's a result of their energies counterattacking with the Veil. Same as demons."

"God, you turn me on when you speak witch geek," said Ronin, pulling her closer. "If we find a room with a bed, I'm not sure I can stop my-self."

Only Ronin could get turned on at a time and place like this.

"Let's keep going," said Marcus. "This manor is about seventeen thousand square feet. We've got a lot to cover."

"Is there a basement?" I hated to admit it, but me and basements sort of went hand in hand.

"No." Marcus flicked his light from my face. "These big houses only have crawl spaces. I don't think your aunts would be kept there. I sure hope not. Just rats and spiders. You don't want to go down there. Trust me."

"If my aunts are there, I'm going."

"They're not there," announced Dolores, who'd been unusually quiet, and I didn't like it. She might be feeling the side effects of that magical coma. I tensed. We had to find Beverly and Ruth fast.

I stared at my tall aunt. "Can you sense them?" Maybe the fact that she was their sister, she had a stronger pull when it came to their witchy senses.

"They're here," she repeated, and that was the only answer I got.

"Keep moving." Marcus turned back around, and we all fell in line behind him.

We kept walking like this for another few minutes, and that's when I smelled it. The sul-fur.

It was heavy and potent and burned my eyes and lungs. I coughed, tasting the bitterness on my tongue like I'd swallowed some sewer water.

"Told you it smelled," came Ronin's voice behind me, and from the disgust I detected in his voice, I guessed he was not opting to sleep over at any haunted houses anymore.

Who are you? Get out of my house! screamed a voice inside my head.

My leg muscles locked, and I was rooted in place. Iris and Ronin crashed into me.

"Tessa? What's the matter?" said Iris.

"Did you *hear* that?"

Marcus was next to me. "You heard a voice?"

"Yeah. Didn't you?"

The chief shook his head, and when I looked over at Iris and Ronin, both shrugged.

"Dolores?" I stared at my aunt. "Did you hear a voice?"

My aunt blinked. "They're here."

Okay, I knew I wasn't going to get much out of her at this point.

"What did the voice say?" Marcus angled his head. I couldn't see his face clearly, but I could imagine the scowl from the uneasy tone in his voice.

"It said to get out of the house."

"That's the ghosts." Iris reached out and squeezed my hand. "Don't worry. If they're talking in your head, that's because they can't do much else. I wouldn't worry about it."

But I *did* worry about it. Why couldn't any of them hear the voice?

I drew a nervous breath and held it, stifling a shiver as we continued on. I had to focus on the bigger picture. I had to find my aunts.

The door to my left slammed shut.

We all screamed. Ronin the loudest.

I think I might have peed.

Iris covered her forehead with her hand. "Oh my God," she panted and gave a nervous laugh. "I almost had a heart attack."

I blew out a breath. "That was intense."

"It's just the ghosts. Let's keep moving." Marcus held my gaze a moment before turning back around. He was tense. I knew he was worried about finding my aunts.

We barely made it ten feet before another door slammed shut. Though we didn't scream this time, it still made us all jerk. I was jumpy, and my nerves were wire tight.

But we soldiered on until a lamp came flying out of nowhere, straight at us.

"Duck!" yelled Marcus, and we all flattened ourselves to the floor. Well, at least I did. Aunt Dolores didn't even move. Iris and Ronin threw themselves against the walls.

The lamp crashed against something behind us. In the darkness, I couldn't see.

"Those bastards are trying to hurt us," I grumbled as I got to my feet.

Get out of my house! came the voice again, and I could tell it was male.

Not until I find my aunts, I said in my mind, unsure that it would work.

You will die. I will take your soul, and you will die.

Not a chance.

I waited, but I didn't hear the voice again. So far, it seemed as though it was only one ghost. Angry, yes, but just one. I could handle one.

We kept going, and after about twenty minutes, we'd explored the entire first floor with the occasional shutting door and more flying lamps, along with two chairs at one point, but we saw no sign of my aunts.

"They're not on this floor," I said.

"Maybe it's the wrong house?" offered Ronin.

I shook my head. "They're here. It's all part of the game. He wouldn't send us here if they weren't. He wanted us to come to this place."

"We should check upstairs," said Iris.

"Yes." I spun on the spot. "I can't remember which way the staircase is." I had a horrible sense of direction. Add darkness in a new environment with many rooms and passageways, and I was lost.

Marcus stepped forward until I could see the smirk on his handsome face. "Follow me."

Again, with the chief leading the way, we stood at the staircase a few minutes later. The stench of rotten eggs was heavier as we climbed the staircase, but I was too busy watching Aunt Dolores climb the stairs to let it bother me. I watched for a sudden loss of balance or exhaustion, but she climbed the stairs like a champ, her determination to find her sisters fueling her long legs.

We reached the landing. Again, it was covered in darkness.

"We should split up," I said. Dolores's quietness was setting off all kinds of alarm bells. She needed to see a healer or at least rest for a little while, not run around in a haunted house. We needed to get out sooner than later. "The house is huge." I glanced at Iris. "We can separate into two groups and meet up again at the staircase in, say… twenty minutes? You go with Ronin, and I'll go with Dolores and Marcus."

I glanced at the chief, expecting him to argue with me, but he gave me a silent nod as his eyes went to Dolores. He was feeling the same anxiety as me. We needed to do this fast.

"And if we find them?" asked Iris.

"Call me. I have my cell phone. And I'll call you if we find them. Uh… we'll go east."

Again, with Marcus taking the lead, we followed him down a long, dark hallway.

Die! Die! You will all die!

Enough with the dramatics. It's not like we want *to be here.*

This is my house. Get out! Get out now, or you—

The voice suddenly cut off, like a radio was turned off or someone had strangled the ghost. Weird.

My boots sounded loud on the dark, polished hardwood floors, but I could barely hear Dolores's tread scuffing next to me.

The hallway opened up into a spacious, two-story-tall room. Large doorways hinted at equally spacious rooms down the hallway. Occasional artwork hung along the walls.

I sent out my senses, again feeling the various energy levels in the house, but I couldn't tell if the forces were coming from my aunts or the ghosts.

Marcus halted and looked at me. "You feel anything? Anything that could help us find them?"

"No." I hated to admit it, but it was true. "Something's here. But I can't tell if it's my aunts. And I have no way of knowing where it's coming from. It's like it's coming from everywhere at once." I was starting to think that maybe Ronin was right, and this wasn't the right house. Or perhaps Samael hadn't brought my aunts here, and he was enjoying watching us scrambling around blindly in the dark.

"It's this way," said Dolores, surprising me as she strolled out of the room.

"You can *sense* them?" I stared at Marcus, seeing the same shock on his face.

"Yes," answered Dolores, in a way that suggested we were idiots if we didn't. "Hurry up. They don't have much time."

I had no idea how she knew this. Must be some sisterly, witchy connection, like twin telepathy, which I heard was a real thing.

"Dolores. Wait." I rushed after her. She couldn't see. I was the one with the flashlight. The last thing I needed was for my aunt to fall down the staircase or crash her head into a wall. She'd suffered enough tonight.

A shoot of light bounced as I ran after my aunt. I could hear Marcus's loud tread behind me, all muscle, of course.

I found Dolores standing before a closed door. "They're inside here. I can *feel* them."

I bounded next to her. "Okay. That's great."

Before I could stop her, she pulled open the door, grabbed my arm, and hauled me inside the room with her. Damn that man-strength of hers. I jerked as the door slammed behind us.

A tug pinged my senses, and the next thing I knew, I was soaring through darkness at an incredible speed, feeling as though my physical body was detaching itself like the shedding of skin. Just when I began to panic, it was over.

I blinked into the bright light, squinting and blinking the spots from my eyes, and looked around.

I stood in a meadow with rolling green hills spread out before me in all directions. Mature trees dotted the landscape with red, orange, and yellow leaves rippling in a soft breeze. More leaves spread on the ground like a textured, colorful gown.

I *knew* this meadow. I'd been here before.

Ah, hell.

I was back in Storybook.

Chapter

22

I spun around, expecting to see Marcus or at least a doorway or portal, but all I saw were more rippling green hills spread in every direction and as far as I could see.

Marcus had been right behind me, but he hadn't crossed over. Somehow, only Dolores and I had stepped through to Storybook. Not somehow. *Samael* had made it so.

And now I was back here. Stuck in Storybook. Fantastic.

But I'd been able to escape before, and I would do it again.

"Don't worry," I said, looking at my aunt, my pulse pounding in my ears. "I'll get us out of here."

"Can you?" Dolores eyed me warily.

"Yes." I called out to my ley lines, knowing that even if we couldn't *see* the portal we stepped through, it was here somewhere. From what I knew, the only way to get to Storybook was with a portal. I knew we'd crossed into this world from that house. Samael had created a portal from one of those rooms. Bastard.

When I realized I wasn't feeling the pull of my ley lines. I tried again. And again. Nothing. Not even the slightest tug of a ley line.

I couldn't reach them this time, and dread filled my gut. We were screwed.

Fury exploded in me in a powerful storm. "Damn you!" I shouted, confident that he could hear me. "What the hell do you want from me!" I kicked the grass, a tantrum igniting in me. "You son of a bitch! Come here and show yourself, you coward! I'm sick of playing your games, you spineless prick!"

When he didn't materialize in the space in front of me, I ran over to a bush of pretty flowers and stomped on them. Next, I saw a glorious maple tree with its leaves a blush red. I pulled off all the leaves I could reach. And then I stomped on them too. After that, I dug my shoes into the lush, perfect grasses, kicking up clomps and making it look like a hungry skunk dug it up in search of worms.

"Tessa, control yourself," snapped Dolores, sounding more like herself. "Your tantrum won't change anything. We're here now."

"Maybe. But it feels good doing it." Because I knew he *loved* this place. If I ruined his pretty grass and flowers, I had a feeling he'd show up. I just had to keep doing it until he did.

I kept kicking up clumps of earth and grass, pacing in a circle and cursing. If anyone saw me, they'd put me in a loony bin.

I was losing my mind. I was angry. Exhausted. Tired of his games. I could handle myself being stuck here but not Dolores. She still needed to see a healer. And I had a strong feeling that Storybook had no healers or doctors. Only fictional characters that Samael created because… what? He was bored? Needed somewhere to relax? Needed to get away? Needed to relive a childhood he lost?

I imagined his stupid face in the orange daisy and stepped on it. Three times.

"Look. Over there." Dolores pointed at something in the distance.

I tore myself away from my death-to-all-pretty-flowers rampage and focused on what she was gesturing at.

"It's a house," said my aunt. "There's smoke."

She was right. I could see a house in the distance. It was too far away to get a description, but I could see a white roof and smoke curling out of a chimney.

"I think Beverly and Ruth must be there."

My insides squeezed. I didn't have the heart to tell her I doubted they were here. I tried not to think about what Samael might have done to my aunts. But maybe she was right. If *we* were here, perhaps this had been his plan all along. Maybe Beverly and Ruth *were* in Storybook as well.

I mean, he'd grabbed Marcus and shoved him here. He might have done the same with my aunts. There was only one way to find out.

"Might as well go check it out." What else are we going to do? Maybe whoever was in that house could help us.

As we made for the house in the distance, it occurred to me that the castles were not visible. At least, the Queen of Heart's castle used to be around here. But we saw nothing but miles of meadows and forests. No castles.

We might have come out in a different area of Storybook. Could be. Who knew how big this world was?

Energy rippled through the grasses, the flowers, the trees, and the air, pulsing around us as we made for the house. Magic. Storybook's magic.

"I'm sorry you're stuck in here with me," I said as we trudged up a slight rise covered in buttercup flowers and black-eyed Susans. "Samael wants me trapped here because his delusional god brain says I took something from him. I'm just sorry you got involved in this mess."

I was sorry for a lot of things. Afraid of never seeing Marcus most of all.

Dolores waded through the tall grasses, her long legs propelling her ahead of me. "It'll be fine."

"Doubt that." Marcus must be having a fit right about now. And I smiled at the thought that he was destroying that haunted house looking for me. Because he looooved me. But then my smile faded at the worry he must be feeling. Iris and Ronin too. Damn it. If I'd known there was a portal to Storybook through that door in the haunted house, I would have kicked Allison through it. One could still hope.

"There's always a logical explanation," my aunt was saying, marching through the foliage like she meant business.

"There's nothing *logical* about being trapped in another world when you didn't ask for it. Or know the reason for it." Apart from the god being a dick.

"Maybe he had his reasons," said Dolores. "You just don't know what they are. We all do things because we have reasons to do them."

269

Rage shook me so violently that I nearly lost my footing. "His *reasons*? There's no reason for him to make my life hell. I had to cancel my wedding because of him." The image of Allison's happy face at the mention of that had me stomping my feet again. At this moment, I wasn't sure who I despised more, Allison or Samael?

I'd figure out a way to get us out of here. If there was an in, there was an out. I just didn't know what that was right now.

And then we'd get those Dark mages to kill Samael.

Good plan.

I lost a bit of time, trudging through the tall grasses and wildflowers, thinking about the mess my life was once again. When I looked up, Dolores was fifty feet away from me. She was marching to that house with purpose, and I could see the anxiousness in the tightness of her shoulders. She honestly thought her sisters were in there.

I ran after her. "How are you feeling? You still have a large welt on the side of your head. Double vision? Nausea? Fatigue?"

Dolores sliced me an annoyed look. "I feel fine. Stop asking."

"You wouldn't be lying to me. Would you?" She still had dried blood around her nostrils and the side of her temple. There was no way she was feeling *fine*. But as Marcus had said, she was a stubborn beast. She would rather suffer in pain than show weakness. Not that it would matter in this place.

Dolores never stopped walking. "Why would I lie about that? We're getting close. See?"

I spotted the house. We were closer. I could see the white roof gleaming in the sun. The siding was a light brown with red-and-white-striped window frames, and the chimney was a sparkling multicolored brick. I'd never seen a house so sparkly and glimmering. From my point of view, it looked like it was made of multicolored glass or some glossy materials. Weird.

"Once we get there, assuming whoever lives there won't try to kill us, we'll take a break." A much-needed break for her. "And then we'll make plans."

"Plans?"

"Plans on escaping this miserable, make-believe world." I had a wereape to get to. A life. Being stuck here twice was bad enough. Hell, I never imagined I'd be back here. Yet here I was.

I wasn't about to give up. I *would* get out. I would.

For that, I needed help. And the only person I could think of to do just that was the size of my hand and had beautiful wings.

"Tinker Bell!" I howled across the meadow. "Tinky! It's me, Tessa. I need your help!"

Dolores stopped and whirled around. "What are you doing?"

271

"Calling my only ally in this place." I just hoped she could hear me.

"And alerting everyone else that we're here."

I blinked at her. "I know. But I'll chance it."

Dolores's face stilled in anger. "You will stop that right now. Think of Beverly and Ruth. The fewer people who know about them, about us, the better. But if you keep shouting at the top of your lungs like a banshee, you'll put everyone in danger."

Okay, she had a point. But I still felt like we needed Tinker Bell. "Fine." I didn't want to get into a fight with my aunt, not in this place and not when she was injured.

When we finally reached the house, I had to stop and blink several times because I couldn't believe what I was looking at.

The exterior walls of the house were made of what looked like gingerbread. White frosting decked the roof peppered with ice-cream sprinkles. Red-and-white candy canes framed the windows and the front door.

"It's made of candy?" Samael was a strange one. "If this is the gingerbread house in the *Hansel and Gretel* stories, there's a witch inside." A witch that ate little children.

"She will help us."

"She's a cannibal."

Dolores gave me one of her infamous pointed looks, and then, without warning, she stepped onto the butterscotch porch and made for the front door. I cursed and ran after her. For a witch who'd suffered blows from a god, she was still annoyingly faster than me.

My aunt didn't bother knocking as she pushed the front door and walked in.

But I wasn't going in there without a weapon.

I searched the ground, found a heavy enough dead branch, and followed her in, holding my makeshift weapon in the air like a sword. Or was that a wand?

The fact of the matter was my magic, *our* magic, was useless in this place. So we'd have to make do with our physical attributes and skills.

It was hopeless.

I ran in after her, my loyal stick with me. Dolores stood in the middle of a space between the kitchen and the living area. There were no seating arrangements apart from a table and chairs next to what looked like a kitchen. Shelves lined the walls with jars, cans, and bags of flour. Next to them stood tall storage cabinets and a long worktable packed with pots and pans. The air was hot and had the scent of banana bread and vanilla. I loved banana bread, yet the smell made my stomach churn.

And the largest antique cooking woodstove I'd ever seen stood at the end of the kitchen area. Large enough to fit a few kids and possibly some witches.

There were no doors or other rooms that I could see. "She's not here. It's empty." I'd left the front door open in case we needed to make a quick getaway.

"There's a fire in the stove," said my aunt, as though the idea soothed her somehow. "She'll come back."

Hopefully not with a couple of kids. "Maybe." Part of me had hoped to find the cannibal witch here. She might have had some information on how to get out of Storybook or even know of a portal. Witches were aware of those kinds of things, even in this make-believe place. Or, at the very least, she could have something to help Dolores and her pain. I took a breath and let it out. "I'm sorry, Dolores," I told her. "I know you thought they were in here." The fact that they weren't only reinforced my feeling that Beverly and Ruth weren't in Storybook.

My aunt said nothing as she admired the stove, her brows knitted together.

I walked over to the table, grabbed a chair, and pushed her into it. "Sit, before you pass out."

"I will not pass out."

I moved over to the long table with the assortment of jars, containers, and dried herbs, looking for something that might help her. Tea would be great. But nothing was here. Guess we'll have to wait for the witch to come back.

"Tessa?"

I spun to the familiar, bell-sounding voice.

A tiny female human, the size of my hand, hovered in the doorway. Transparent, butterfly-like wings fluttered behind her as she drifted closer. Her green strapless dress contrasted against her fair skin, matching the green flats on her feet. With her blonde hair up in a bun, she had the cutest pointy elf-like ears.

My shoulders slumped. "Oh. Thank the cauldron. I wasn't sure if you'd heard me."

The tiny fairy floated at my eye level. She smiled and said, "I heard you. You do have a *very* loud voice."

I cringed. That meant if she heard me, others had also heard me. It didn't matter. I needed to focus on the more important matters.

Bursts of wind patted my face as the fairy glided in the air in front of me. "Tinker Bell. I need your help to get us out of here."

A cute frown pulled the fairy's face. "But why are you back?"

"Long story. But my aunt and I need to find our way back home."

The fairy looked over at my aunt, and her lips parted, something like shock crossing her pretty features.

"Tinker Bell?" I cast my gaze at Dolores. She was standing and staring at the fairy with a deep loathing. What was that about?

When I looked back at the fairy, her face was ashen. Tension slid through me at the fear I saw move over her face and creep into the stiffness of her flying.

"Tinker Bell?" I tried again.

The fairy looked at me. She clamped her jaw and hesitated, struggling with something she was about to reveal. "That's *not* your aunt."

I felt like I'd been kicked in the gut with a size sixteen boot. "What?" A nauseating mix of dread and fear shook my knees.

I looked back at Dolores. The touch of triumph in her eyes and arrogance curving her lips rang alarm bells in my mind.

"I regret ever creating that miserable flying bug," said Dolores, her voice deeper, her skin rippling like I'd seen Marcus's do many times when he was about to beast out into his alter ego, King Kong.

The pulse of magic thrummed heavily in the air and coated my skin like a thick mist. Whatever magic this was, it was ancient and powerful.

I stared in shock and disbelief as the witch, I thought was my aunt, slowly morphed into a taller, more masculine shape until glittering black eyes peered from within a cold, pale face. His expression was mild, amused, cold, and vengeful.

Samael.

Well, crap.

CHAPTER
23

What does a witch do when she's facing a powerful god? She goes crazy on his ass.

"You son of a bitch!" I howled, waving my stick at him as I imagined smacking it across his stupid face. "You tricked me. You've been lying to me this whole time." I realized like an idiot that we were never with Dolores. It had always been him, disguised as my aunt. "The cemetery? That was you?"

"Indeed." Samael's teeth showed as his lips curled into an ugly smile. His blond hair was slicked back, making his sharp features stand out. This time around, a red, three-piece suit clung to his lean frame with a neat white tie.

And… yup. The cape was back.

It took every ounce of strength to stay put and resist the urge to rush over and kick him in the throat. "You sick bastard." I caught sight of Tinker Bell as she flew over to the table and hid behind one of the chairs. "Why? Why did you do this?" Because he was a sick son of a bitch.

Samael's smile was like he'd won a poker game, stealing all my chips and my date. "I had to get you to follow me."

"Get me to follow you here?"

"Yes."

"To trap me again. Is that it?"

Samael's eyes widened. "How perceptive of you."

"Screw you." Rage flared inside me. I was furious for letting myself believe this was Dolores. How could I not tell this wasn't my aunt? I was a fool. And I'd paid for my folly. "What happened to the castles?"

"I got rid of them. They bored me."

"Like a kid losing interest in his toys."

His right eye twitched, his expression darkened as he angled his head. "I told you before. You needed to play your part in this game."

"You mean your demented games. No thanks."

"I had to bring you here."

"Why?" I took a step forward, losing all sense of reason, along with my fear. All I felt was fury. I was going to hit him. I knew I was. "What is it about me that has you so stalkerish? Why the obsession? I took nothing from you."

Samael seemed to catch my intention as he casually glanced at the stick in my hand. "Oh, but you did. You took something precious from me."

Okay, now I was infuriated and confused. But more infuriated. "What is this crap flowing out of your mouth. I took nothing from you, you crazy bastard." I heard Tinky's intake of breath at my choice of words. Yes. This was not the polite way to speak to a god. But at this point, I had nothing to lose.

Anger pinched his eyes. "Oh, but you did."

I knew that was a lie. He was just toying with me to give me a reason why he wanted to put me here again. "Why not just kill me?" I took another step closer. "You've had many occasions to do it. You could have killed me while I slept when you pretended to be Marcus—which is really pervy, by the way."

"Yes." Samael sighed dramatically. "Unfortunately, I cannot."

That was interesting. "Why? Because I'm soooo *irresistible*?"

The god raised a questionable brow. "Not in the least. Because my mother made it so. She put a spell on you that prevents me from being able to kill you. And I've tried. Many times. But unfortunately, I cannot break the spell."

I frowned. Lilith put a spell on me to protect me from her son? Why hadn't she told me? But it explained why he'd sent the scarecrow and the jester. Because *he* couldn't kill me.

Samael raised his hands. "And now you're here. And you'll stay here… forever."

"Not going to happen."

The god laughed, and I inched closer. The grip on my stick tightened. "What happened to my aunts? Where are they? What did you do to them?"

"As much as I would have loved to rip apart their old, disgusting bodies, I had nothing to do with their disappearance."

"Liar."

"Maybe. Maybe not."

I pointed the stick to his face. "You tell me what you did to them." My throat contracted as I swallowed, my fear redoubling.

"Or what? You'll flog me with your little stick?" The god laughed. "I am a god. You're nothing but a weak, mortal female."

"Fine. I'm mortal and weak. You still haven't told me why you want me here, in this place." I watched his face. "Oh, I get it. You're *in love* with me."

Samael looked like he might puke. "I am *not* in love with you."

"Oh, yes, you are," I pressed, enjoying seeing the disgust for me on his face. I didn't think I was that gross, but whatever. To each his own, right?

Samael's face rippled in revulsion as his eyes rolled over me. "The thought of loving a despicable, weak creature such as you is repulsive. Gods don't fornicate with mortals."

"Sure they do, but keep telling yourself that, lover boy." I winked at him, and my smile widened at the displeasure I saw on his face.

Samael started to pace the room. "You took something from me," he said again like he was testing the words on his tongue.

I shook my head, following him with my eyes. "I didn't."

"You see," he began, admiring the walls of his gingerbread house. "I was next in line to rule the Netherworld."

"I thought Lucifer ruled the Netherworld."

"There are different levels to the chain of command. In your world, it is like a lieutenant. A commander in chief. Without Lilith to stand in my way, it was to be mine. All that power *was* to be mine. But when you released my mother from her prison, well, she was once again at her post."

Oh crap. Now things started to make sense. "You're pissed at me because you lost your promotion?" Of course he was. With Lilith back, he was nothing more than the prodigal son—a discarded leader who had been at the post while his mommy was away. And now she took it from him.

And all because of me. Oopsie.

"So *that's* why you wanted to kill me?" Okay, now I began to understand his deep loathing of me. "I had no idea that releasing your mother would do that. How could I? It's not like I'm involved in the Netherworld's politics. I didn't know."

I took a chance and looked over at Tinker Bell, who was staring at me with her wide eyes filled with fear as she kept glancing from me to the god. She couldn't help me. Not now. Not against the god who'd created her.

The god turned his burning glare to me. "Without you, Lilith would have never been released," he voiced with barely controlled rage. "Without you, *I'd* still be in command. You did this to me. You. And you're going to pay."

A bout of foolishness took over, and before I knew what I was doing, I hit Samael over the head with the stick as hard as I could, snapping it in half with the effort. Maybe I could render him unconscious.

The god stumbled back, and victory filled my gut. I'd hurt him. Yay! Look at me go!

And just when I thought it had worked, and I was ready to do some damage to his godly junk, he straightened and smiled at me.

Uh-oh.

"You hit like a girl," said Samael.

"Funny, I was just about to say the same thing to you."

Samael's face creased in amusement. "I'll give you points for creativity, but you fail in strength. You're a weak female. Without strength, you have nothing. Whereas I *am* strength and power and darkness. But I am less inclined to tolerate the stupidity behind these mindless affronts. You will pay for what you took from me."

A tiny whimper sounded from Tinker Bell. Ice licked my spine as I felt my bravado from before, evaporating. I took a step back, the remaining part of the stick feeling heavy in my grasp. "You said it yourself. You can't kill me. Lilith's spell protects me."

Samael's face crinkled into a wicked smile as he said, "From killing you, yes. But not from pain. Lots and lots of delicious, unimaginable pain." A dark glee simmered in the backs of his eyes, unholy and absolute. And then he raised his hand and snapped his fingers.

I wasn't sure I was ready for this. Not sure I knew how much it was going to hurt.

But it did.

A sharp pain struck my body like an electric shock. I screamed. And then I screamed again. Every nerve in my body was alight with fire, scorching me from the inside. My stomach twisted as undulating surges of pain grew and grew until I felt like nothing was left of me but my clothes. A band tightened around my chest, and I couldn't breathe. That, or all the air had disappeared.

The god's power pressed me down while I struggled and screamed uselessly, my mind too full of terror to focus or defend myself. Magic burned through my skin and insides, sending searing pain soaring through my body and making me crumple in agony.

Laughter, rich, deep, sick, and mocking reached my ears. The bastard was enjoying this.

Some of the pain was released, and I took a gasping breath.

"The thing with Storybook," said Samael as he appeared before me. "Is that mortals, like you, can live forever. You won't age. You'll stay young and fresh. Isn't that wonderful?"

"Go to hell." I realized that wouldn't really do much since he was the son of hell.

Samael chuckled again at my obvious pain, ticking me off all the more. "You will never die, Tessa Davenport. You will live forever. And you will feel pain *forever*."

I barely had time to brace myself as the pain hit. It was like being beaten down by a giant hammer at my head and body while I shrieked against it. Excruciating pain surged and then nothing.

I blinked through tears and saw a smiling Sa-mael. He didn't want to kill me. He wanted me to suffer tremendous agony while he relished in it.

Sobs caught my attention, and I raised my head to see Tinker Bell hovering in the air before my eyes, a manic expression on her face.

"It's okay," I wheezed.

The fairy turned toward her Creator. "Stop. Please stop. You're hurting her."

Samael glanced lazily at the fairy. "Don't make me regret the day I made you."

"Tinker Bell," I panted. Every word sent a jarring pain inside my skull. "You should go. I don't want you to see this." I didn't want anyone to see this.

The fairy made fists with her hands. "No. This isn't right. Tessa is my friend."

"Get another friend," said the god as he chuckled.

She yanked out her tiny dagger. And then the next thing I saw, she zoomed at him like a massive, angry wasp.

"Tinker Bell!"

An invisible force swatted the fairy, and she hit the side wall with a horrible crunch. My breath caught as she plopped to the floor, her wings bent awkwardly.

Fury soared. "You bastard. Why create things if you're only going to destroy them." I didn't know if the tiny fairy was dead, but she was undoubtedly unconscious.

Samael sneered. "Because it's fun. Just like in-flicting pain on you gives me"—he shuddered in delight—"great satisfaction."

"Fuck you," I said, my voice hoarse, lips trembling as hot tears fell freely down my face, past my chin.

Samael giggled. It sounded juvenile. "The forces of the worlds granted you a mighty gift, Tessa." His voice took on an edge of vicious, spiteful satisfaction. "Being of two different worlds. It allowed you to borrow magic from demons and cast elemental spells."

And ley lines, but he didn't say it. Maybe he didn't know about them. Good. Because if I were able to use them and get out of Storybook, they might come in handy again.

Samael halted, clicking his heels together. "You know, I'd always wondered how you managed to escape. I didn't think it possible for anyone to leave."

I smiled at him, tasting blood in my mouth. "But I did."

"Yes. Because of the ley lines." I stiffened, and he smiled at what was most certainly shock and fear on my face. "That was unexpected. Good play on your part."

"I wasn't playing." A cold panic started to form in my gut. I'd been holding on to the idea that the ley lines might help me leave again. But if he knew about them, I was pretty sure they'd be useless to me now.

"You won't be able to use them anymore," he said, like he'd pulled those thoughts from inside my forehead. "There's nothing you can do. You will stay here. And you will suffer like you've made me suffer."

My lips parted, but nothing was coming out. My body shook with pain. My head lolled to the side because I didn't have the strength to keep it straight.

Before I knew what was happening, I heard the sharp sound of flesh smacking flesh. When the pain hit, I realized it had been my flesh. *My* face.

The world lurched, and I hit the cold floor again. A pained sob escaped me as I lay in a crumpled heap, my breath a whisper and my lungs burning with every intake of air.

Someone screamed. Tinker Bell? Me? I didn't know.

I tried to move but couldn't even feel my legs or arms anymore. I strained to keep my head up. I blinked but couldn't stop the darkness that crept into my vision.

Would this be my life? To suffer at the hands of this god… in perpetuity?

Dismay, fear, and guilt were all the emotions that ran through me. I would never see my

287

family and friends again. I would never look upon Marcus's handsome face.

No. I would be here. Suffering. All because I'd let out the goddess of hell from her cage.

I closed my eyes and thought, *Let it end. Just let it end.*

CHAPTER
24

I lay there in a crumpled heap, sobbing in agony and sorrow, thinking I better get used to this since this was what my future looked like. I went deep inside myself, where there was nothing, just a profound darkness and despair.

Tears fell freely down my face as a pained weep escaped me. My breath was a whisper, and my lungs burned with every intake of air.

After a few moments, I didn't feel much of the pain as I went numb, body and mind.

I would rather die than feel this kind of hurt forever. The thought of never seeing Marcus again was a different kind of anguish. Deeper and unbearable.

When the pain stopped completely, I thought I had imagined it. Maybe I'd gone so far deep inside my psyche that I was in a waking coma or something. Blinking through tears, I spotted a tall, redheaded goddess.

Okay, *now* I was going crazy.

"I'm disappointed in you, Samael," came Lilith's voice. "So disappointed in you. How could you do this? I thought you were done with your games."

Okay, maybe I *wasn't* imagining this. Maybe Lilith *was* here?

With the pain gone, I felt a little daring come to me. I propped myself up on my elbows, and a dizzy spell hit. But otherwise, I could see very clearly. Yup. That was the goddess.

Lilith stood in the tiny gingerbread house with her arms crossed over her chest, looking livid. I didn't think I'd ever seen her this angry. But it was more than that. Disappointment crossed her face. "You thought you could take Tessa away and hide her here? You thought I wouldn't find out?"

"Get out," seethed Samael, and I swear I saw fear reflecting in his black eyes. Good. Fear looked good on his stupid face. "This is *my* world. I made it. It's *mine*! Leave!" he shouted as he stomped his foot.

Oooh. Temper, temper.

"That's my little demon witch," said his mother, and she uncrossed her arms and stepped forward to where I was lying on the floor. "I told you to stay away from her. I told you not to touch her. But you didn't listen. You never listen to me."

Fury slipped over Samael's brow, born from frustration. "You're not taking this away from me. You can't. *I* made this. *Me*. Not you. Not Father. *I'm* the one gifted with creating worlds. Something you lack, dear mother."

Lilith shrugged. "Maybe. But if you had listened to me, I wouldn't have cared about this…" She raised her arms. "This charming little world you've got going here." Her red eyes settled on her son. "I can't let you keep it."

In a rage, Samael grabbed the table and threw it at his mother. It was about an inch from her face when it vanished.

Wow. And here I thought I had problems with my mother. I took that distraction to search for Tinker Bell. She sat up against a wall, her left wing bent at an odd angle. Crap. It was broken. I could see some blood trickling down her nose, but otherwise, she was okay. She was alive.

She caught me staring, and I lifted a finger to my lips. The last thing I needed was for them to notice the fairy and decide to end her because they felt like it. Gods. You just never know with them. Tinker Bell was safe where she was. For now.

"You took everything from me, you stupid bitch," shouted Samael. "You should have

291

stayed in your prison. Everyone knows it. You don't have what it takes to rule. Females are too emotional. They're not fit to govern."

What a douche.

Lilith was shaking her head. "All you had to do was leave Tessa alone. It was simple. And you couldn't even follow those instructions."

"I don't have to listen to you." Samael's body shook with rage. "You're nothing. You're just a whore."

Tightness pulled Lilith's face. "Careful. I'm your mother. You better start showing me some respect."

"Respect?" Samael gave a mock laugh. "You don't deserve my respect. I hate you."

I'm not sure how I would feel hearing my son speak to me like that, but Lilith was taking it like a champ. I couldn't see much emotion on her face. Words like that must hurt. Even if she was a goddess, she wasn't without feeling, but I couldn't see it.

Yet I knew she loved her son. I'd seen it in her eyes when I'd tried to summon Loki and even before that. She'd kept his identity secret because she wanted to protect him.

Lilith tsked. "You know, when you get like that, part of me wants to throw you over my knee and give you a good spanking."

"Amen," I laughed, playing it out in my mind as it gave me immense satisfaction, but immediately regretted it when Samael's attention flicked to me.

Samael glanced back at his mother. "I'm not giving up the witch. We haven't finished our game."

"Yes, you have," said Lilith.

Samael threw his hands up dramatically, his cape swishing behind him. "What is your fascination with her? Are you lovers? Is that it? You want to *screw* her."

"You're an asshole," I said and pushed to my feet. Though I did sway for a moment, I managed to get my footing. I felt terrible for Lilith for having such an ungrateful, selfish child. If she had other children, I hoped they were a little nicer.

Samael's face stretched into a smile that reminded me of the scarecrow dude he'd sent to hurt me. "I'm not finished with you. We have lots to do, you and me."

I looked over at Lilith, hoping she'd come here to stop him, to take me home.

Samael caught me looking. "She can't stop me." The god laughed, his eyes gleaming with a manic glee. "She's nothing. She's not as powerful as me. I have my father's blood, his power."

Lilith sighed, and I noticed she looked a little defeated, crushed. "I'm taking Tessa back to her world. And you will never hurt her again."

"No!" Samael stomped his feet, pacing around the gingerbread house. He kicked one of the chairs, which crashed next to the wall where Tinker Bell rested. But it didn't touch her.

"Yes," said Lilith. "You've had your fun. And now it's over."

Samael whirled around and came dangerously close to his mother. Both were tall, but he was slightly taller than her. He leaned forward until his nose nearly brushed against hers. His expression became almost grotesque. "It's over when I say it's over. And I say I'm not finished playing with the witch."

"You are done, Samael. It's over."

He leaned back, laughing a disturbing, high-pitched laugh. "And when I'm finished with her, I'll kill her. And then… then I'll kill you!" He started to laugh again.

Yeah, this guy was crazy.

The goddess sighed, sadness heavy in her expression. "It's our fault," she said, her voice holding layers of emotion. "We've spoiled you, and look what you've become."

Samael raised his arms like he was about to offer himself to another god. "A powerful god. The *most* powerful god in the worlds."

"A spoiled little boy," said Lilith. "That's all you are. A boy. An immature little child."

Samael looked to the ground for a moment, emotions playing along his jaw and forehead. He pointed a finger at Lilith. "Careful, Mother. If you try to stop me, I'll kill you!" he shouted.

Lilith glanced at me. "If you ever have kids with that glorious wereape, don't spoil them too much. Because when you do, they become monsters."

"I'll keep that in mind." We'd never discussed kids, but I knew someday we would have them.

Samael looked at me, his eyes gleaming with fever. And then he smiled.

Uh-oh.

The air cracked and hissed like an electrical storm as massive amounts of power and magic rushed around us. The floor shook, the gingerbread house walls trembled, and clumps started to fall around us. The floor heaved around my feet. I stumbled several steps back and watched as segments of the roof collapsed, and giant chunks of icing splattered the floors. The gingerbread walls shook, loosening up.

Shit. The house was going to cave in on us.

Tinker Bell!

I staggered over to her and scooped her up in my hands as gently as I could in a hurry. Shielding her against my chest, I spun around.

Lilith and Samael faced each other, arms splayed at their sides like they were about to duel. Lilith's hair floated around her like she was underwater, great bouts of power emitting from her. A rush of energy flooded the house. It was both hot and cold, and I couldn't tell which was Lilith's and which was Samael's.

My breath came fast as another torrent of energy surged, larger this time, with a force that shook me.

Lilith's magic, her goddess magic, was red coiling around her arms like bracelets, the same color as her eyes. She smiled at what she saw on my face, probably a combination of shock and intrigue.

A burst of energy boomed around us, and Lilith rocked back as though a violent, invisible wave smashed into her. Samael crouched, a victorious smile on his stupid face.

Lilith straightened. Her face deadly calm. Raw force lashed out and hit Samael. The god staggered back, shaking his head as if he'd been dazed.

I had no idea who was stronger, the mother or the son. Both seemed to have acquired significant amounts of power, but I was rooting for Lilith. She'd put a protective spell on me to keep her crazy-ass son from killing me. And now she'd shown up here, saying she was taking me back. A foolish part of me wanted to help her win. But what the hell could I do? I couldn't even do magic in this world.

Samael lunged with inhuman speed at Lilith. The gingerbread house shook as he slammed her into the wall next to the kitchen. Chunks of bread and icing fell around them like snow.

Samael pinned his mother by the neck. And I was disturbed by the triumphant smile on his face. Lilith's face was screwed up in a vicious snarl, muscles from her neck and shoulders bulging as she struggled under her son's hold.

In a blur that was almost unnoticeable, Lilith moved fast, knocking Samael's hold on her. She kicked him in the gut with a powerful blow, and Samael staggered back, his black eyes wild and frantic with a visible smile on his face.

"I think you guys need some family therapy," I said, though neither of them heard me.

Lilith lurched herself at Samael. Matching the god in speed and agility, she leaped in the air and hit him with a powerful kick to the jaw. Impressive. I had no idea she could fight like that: a goddess of many talents.

The air was filled with the sounds of grunts and fists hitting flesh. I even saw some long red strands of hair drifting in the air. Samael's face was creased with effort as he slammed Lilith into the kitchen cabinets, bread and candy shards exploding from the impact.

A massive clump of icing fell at my feet, making me jump.

"Maybe we should get out?" said Tinker Bell, looking up at me.

"Did I ever tell you how smart you were?" I told her, gauging the distance between me and the front door, which stood ajar.

A smile formed on the fairy's lips. "No."

"Well, you are. Hang on." I glanced over at the gods, seeing them still battling, and then rushed out the door. Only when I got about fifty feet away did I turn around.

"What do we do if Samael wins?"

I looked down at the fairy resting in my hand. "Pray that he doesn't." Because if he won, I'd never see my family again, or Marcus.

I took a moment to observe the tiny fairy, and now that I could, I saw traces of pain across her face. I knew she was holding it in. She was pale, more so than usual. Her wing was broken, and I had no idea how to fix it.

There was a sudden sonic boom, and I staggered back with the impact. I watched as the walls of the gingerbread house fell as though it were made of cards, until nothing was left.

Well, the only things standing were Lilith and her son.

The next thing I saw was Lilith raising her hand. Something shot out of it, but I couldn't tell what that was.

"No!" screamed Samael.

And that's when things got a little weird.

Samael, son of Lilith and Lucifer, started to *shrink*.

His body rippled, not unlike before when he had been in the shape of Aunt Dolores as he'd morphed back into himself. But this was a bit different. Not only was he shrinking, but his face changed. It went from a thirty-year-old man to a teenager to a young boy and continued until he was about four feet tall. And then he was gone. I couldn't see him anymore.

"Did you see that?" I asked the fairy.

"Yup. Do you think she killed him?"

"Good question." I started forward, not sure if a mother was capable of killing her own son, and halted at the clumps of clothes above the rubble of gingerbread and candy cane.

A baby lay over the pile of dark clothes. A cute, chubby, wriggling infant that couldn't be more than a year old.

"Holy shit."

Samael, the grown-ass god, was now a cute little baby.

Lilith walked over to her newly transformed child, wrapped him up in his shirt like a blanket, lifted him up, and held him close to her breast. "This is my favorite age for him," she said, all smiles as the baby Samael grinned at his mother and touched her face.

"Uh, does that mean you've done this before?"

Lilith kissed her baby's fingers. "Yes. When he becomes disobedient and unbearable, I change him back to a baby. I much prefer him like this. Isn't he beautiful?"

Tinker Bell and I shared a look before I answered. "He is adorable. And look at those cheeks."

"I know." Lilith rubbed her head playfully against her baby's belly. Samael let out a garbled laugh.

I couldn't believe I thought he was cute when only moments ago, he'd inflicted me with excruciating pain. But he was adorable. Damn him.

Funny how something so small and cute could grow up to be a monster.

I watched mother and child exchange their love for a moment. "Are my aunts okay?" I remembered them being missing. Samael could have killed them out of spite. Lilith had put a protective spell on me, not my aunts.

Lilith made faces at her son. "They're fine."

I let out a breath of relief. "Thank the cauldron. So now what? You take me back?"

"Yes," answered the goddess. "But first, I'll destroy this world. Then I'll take you back home."

Tension soared anew. "But…" I stared at the tiny fairy. Her expression went a little green, and I could see the tears brimming in her eyes. "If you do that, what happens to the inhabitants of Storybook?"

Lilith shrugged as she started to rock her baby in her arms. "They'll cease to exist. Who cares."

"No." A foolish part of me wanted to slap her. It infuriated me how she could be so loving one moment and utterly insensitive the next.

"Tinker Bell comes back with me. I'm not leaving without her." I knew giving the goddess an ultimatum was a no-no, and she could decide to end me with this world her son created. But she was all smiling, staring lovingly at her baby boy. Nothing else mattered to her at that moment, and for the first time, Lilith looked mortal to me. A mortal mother in love with her baby. It was beautiful to watch, but I still wanted to get the hell away from here—with Tinker Bell.

"Fine." Lilith kissed her son's head. "What do I care? You want to take it with you, that's your choice." She lowered her head and began kissing her son all over his face.

I smiled at Tinker Bell, knowing that Ruth would go bananas over her. She slumped against my palm, relieved that she wasn't about to die.

"Okay, then," I breathed. Something occurred to me. "Oh. And the eight paranormals who crossed over by mistake." Scarlett was one of them.

"Yes, yes, fine," answered Lilith, staring lovingly at her baby boy.

That had been easier than I thought. "So when do we leave? Could you—"

With a scent of spices, the world around me vanished.

CHAPTER
25

A moment later, I stood in Davenport House's kitchen.

"Wow. That was fast." And I didn't even feel nauseated or anything.

"Ah!" howled Beverly as she fell from her chair in an unattractive tangle on the floor, both legs in the air.

The mug Dolores was holding exploded. "Tessa? How did you just appear in our kitchen?

"Lilith brought me back," I said. "Long story." I could feel the tears threatening to come as I glanced at my aunts, all alive, all seemingly unharmed.

"Oh, hi, Tessa," said Ruth as she walked into the kitchen with a jar of something in her hand. "When did you get back? Marcus said that you—"

Ruth's eyes widened as she stared at what I held in my hand. Her lips were moving, but no words were coming out. Her blue eyes swam with tears. "Tinky? Is that you?"

Tinker Bell raised her hand and said words that sounded like the chimes of bells. Right. I'd forgotten about that. Now that she was here, I couldn't understand her. But I didn't care. Not when I looked into Ruth's face and saw the happiness, the joy that brought tears to my own eyes.

I swallowed hard. "She's injured. I think her wing is broken. Do you think you can help her?"

That seemed to wake Ruth from her temporary stupor. "Yes. Yes. Put her gently on the island, and let me take a look at her."

I did what I was told and watched as Ruth gently pressed her fingers against Tinker Bell's wing. She leaned back. "It's broken. But I can fix it."

"How?" I asked, amazed.

"Well, I'll need to make a brace for it." Ruth looked at the fairy. "You won't be able to fly for a few days, but it will heal. Fairies heal faster than we do. And I have a few tonics that should triple the healing process. Then you'll be able to fly. Just as before."

Words flew from Tinker Bell's mouth, and she clapped. Her face was bright and smiling.

"I wish I could understand her," I said, knowing that was pushing it. I'd gotten used to being able to communicate with the fairy over in Storybook.

"You will." Ruth looked at my confusion and said, "I'd been working on a translation potion before... well, before Tinky went back to that *other* place." She made finger quotes. "It'll make it so you and everyone else can understand her."

I stared down at the fairy. "Good. That would be amazing."

"Who broke her wing?" Ruth's face went tight with anger.

"The god that sent me those dead roses," I told her.

"What happened to you, Tessa?" Beverly was back on her feet, her face red. "We've been worried sick. Marcus said you were at the Crane family manor with Dolores, and you just disappeared."

"That *wasn't* me," snapped Dolores. "I was here the whole time." She muttered words, and the broken pieces of her mug rose from the floor and moved over to the garbage bin and dropped inside it.

"About that," I said, "Where were you? You weren't here, and it looked like you'd left in a hurry. That's the only reason I thought faux-Dolores was Dolores."

"Gilbert called us in a fret," answered Beverly. "Apparently, a group of forest gnomes got into his store. They trashed the place. We rushed over to help him. Customers were running out screaming."

I was glad they were okay, but that couldn't happen again. "You guys need cell phones."

Dolores dismissed me with a wave of her hand. "I am not using any trinket that gives off radiation."

"Yeah. We don't want brain tumors," said Ruth as she measured Tinker Bell's wing with a tape measure.

I was just about to tell them the amount of radiation emitted by the cell phone was minimal, when Dolores cut me off.

"So what the hell happened to you? We've been going out of our minds trying to figure this out." My tall aunt bore her dark eyes into me with that expression that meant she wasn't going to let me go anywhere until I spilled the beans. And I *really* needed to see one person right now.

So I told them everything—from finding them missing and faux-Dolores in the cemetery to finally Lilith changing her son into a baby.

"I can't believe how rude he was to his own mother," said Beverly as she grabbed her chair and sat. "That's why I never had children. They grow up to be miserable little brats. And they destroy your body. I'd never let anything destroy this superb, glorious physique. Children are a huge no-no when you have a body like mine."

I raised a brow. Why did that not surprise me? "Not all children are brats. I'm pretty sure most kids are good." The way they turned out had a lot to do with their parents, yes, but also their environment.

Beverly tsked. "You're so naïve. Are you going to have kids with Marcus?"

I decided not to get angry with her. "Yes. Eventually. But not for a few years." And not until I was sure no more gods or any other beings were lurking around wanting to kill me. Nope. I had to make damn sure my life was boring enough to raise me a couple of wereape-witchlings.

Beverly made a disgusted sound in her throat and shook her body like the idea of having children repulsed her.

Ruth clapped her hands. "Yay! I *love* babies. All of them are miracles. They're so cute and delicious."

"Why do you say it like you want to *eat* them," chuckled Dolores.

Ruth made angry eyes at her sister, which made her look slightly constipated. "I love babies. Because babies love you unconditionally. Not like snotty older sisters."

306

"But if I *were* to have children," said Beverly, grabbing her glass of wine. "I would be an excellent mother."

Dolores snorted. "Oh, please. Your childbearing days have been over since the Ice Age."

Beverly lost some of her smile as she took a sip of wine. "I don't know what you mean. Lots of women have babies in their forties."

Dolores threw back her head and howled. "Ha. The last time you were in your forties, horses pulled buggies and coaches."

I looked out the window. It was pitch black outside. "How long was I gone?" I still wasn't sure about the time difference between here and Storybook.

"A few hours," answered Dolores. "Not too long."

My heart thrashed as I looked at Ruth. "Hildo won't be happy." I'd noticed that the cat was gone, but he liked to prowl around outdoors at night.

"Don't worry about him," said Ruth as she released the measuring tape and wrote something on her pad. "I'll deal with him. He'll just have to accept that Tinky is part of the family now."

A big sob, well, big for a tiny fairy, erupted from Tinker Bell. Her lips moved as the sound of ringing bells filled the air like wind chimes. I didn't have to understand her words to understand that. She was overwhelmed with happiness. I was too.

Even though Tinker Bell had decided to stay in Storybook, I'd always felt a little sorrowful that we'd left her behind. But now, she'd always be with us. Part of our family.

I felt another spell of emotions spring up inside me. I didn't want to break down and cry. I was too happy to cry. And I wanted to do some *other* things that involved a *different* kind of crying. "You good here? I need to check up on Marcus." He was most probably out of his mind with worry. I pulled out my phone, seeing that I still had battery life. "I should call him."

"Why?" Dolores walked over to the counter, grabbed a chocolate cake, and set it on the table. "He's over at the cottage," she said as she sliced a piece and placed it on a small dessert plate.

I eyed the cake. It looked dangerously good, like a few extra pounds around my ass and hips that I didn't need. "Well, that's a relief." Instead of calling the chief, I quickly texted Iris to let her know that I was alive and fine and that I'd tell her all about it later.

Yanking my eyes from the evil cake that was calling my name, I made my way to the back door. "I'll see you later, Tinky," I told the fairy.

Tinker Bell waved at me, her face flushed with emotions. I could tell she was trying really hard to reel in her feelings, but it wouldn't last. She was about to explode into a sobbing mess.

"Does that mean the wedding is back on?"

I spun around at Beverly's question. "Oh, right. I guess?" Now that Samael was a tiny baby, nothing was stopping Marcus and me from getting married.

"You better go over there quick and revive your man. Lots of reviving." Beverly winked at me.

"I'll see you later."

With my heart in my throat, I dashed across the backyard, sprang onto the front porch, and barged through the front door.

Marcus leaped up from the couch. Papers were strewn over the coffee table, and the ones he held slipped from his fingers.

He stood there, jaw clenched, his expression shifting from shock and fear to something I didn't understand. He went to say something, his emotions showing more than usual, playing on the tension in his shoulders.

"Tessa?" Marcus moved away from the coffee table.

He'd put so much emphasis on my name like he thought he'd never see me again. My insides clenched painfully as emotions cascaded over me in a rapid, fluid torrent.

I didn't care that this was probably a cliché move, but I ran across the room and threw myself into his arms.

Yeah, clichés are fun.

KIM RICHARDSON

Marcus caught me easily, pulling me up into him and holding me close. I buried my face into his warm chest, his musky scent familiar and exhilarating. His muscular arms wrapped around me protectively as though he never wanted to let me go. His body shook with the last of his emotions, his fear of losing me, of what had transpired.

My mouth opened, wanting to say something, but his lips sealed on mine and captured my breath. The dread of Samael, of Storybook, of never seeing Marcus or my friends and family that hung around me like a dark, ragged blanket vanished, obliterated in a rush of lust, need, and love. He grabbed my butt and pulled me closer.

It was a desperate kiss filled with emotions and the things he'd wanted to say to me. I felt the loss he'd felt at the thought of losing me, the ache, and it brought tears to my eyes.

I tasted salt in the kiss. We kept kissing like that in a tight, desperate embrace, Marcus still holding me up, wrapped in his arms like he was afraid he would never see me again if he let me go.

After a moment, he pulled back, his gaze molten. "You just disappeared in front of me," he said, his voice rough with a need that had my heart pumping and my knees weak.

310

"I know." My voice came out in a muffled squeak. A single tear fell over his cheek, and I brushed it away with my thumb.

"How?" Marcus looked at me. He looked so vulnerable. I'd never seen him looking like this before.

I knew what he was asking. "Lilith. Lilith saved me. Samael took me back to Storybook to keep me there forever. Lilith showed up and stopped him." I took a shuddering breath, doing my best not to start wailing at all the emotions that fluttered over the chief's face. I decided not to mention torture for now.

Marcus frowned. "Lilith?"

"I was surprised to see her, knowing Samael is her son. But she did the right thing." And I would be eternally grateful.

The chief sighed. "I've been putting some money together. I think we'll have enough to hire the Dark mages."

"You won't need to anymore." I wiggled out of his arms, and the chief set me on the floor.

"What do you mean?" He rubbed my arms up and down.

"Lilith changed Samael into a baby. It was crazy to watch. Apparently, it's not the first time she's done this. He becomes an uncontrollable psycho god, and Mommy puts him in diapers. He won't be showing up anytime soon." Not in our lifetime. "He'll never bother us again. Ever."

Marcus sighed, the last of his tension releasing in the slump of his shoulders. "That's the best news I've heard in days."

I grinned. "We can finally put all that behind us and move forward."

"With the wedding." He moved his hands around to my back, grabbed my ass, and pulled me hard against him.

"Yes, with the wedding." The thought that we could finally get married had my stomach doing a break dance.

"And other things," he purred, his voice deep with desire, still squeezing my butt.

I flashed him a cheeky grin. "Lots and lots of things." We both had a lot of tension to let go of. And what better way to release all those pent-up emotions than having a go at some horizontal tango?

"Your muscles are all tight," I told him, rubbing my hands over his shoulders. "You need a little release."

Marcus raised a brow. "What kind of release did you have in mind?"

"The dirty kind."

The chief let out a feral growl. "My favorite."

"Mine too."

In a flash, the wereape pulled off his T-shirt, jeans, and underwear to stand in his naked glory, his long, perfect manhood pointing in my direction.

"I've been practicing. Watch this." I attempted to pull off my T-shirt in one clever arm pull, and got my arm and head stuck halfway. Not the sexy striptease I was hoping to accomplish.

Marcus chuckled. "Better leave that to me."

"I *was* trying to seduce you with my uber-striptease skills," I said through the fabric of my T-shirt.

"No need."

I shrieked in glee as my T-shirt, jeans, and panties disappeared.

Marcus wiggled his brows. "Much better." He crushed me against him again, letting me feel the hardness and hotness of his skin on mine. My body snapped to attention as if it had been asleep for years and suddenly woke up.

Marcus grabbed my butt and hoisted me up on his hips, and I wrapped my legs around his waist. He swung me around and carried me to our bedroom. My heart thumped as he lowered me on the bed, his big body on top of mine, all the while sending tiny kisses along my jaw, neck, collarbone, and earlobes. The wereape knew how to turn me on.

Delicious heat pounded through my core, my fingertips, and everywhere. He dragged his mouth from my lips, staring down at me as passion flashed in his eyes.

"I love you," he muttered as he buried himself inside me.

"I love you too, gorilla man."

And with our bodies aligned and hearts pounding as one, we rode it out together until the early morning.

Chapter
26

I woke up a few hours later feeling glorious, relaxed, and ravenous. Of course, all that cardio workout last night would do that to a person.

I needed carbs. Lots and lots of delicious carbs. Ruth's famous chocolate-glazed doughnuts sounded about right. *Three* chocolate glazed doughnuts.

I turned and saw the pillow where Marcus's head had lain last night. After our Olympian-worthy, carnal cardiovascular workouts, I'd dozed off watching him sleep. The man was gorgeous even as he slept. And no, that was not being a stalker. Okay, maybe just a little bit.

I peered through the window, seeing a bright blue sky with no clouds in sight. It was a beautiful morning.

The thought of Ruth's doughnuts had me swinging my legs out of bed and running into the bathroom. I was practically drooling as I imagined how good those doughnuts would taste on my tongue.

After doing my business and brushing my teeth, I pulled on a clean pair of jeans, a bra, and a T-shirt before heading out.

Just as I'd made it across the hall to the open area that included the kitchen and living room—I froze.

A mannequin stood in the middle of my living room.

It sported a white gown with too many layers of fabric and lace and covered in white fur. It was Mrs. Durand's wedding dress. But what the hell was it doing in my living room?

"Oh, hi, sweetie," said my mother, who popped out of my kitchen like a jack-in-the-box. Damn. I'd never even seen her there. She was developing stealth skills.

I swallowed. "Uh. What's *that* doing here?" I pointed at the mannequin in case it was lost on her.

My mother sighed as she walked over to the dress. "I know. I know. It's not ideal."

"Not ideal? It's a monstrosity. And you still haven't told me why it's here in my living room."

My mother went to touch the gown but then withdrew her hand. "Well, we don't have a lot of options. We must make do with what we have."

I walked over, shaking my head. "You've lost me." My stomach rumbled noisily. It sounded like I had a gremlin living in there. It was too early in the morning for my mother's antics. And I was too damn hungry.

"You need a dress. You can't get married in jeans, Tessa, though I know if you had a choice, that's exactly what you'd do."

I frowned at her. "I wouldn't. Give me a little credit." A pretty summer dress would have been fine with me. "You're still avoiding my question."

My mother beamed at me. "Because you're getting married today, silly."

My stomach fell to the floor around my feet. "Excuse me?"

"Yes. Today."

"Today!"

"In four hours."

"In *four* hours!"

"Beverly called me last night," continued my mother, oblivious to the panic attack I was having. "She said the wedding was back on. Thank goodness for that too. I don't think the flowers would have lasted another day. Even with the spells."

My stomach lurched, and I was glad nothing was in it because it would have come out. It wasn't that I *didn't* want to get married. I'd hoped to have a day or so to prepare for it mentally.

"But what about all the guests? I thought we'd told them the wedding was off?"

My mother waved a hand at me. "Don't worry about that. Dolores has been on the phone all morning, setting things straight. Word travels fast in the witch community. All the guests have been informed."

My head started to spin, and I felt dizzy like I couldn't find enough air to fill my lungs. "I need to sit down."

"Don't be nervous, Tessa. It's going to be the most beautiful garden wedding you've ever seen."

I let myself fall into the couch. "Easy for you to say. You don't have to wear some poor animal's hide. I thought you hated this thing. I thought you were against me wearing it."

My mother looked back at the dress. "I was. I am. But there's no time to go shopping for a dress."

I rubbed my face with my hands. "I'm not wearing that."

"Okay. Hear me out. We'll make some adjustments to it."

"How about we burn it." I had the sudden urge to scratch my arms as an itch formed, like hundreds of fleas crawling over me.

"Stop that," ordered my mother, her eyes narrowing. "You don't want to leave marks over your skin and look like a leper." She sighed and glanced back at the gown, her hands on her hips. "We can get rid of all the fur. And some of the lace. If we can remove these horrible sleeves and give you cap sleeves, that will make a world of difference. The material is quite nice, excellent quality. We can make it beautiful, Tessa."

"I hate it." I was grumpy. That's what you got when you were hungry. Tessa-Zilla.

"It's not *that* bad," commented my mother, her face grimacing and her hands tracing over the dress but never touching it. Guess she thought it had fleas too.

I snorted and leaned back on the couch, crossing my arms. "Right. I remember you telling Mrs. Durand I would never wear this dress."

"Things change."

"Not when you're talking creepy wedding dresses," I said. "And Mrs. Durand said it was okay to tear up her family heirloom like this?" The memory of the shock and distaste she held for me after I'd laughed at it was still very fresh in my mind. Not to mention giving me the cold shoulder in Marcus's office. I didn't think she still wanted me to marry her son. Not when Allison was back in town.

My mother laughed. "Not at first. Marcus was over there this morning to tell his parents the good news. And without a dress, she knew you'd be stuck. But Marcus told his mother if you didn't want to wear it, that was your choice. He would never ask you to do something you weren't comfortable with. And then Katherine suggested that you could… *alter* it. So there you go. Everyone's happy."

I pursed my lips. "How do you know this?"

"Because he's the one who brought over the dress this morning. He called me."

"Hmmm." He had the tendency to leave earlier than humanly possible. "But how are we going to alter the dress? I don't know anything about sewing, and you're not exactly a seamstress."

My mother raised an annoyed brow. "My sisters are going to help."

As if on cue, the front door burst open, and Dolores, Beverly, and Ruth all came strolling in.

A flutter of wings reached me, and Tinker Bell flew past them to settle on the coffee table next to me.

"You can fly?" I stared at her wings, and both were up and functional. Ruth had said it would take time. Obviously, fairies healed way faster.

"Ruth fixed it," said the fairy. She gave a flap of her wings to show me. "Good as new."

"I can understand you!" I reached out, wanting to squeeze her, but thought better of it and pulled my hands away as I realized I might break her other wing in my excitement.

"My translation potion was ready this morning." Ruth came over and set a plate filled with golden Belgian waffles and a cup of steaming coffee in front of me. I was spoiled. It wasn't her chocolate-glazed doughnuts, but it was good enough. I needed carbs, and carbs I *would* have.

I grabbed a waffle and took a bite. "Wow," I said, my mouth full. "So good." I did a little dance with my feet.

Ruth beamed. "I knew you'd be hungry."

"Yeah, with all the commotion we heard last night," said Beverly as she set her purse on the kitchen island and sashayed into the living room.

I stopped mid-chew. I wasn't sure if she was joking or not. Could she really hear us? It wasn't the first time she'd stated that, with Marcus and me living only a few feet from the big house. The idea was mortifying. I swallowed and tore into my waffle.

"Urgh." Beverly stood next to the manne-quin. "Would you look at that?" She touched the fabric of the dress with her finger. The look on her face was like she was sniffing sour milk. "This thing belongs in a petting zoo. Looks like something Katherine would wear," she snick-ered. "The woman has always had *dreadful* taste in clothes."

"But not in men, right?" Dolores dumped the books she'd been holding on the coffee table next to the plate of waffles. It was no secret that Beverly had dated Mr. Durand before Katherine. "Martha was kind enough to give us some of her altering spells. Should be easy enough to make it the way you want, Tessa." She looked at me. "But are you sure? You don't have to wear it. I'm sure we could find something else."

Beverly flicked a strand of her blonde hair from her eyes. "I wouldn't be caught dead in another woman's wedding dress."

"No. Just in another woman's bed with her husband," scoffed Dolores.

Beverly spread her red lips into a knowing smile. "Touché."

I opened my mouth to answer Dolores, but my mother got there first. "No, she doesn't have time to shop for a dress. She's getting married in less than four hours. *This* is the dress. We'll just have to make it into something my daughter will be happy to wear. Right, Tessa?"

"Hmmm," I said as I swallowed the last of my waffle and then reached out and grabbed another. If I ate enough of these waffles, maybe the dress wouldn't fit. Yeah, that was the plan.

Tinker Bell laughed. "You eat like a pig."

I smiled, thrilled that we could carry on a conversation on this side of the world. "I know. But it's hard not to when you taste Ruth's cooking. Here, try some."

The fairy walked over to the plate and pulled herself a piece of the Belgian waffle. She popped it into her mouth, and I laughed as her eyes rolled in the back of her head. "What *is* this? It tastes amazing."

I laughed harder. "I know. Ruth's Belgian waffles."

"I have a feeling I'm going to lose my figure living here," said the fairy, a chunk of waffle stuck to her cheek.

"I know that too." We both started laughing as we continued to eat our waffles. It would have been an enjoyable, perfect morning, except for that horrid dress that looked like it could pick itself up and run away.

"We should get started." Dolores flipped through one of Martha's books. "We'll need at least an hour for the dress. And there are still all the tents and chairs to set up. And the caterers will be here in two hours."

"And the garden arbor," said Ruth. She looked at me and added, "Me and Tinky added a spell to the pink and white roses weaved in the trellis so that they keep shooting golden fairy dust."

Ruth held her palm out to the fairy for a high five, and Tinker Bell jumped into the air and smacked my aunt's palm. God, these two were cute. My gut warmed at seeing them and seeing Tinker Bell with us. I could have never left her behind. Never. She was part of the family now.

Something occurred to me. "Where did you sleep?" If she was to live with us, she deserved her own room or space. She didn't need *much* space, but she needed her own space.

"Your house made me a room," said the fairy, her face brightening. "Right next to Ruth's. There's a small red door. That's my room."

I felt another wave of emotion rush in, and I blinked fast. "House is great." I tapped my hand on the wall. "Thanks for that, House."

I heard a soft rumbling of pipes inside the walls, and I knew that was House's way of saying, "You're welcome."

"How are you wearing your hair?" My mother appeared, and I had no idea how long she'd been standing there, listening to our conversation.

"Uhh…"

"Uhhh-up or uhhh-down?" My mother flashed me her familiar annoyed frown. "What about half-up? That would look very pretty and classy."

I really hadn't given it much thought, not when I had a god on my ass who wanted me dead. Well, wanted to induce torture forever. "I'm not sure it'll matter, if I have to wear the dead animals."

"Stop saying that," snapped my mother. "I told you. We'll take care of the *fur*."

"It's already done." Dolores stood next to the now fur-less gown, her arms filled with white bundles of fur. She sneezed. "I'll need a shower after this."

I stared at the gown. Without the fur, it didn't look half-bad. A little old-fashioned, but with my mother's and aunts' help, I could start seeing the bigger picture.

My mother clapped her hands together. "We're getting somewhere. I had no idea what was under all that."

"That's what he said," chuckled Beverly.

"Okay, Tessa. Now it's your turn." My mother grabbed my hand and pulled me to my feet.

"What are you talking about?" I yanked my arm out of her grip.

My mother gestured toward the dress. "You need to put it on. Strip."

"What? Now? No. I don't think so." I knew eventually that grotesque cloth would have to touch my skin. I'd hoped it wouldn't be so soon and early in the morning.

My mother propped her hands on her hips. "Don't you start."

"Don't *make* me start."

"Tessa." Ruth appeared between us. "You have to put it on so we can start the tailoring spells. You have to be *wearing* it."

"It's been dry-cleaned, so you don't have to worry about any… unpleasant smells," said my mother, still with her eyebrows raised expectantly. "Tessa?" My mother snapped her fingers at me. "Come on. We don't have all day."

Tinker Bell laughed, and I gave her a look before removing my T-shirt and jeans. "I swear, if I get hives, I'll never speak to any of you ever again."

"Don't worry," said Ruth. "I've got an ointment for hives. It'll clear those suckers right up."

Of course, she did.

I watched as my mother and Dolores removed the gown from the mannequin. Then they held it out for me, and I stepped into it. I shoved my arms through the sleeves, the bodice wrapping around my chest as my mother moved behind me and pulled up the zipper. She was halfway when she began to tug. Then curse.

"You gained weight," said my mother, and I could sense her disapproving frown.

My body jerked forward as my mother kept tugging the dress's zipper. My face flamed, and the last thing I wanted to talk about was my weight. "I *didn't* gain weight. I'm bigger boned than Mrs. Durand." My jeans had been a little tighter around the waist lately. "Can't you adjust that with Martha's spells?"

"It would have been easier if you stuck to salads the weeks before your wedding," snapped my dearest mama. She let out an exasperated sigh. "You've got back fat."

I cringed, mortified. "I've got *back fat*?"

My mother sighed again. "This is hopeless. I can't get it to fit."

"I've got it." Tinker Bell sailed toward me. She took out her wand and then disappeared behind me. A swell of magic pinged at my senses. "There. That should do it."

I blinked, and the fairy zoomed back into my line of sight, hovering at my eye level. I felt another overly aggressive tug on the gown and then the sound of the zipper finally making its way to the top.

"Thank you, little fairy," said my mother. "I thought we were doomed."

I rolled my eyes as Tinker Bell giggled. "Now what?"

"We will remove the sleeves." Dolores walked forward, a book balanced in her arms, her expression serious and determined. She glanced at the book and then chanted, "I call upon the power of the elements. What you were, you are now another. Make this gown to what we want to see, and take these sleeves and make them flee."

A burst of magic welled around me, prickling over my skin. The scent of roses and vanilla filled my nose. Obviously, this was one of Martha's spells. It wasn't unpleasant, just different from what I was used to.

As the magic wafted away, I saw Tinker Bell's face, her eyes round, her lips pressed tight, and she looked like she was trying hard not to laugh.

"Now, *that's* my kind of dress," said Beverly, and she gave me a wink.

"What?" I asked. My eyes went to my mother, who looked like she was about to faint.

Dolores's face went tight. "Oops."

My face fell. "Oops? What do you mean, *oops*?"

I glanced down at the gown, and my breath caught.

"Why can I see my thighs?"

Because the skirt had vanished, and I was standing in my underwear.

Ah, hell.

CHAPTER
27

After another hour of trying out Martha's tailoring spells, Dolores, with the help of Ruth, Beverly, and Tinker Bell, managed to make Mrs. Durand's dress look beautiful.

Once Dolores had been able to *magic* back the skirt, the horrid fur monstrosity was now a flowing, capped-sleeved, A-line, floor-length dress with a lace bodice. It was a gown that I wasn't embarrassed to be seen in. Better yet, married in.

"There." Iris stepped back with her eyeshadow palette, admiring her work. "Just a bit of a smoky eye to add some dramatic effect. You look beautiful."

"Thanks." I blinked and stared at myself in the full-length mirror that House had graciously added. "Wow. I look nice." I wasn't used to seeing myself all done up with makeup. Going with my mother's advice, they'd done my hair in a half-up style. It was soft and romantic and really pretty.

"You look *better* than nice." Iris set her palette on the dresser, her off-the-shoulder, black silk dress flowing with her. "You're gorgeous."

I let out a nervous laugh. "Not quite." I'd never be gorgeous, but I'd settle for pretty, especially on my wedding day.

My wedding day.

"This is really happening," I muttered. Butterflies filled my stomach, and Ruth's waffles churned. Damn. Why did I have to eat four of them?

"Yup." Iris blinked at me. "You nervous?"

Yes. "No."

"Yeah, you're nervous." Iris joined me and faced the mirror. She stared at my reflection. "But it's okay. It's totally normal. I'd be nervous if this was my wedding day. I think all brides are nervous at one point."

I sighed. "When I was in Storybook, I thought I was going to die there. I thought I'd never see this day."

"But you're here, and you're going to marry the chief. Just like you were supposed to."

Music wafted through the window with the echo of happy voices.

"Tessa! Where's my daughter?" came my mother's frantic voice.

"In there with Iris," was Ronin's answer from somewhere in my living room.

The sound of steps echoed, and then—

"Tessa. It's time." My mother stood in the doorway of my bedroom. "You're not ready yet? How long does it take a person to do her makeup?"

I glanced at my mother. "I'm ready, Mother. You can't hurry a bride on her wedding day."

My mother pressed her hand on her hip. "Yes, I can." She strolled into the room and held my cell phone to my face. "I can't make this thing work. Your father is waiting."

I grabbed my cell phone, swiped the screen, and tapped on the WhatsApp video call application. After a single ringtone, my father's surprised face appeared on the screen. "Hi, Dad."

My father beamed. "Tessa. I can see you! I have to say I'm impressed with these human contraptions. This is like fiend mirroring, where you can have a two-way conversation with another demon miles away."

"And you'll be able to see the wedding live," I said. The idea came to me earlier today when my mother became distraught and quiet. When I'd asked her what the matter was, she'd told me that she felt guilty that my father would miss the wedding, seeing that he was a demon and all and couldn't step out into the sunlight. So a live video chat from the comfort and protection of my mother's house was the perfect solution. Naturally, my dearest mama was the designated videographer.

"You look lovely, Tessa," my father was saying.

"Thanks, Dad. Here." I gave my phone to my mother. "Have fun."

"Just a second, Obiryn." My mother gave me one of her impatient looks. "It's time, Tessa. We're all waiting."

"I'm coming." I watched my mother leave and took a deep breath. "Well, you heard the lady. Let's go."

I stepped into the living room, seeing my half-vampire friend stand up from the couch.

"You're rocking that dress, Tess," said Ronin, in a dark gray suit of some soft, silky material that looked as expensive as his car.

I smiled at him. "You're rocking that suit too."

Ronin pulled on his sleeves. "I'm the hottest thing on two legs, baby."

Iris rolled her eyes. "He's been saying that all morning."

I laughed, feeling grateful to have such good friends to make me laugh on this day. I was a bundle of nerves, and the small spells of laughter did lessen the tension.

Ronin held the front door open for us, and I followed Iris onto the porch and took in the view.

The backyard, Davenport House, and cottage grounds had been transformed into a magnificent garden wedding.

Twelve long tables stockpiled with food, wine bottles, and grill stations rested below white garden pavilions. The air was heavy with cheerful conversation from all the guests, and Louis Armstrong and Ella Fitzgerald's "Love Is Here to Stay" boomed from wireless speakers.

From the porch, I had a clear view of the raised platform tucked under a white-painted garden arbor and decorated with pink and white roses at the end of the row of white wood chairs. The chairs' backrests were adorned with gold and white ribbons, my mother's touch. From my vantage point, I could see golden dust sprinkling down from the roses on the arbor, Ruth's and Tinker Bell's doing. It was enchanting and beautiful, adding a fairy-tale touch I loved. A long white drape with pink and white rose petals was placed in the aisle. Each aisle chair had a bouquet of pink and white roses tied to it, fastened with white and gold ribbons.

It had the same vibe as my mother's wedding, only with grandeur and a hell of a lot more guests. No doubt a result of the Durands. My insides tightened at the idea of facing them.

"Are all these people your relatives?" asked Iris as she and I stepped off the porch.

"Never seen them before. Probably Marcus's side of the family."

I spotted Mr. and Mrs. Durand standing beside a row of chairs next to the platform. It was nearly impossible to miss Mr. Durand's big, imposing frame. The light-beige suit could barely hold all his muscles. He looked sophisticated and dangerous, like a 1940s' mob boss. Casting a quick look around, he appeared to be the largest male here, apart from his son.

I caught Mrs. Durand's stare from across the yard. Her eyes went to my feet. Yes, my *feet*. I might have agreed to wear her dress, though you'd barely recognize it anymore. She would just have to deal with the fact I was going barefoot. So she could suck it.

I wiggled my toes in the grass, enjoying the feel of it squishing under my feet, the coolness of it, the sense of nature.

But then her face blossomed into a genuine smile, and I felt myself smiling back.

Huh. *That* was unexpected. Guess something as simple as wearing that dress made up for any past squabbles.

I couldn't see Allison anywhere. I'd thought she might have invited herself to crash the wedding. I was really hoping she did. I was in the mood for a gorilla Barbie ass-kicking. One could only hope.

I moved along and spotted Beverly. She looked absolutely stunning in a low-cut, mermaid-style, teal dress, her blonde hair gleaming in the sunlight. Three men surrounded her, all handsome, and all wereapes, if their muscles and sheer size were any indications. With Marcus's relatives and close friends, there was enough muscle and testosterone to go around and set off a nuclear explosion.

I grinned at the three men battling for her special attention. She caught me staring and gave me a wave. She looked positively delighted at all the interest she was getting. She looked happier than me at the moment.

A black cat rushed between Iris and me with a fairy riding on his back, no less.

"Hildo?" I stared, flabbergasted, as he stopped with Tinker Bell sitting comfortably on his back like she was riding a pony. "I thought you hated her."

The cat shrugged, his yellow eyes gleaming in the sun. "We made up."

I stared at him, not believing a word. "Really? That was fast."

"I promised to make him breakfast and lunch for a year," answered the fairy. "And he agreed to be friends."

Before I could ask more questions, the cat bounded away, and I could hear Tinky's laughter in his wake.

"I never saw that coming," I said, still uneasy about the tiny fairy riding on the feline when only a few weeks ago, he wanted to feast on her.

"I think it's cute," said Iris.

"Until he eats her."

We continued on. My mother was next to one of the pavilions, my cell phone in her hand as she showed off her hard work with the flowers to my father.

"I received an invitation to be here!" shouted a voice.

I turned in search of the ruckus and found Gilbert standing with his face set in a grimace and his hands on the hips of his beige, brown-striped suit with an orange bow tie that looked like it belonged to the '70s.

"Not to promote this silly medieval festival during my niece's wedding!" yelled Dolores, towering over the small shifter, her long navy dress grazing her ankles.

Gilbert rocked back like she'd just shot him with a twelve-gauge shotgun. "The medieval festival is not silly! Everyone *loves* it. You're just jealous because you didn't think of it first!"

Dolores stomped her foot, reminding me of Samael. "I am not. You miserable little chicken. One more word about this festival to the guests, and I'll throw you off my property!"

Gilbert batted his arms around like he was about to take flight. "You wouldn't dare! *I'm* the *mayor*."

A coy smile spread over Dolores's face. "Watch me."

I clamped my jaw to keep from laughing and turned to find Ruth standing next to a long table with the most beautiful wedding cake I'd ever seen.

It was a six-tiered cake in a flourish of white and gold sugar flowers, trellising upward through the layers. It was both glamorous and bohemian, with delicate sugar-flower wreaths and organically placed leafy vines.

But the best part was the tiny, golden candy fairies that flew around the cake, spreading golden sugar dust in their wake.

"Wow, Ruth," I said, marveling at my aunt's talent in her tiny fingers. "You weren't kidding. This is the most beautiful cake I've ever laid eyes on."

Twin pink spots appeared on my aunt's cheeks. "Well, I'm glad you like it." An apron with the words FAIRIES RULE covered her yellow and white-polka-dot dress.

I spied Iris, trying to catch one of the candy fairies, but they kept ducking and zooming past her hands. Ronin was cheering her on. Seemed like they were spelled to avoid capture.

Ruth leaned forward, her eyes wide, and whispered, "Inside, it's your favorite. Chocolate, caramel, with *raspberry* cream."

Yum. "Don't tell my mother, but I have a feeling this dress won't last through the evening."

Ruth giggled, wiping her hands on her apron. "Don't worry. There are spells for that too. You eat as much as you like."

"Trust me. I will."

I moved away, Ronin and Iris with me, my bridesmaid and bridesman at my sides. Together, we made our way slowly toward the platform at the end. Unlike traditional weddings with fathers walking the aisle with their daughters, Marcus and I agreed we wouldn't have that. First, well, because my father couldn't be here physically, and I didn't want Mr. Durand to do it. He'd offered, but that would hurt my father.

So I was to arrive at the platform alone to my waiting husband-to-be. I cast my gaze around the yard, not seeing him. He wasn't on the platform waiting either.

My heart quivered like a scared little squirrel. Was he having second thoughts? Dread felt heavy in my stomach, and my legs were like wooden beams as I forced them to keep walking.

The music changed to a more ceremonial type, the cue to be seated, and the guests filed around and took their seats. My aunts and mother sat in the front row to the right, and Mr. and Mrs. Durand took the left side, accompanied by another couple I didn't know.

And still, no Marcus.

I saw the witch called Alastor, who would officiate the wedding ceremony climb up to the platform. His long white hair and beard reminded me of that Gandalf stripper. He was tall, and I was sure he had once been broad-shouldered and strong, though now was reduced to purely bone and sagging skin. He was dressed in what looked like some kind of golden fabric with the texture of leather but the supple sweep of silk, which hung loosely on his body.

But my wereape was nowhere to be found.

My stomach dropped, and I felt sick. "Where's Marcus?" I mouthed, trying to keep my calm and wits about me.

"I don't know," whispered Iris. The worry in her voice only made me feel worse.

I felt eyes on me, and then, in a collective movement, those seated all turned to look at me.

I was in hell.

"You want me to go look for him," murmured Ronin in my other ear.

I shook my head, not trusting my voice. If Marcus had second thoughts or cold feet, the humiliation would be bad enough, but my heart… well, let's just say no amount of Krazy Glue could fix it.

He wasn't here.

And just when I felt the tears on their way, my eyes found Marcus as he strolled across the grounds and stepped up to the platform.

My stomach exploded in a few somersaults and high jumps.

He was wearing Beast's outfit.

A blue Victorian jacket decorated his broad shoulders over a golden satin vest, a white shirt, and tight black dress pants that hugged his muscular legs.

The only difference from the times I'd seen it on him before was the addition of the vest and a white shirt.

I wasn't sure what was more overwhelming—him standing there looking like a fairy tale come true or the fact that I thought he'd changed his mind only a few seconds ago.

"Wow, he looks stunning," said Iris. "Really hot."

Yes, no one apart from Tinky and me had feasted our eyes on the chief in Beast's costume. I thought he was going to wear the traditional suit or a tux.

This was *wayyyyy* better.

Ronin stared at Iris. "You think he looks hot in that Beast costume? Well, I happen to have a Count Dracula outfit in my closet."

Iris's mouth parted. "Can you wear it tonight?"

The half-vampire smiled sensuously. "Oh baby, it's on tonight."

I pulled myself away laughing as I climbed up to the platform, careful not to trip, my heart on the verge of exploding. I nodded to Alastor as Ronin and Iris took their spots slightly off to the side.

The tall man standing next to Marcus, I guessed, was his best man. And since there was a definite family resemblance in the thickness of his shoulders and the square jaw, he was probably a cousin or something. Sorry to say, but at this moment, I didn't care who he was. All I cared about was Marcus and how good he looked.

The knowing smile he gave me as I reached him told me he knew it.

I faced him, the grin on my face spreading. "Good choice."

Marcus's gray eyes glimmered. "I know."

"I almost thought you wouldn't make it," I told him.

Marcus looked away, seemingly embarrassed for a few seconds. "Sorry. I was having issues with the vest. It's fine now."

"It is *fine*."

"Are you ready for this?" asked the chief.

I licked my lips, my pulse racing. "Ready to spend the rest of my life with you? Hell ya."

And I was ready. Ready to begin our journey together and see where life took us. Together. As one.

With my best friends next to me, and my wonderful witchy aunts, mother, and father, I couldn't ask for anything more.

Marcus never stopped smiling as he took my hands in his, his rough callouses sending tiny goose bumps over my skin. "This is your last chance to run."

A nervous laugh, louder than I'd anticipated, escaped me. I clamped down on my nerves. "You know I'm not the running type. Gives my thighs cramps."

Marcus chuckled, and then his face got all serious. His eyes held a fiery passion full of love, compassion, and promise.

It was a miracle I wasn't a sobbing mess. Thank the souls I could control myself. Sometimes.

I was standing in Marcus's mother's magically altered wedding dress that I'd sworn I'd never wear, about to say yes to the very best of men.

I was a very lucky woman.

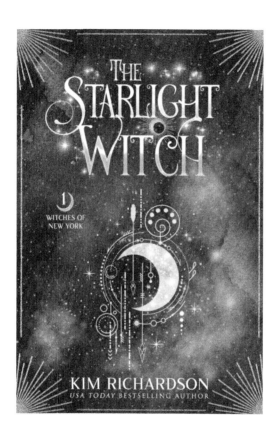

Accepting my new gig could be my doom…

After fifteen years of marriage, I catch my husband cheating on me. What do I do? I laugh, which probably wasn't the reaction he expected.

And then I laughed some more.

So, when a job comes my way from The Twilight Hotel—a paranormal hotel in midtown Manhattan that serves as a sanctuary and residence—I take it.

Cue in tattooed, sexy as sin, grumpy restaurant owner Valen, who can't do drama or high-maintenance women. The problem? He's cruel and dangerous. And he's hiding something.

Rumors arise of a dark spell that would mean the hotel's closure, and I don't know who I can trust. Do I have what it takes to fight this new evil? We'll see.

Brace yourselves. It's going to be a bumpy ride.

ABOUT THE AUTHOR

Kim Richardson is a USA Today bestselling and award-winning author of urban fantasy, fantasy, and young adult books. She lives in the eastern part of Canada with her husband, two dogs and a very old cat. Kim's books are available in print editions, and translations are available in over 7 languages.

To learn more about the author, please visit:

www.kimrichardsonbooks.com

Printed in Great Britain
by Amazon

20267016R00202